THE VANISHING CASTLE

A SIMARRON MYSTERY

Marlena Cannon

Cover design by Marlena Cannon

Copy/line editor: Wren L. Helgren of Helgren Editing

Published by Makenwak Books
3971 Hoover Rd. #52
Grove City, OH 43123

The story, all names, characters, and incidents portrayed in this production are fictitious. No identification with actual persons (living or deceased), places, and products is intended or should be inferred.

Library of Congress Control Number: 2025913945
ISBN: 979-8-9987182-0-5

Printed in the U.S.A.

To my inner child, and yours.

Chapter One

Checking my pocket watch, I scuffed the moisture off my hooves as I entered the brick building. Inside, a framed newspaper article announced the founding of the Magic and Alchemy Safety and Health Administration just ten years ago. But the smell of dust, lamp oil, and crumbling paper told a different story, one far older. I caught a dim reflection of myself in the glass—enough to see that my auburn mane looked presentable—but I smoothed it down anyway while I waited.

My gaze restlessly traveled the shelves containing old books and magical oddities, including a globe of the world adorned with dynamic swirls of clouds that flowed over the model. The morning light streamed in from a pair of narrow, floor-to-ceiling windows, brightening the dark wood and heavy silence of the interior.

I glanced at my pocket watch again—one minute until my appointment. Inconveniently, the desk positioned outside the director's office was unoccupied. Not a secretary in sight. Oh, no—they didn't expect me to interview for a secretary position, did they?

An indistinct figure moved beyond the glass-paneled door. I shifted from hoof to hoof. What was I to do in this situation, knock or wait one more minute?

By the time I worked up the nerve to announce my presence, two more minutes ticked by. Dread slid its icy fingers into my chest, warning me that I was now late, and gave me the final push to act.

I reached forward to knock, pausing when I heard footsteps shuffle to a halt on the other side. I backed up awkwardly, my hooves clattering on the wood floor as the door swung outward.

"Hello, you must be Simarron! I'm Ken Moosekind, Executive Director of MASHA," said a squinty man with a bushy mustache whose robes smelled faintly of tobacco. "Come in, lad, and mind your head." He retreated behind his cluttered desk.

I ducked my head slightly, entering the office: a place of organized chaos. Books and files sat piled atop cabinets and shelves—even on the floor. Wood scraped on wood as I moved aside a chair and settled down on my haunches opposite the director.

Director Moosekind shifted a stack of papers aside. "So, Simarron, you want to join MASHA as a magical safety inspector, do you?"

"Yes, sire—I mean Director," I said, adjusting my collar.

He nodded. "Right then. Tell me, what's your background? Have you ever worked for a government agency?"

"I was a letter carrier for the Centaur Post, sire—Director. It taught me a thing or two about organization and diligence." I had also built up my endurance by traveling long distances and could carry a heavy load with ease, but I didn't mention those qualities. I wanted to avoid being compared to other centaurs in the city.

Director Moosekind's gray eyebrows climbed up his face, revealing his small dark eyes that sparkled like gems—like those with Sireliad heritage. "A letter carrier, you say? I suppose that does require some level of discipline and attention to detail. Do you have any experience with magic?"

"I don't use magic, per se." I paused. "Well, one time I had to deliver a parcel that was magical in nature. I had to wear spelled gloves, and keep it separate from the other deliveries to prevent magical interference."

"Good. We need someone who can follow proper procedures," said Director Moosekind. "How old are you, Simarron?"

"I'm twenty-five."

"A respectable age. Well, I'm sure we would be glad to have your help."

Surprised, I didn't respond right away. Did I pass? Was I hired?

"Thank you, Director," I said at last.

"Unfortunately, all we have for you is a desk in the old records storage, but I hope you'll find it suitable," the director continued, standing up.

"I'm sure it will be fine," I replied, rising to all fours. At least it wasn't the old stables.

"If you'll just come this way," he said, exiting the office and heading down a narrow hallway to the left of the lobby. I followed, navigating my large body as nimbly as I could in the confined space.

"Where are you living?" Moosekind asked conversationally.

"I'm looking for permanent accommodations," I said, not wanting to disclose that I was staying at a boarding house for centaurs in The Docks.

"Check the ads in *The Mercury* for rooms available, but stay away from Sunset Bank," he advised.

"Will do. Thank you, Director." I accidentally bumped into a stack of filing boxes, sending papers scattering. Apologizing, I attempted to set them right, but Director Moosekind waved me off.

"Not to worry. The secretary will put them away," he assured me as my face burned.

I nodded, grateful that I didn't have to embarrass myself further by kneeling to reach the papers. Reaching items flat on the floor was always difficult.

"As Executive Director, I report to the Board of Alchemists on Gold Row and am tasked with executing their decisions," he continued. "For day-to-day operations, however, you'll be working under Administrator Hereswith."

We paused at an open doorway and he called to the person inside. "Mina, meet Simarron."

"Is that the new safety inspector?" inquired a deep, feminine voice. Her head was bent over her desk, the ends of her black hair—cut just above her shoulders—sweeping forward as she worked.

"A centaur!" Mina's eyes widened as she looked up. Judging by her features, I'd guess she was a Sireliad like Moosekind. Among the lineages of two-legged folks in these parts, the Sireliads had the most captivating eyes—alive with shifting flecks of color, like precious minerals. She was staring at me and I dared to meet her gaze. Her dark irises sparkled with copper, framed by the elegant, tapering shape of her eyelids. At her temples, delicate metallic lines, tinged greenish-blue like oxidized bronze, traced beneath her golden skin.

I looked away first. "Simarron, at your service."

"Mina Hereswith. Pleased to meet you," she replied coolly. She wore high-waisted trousers, a high-collared shirt, and a practical coat, suggesting that the administrator's duties required constant mobility. In stark contrast, the director's attire consisted of traditional robes, signifying a more desk-bound role in a higher-ranking position.

"Nice to meet you, mare." It was probably the worst thing I could have said. People in the city of Kami-Nihkia were referred to by their titles. I knew that, but in my nervousness, I had slipped up.

Her red-painted lips twisted. "You may call me Administrator Hereswith."

Mortified, I realized I had so far arrived late for my appointment, created a mess, and offended my potential new supervisor. Now I didn't know what to do . . . shake hands? Centaurs clasped each other's forearms, and I hated it.

Again, Director Moosekind rescued me from my clumsiness. Clearing his throat, he announced, "Right then, that's introductions." He bowed slightly to me and to Administrator Hereswith.

"I am new to this city and still learning some of the local customs," I mumbled in apology, glancing down as I bowed. Great, the top button on one of my hoof spats was unbuttoned. I was truly a mess.

"Indeed," said Administrator Hereswith with a slight dip of her head that caused her glossy black hair to swing forward and back. A sharp, clean scent like peppermint wafted forth. "I had not met a professional centaur before. This job requires certain traits and attitudes that most centaurs—really, most people—in this city are lacking."

We filed into her office as she continued to explain the job. The ban on alchemy in the city was lifted ten years ago, but only on the condition that the alchemy community take formal responsibility for overseeing its own practices. In response, the Magic and Alchemy Safety and Health Administration was formed as an independent guild-like body, answerable to the Council of Governors, Kami-Nihkia University's board of wizards, and the alchemists of Gold Row. Together, they established the first set of standards and regulations for safe magical practice. This was enforced through permits for certain magical activities and regular safety inspections.

I listened intently, glancing curiously around the room as she began talking about recognizing and reporting noncompliance issues, such as improperly labeled or stored ingredients, faulty or missing safety equipment, and improper magical waste disposal. Nestled on the shelves were heavy tomes, their covers worn with age. In contrast, a sleek, modern lamp hung from the tall ceiling, its green glass shade designed to temper the bright glare of meteor crystal. Scattered among the books and office paraphernalia on the administrator's desk were curious artifacts—most notably, a pen stand topped with a glowing eye that glared back at me.

Administrator Hereswith was saying, "In fact, mishandling meteor crystal can cause severe poisoning. So you see, attention to detail and communication skills are of the utmost importance."

"This work has its difficulties," Director Moosekind added. "Alchemists are a highly competitive bunch and some feel that MASHA is overreaching or even spying on them. However, we must come together and keep matters in check or risk the ban being reinstated."

"Yes, though that's different from the challenges I was referring to," said Mina, her tone dry. "Alchemists call us spies, the university treats us as amateurs, and the council sees us like an unstable experiment after their Bureau of Magical Inquiries disbanded. We catch it from every side."

As she spoke, the pen stand on her desk slowly rotated, pointing its glowing eye directly at a letter in the administrator's inbox. She reached for the letter, unfolded it, and scanned the contents with a sharp gaze.

"This is a request for an alchemy workshop permit from Professor Ashmin," she announced, holding the letter up so that we could see the university's official seal. "Your first assignment."

"My first assignment," I repeated, trying not to sound too surprised. They were really going to hire me.

Mina placed the letter back on her desk. "We'll conduct a full review of the facilities and past compliance history. Ensuring every workshop operates within our guidelines is vital to maintaining public safety and trust in our oversight. We must be thorough."

"Thorough, yes, but I'm sure you won't give Kari Ashmin too much trouble. She is on the Board of Alchemists, after all. But first things first, let us show Simarron where he will be working," said Director Moosekind, leading us to an adjacent room.

The records storage, as promised, contained a desk, and several tall wooden filing cabinets sat against the wall to the left. A parade of dusty old portraits of stern-looking officials from days past lined the windowless walls—storage masquerading as decoration. I pulled open a drawer labeled "600-699" to find a stack of papers stored lying flat, further sorted by metal dividers etched with arcane symbols.

The rolltop desk slid open with a satisfying clack, revealing a pen and inkwell, drawers of paper and envelopes, and other writing supplies. It was a bit too low for comfort, for I preferred to stand while working. The counter on the opposite wall, however, was the perfect height to work at. And although it was an outdated relic like the portraits, I quite enjoyed the look of the armillary sphere. Honestly, it might have been what truly sold me on the job, symbolizing a position where I could examine intricate details and measure things. In this office, I was a civilized centaur of reason and intellect.

Administrator Hereswith held out a volume titled *Magic and Alchemy Safety and Health Administration: Rules and Regulations*. "You can start by reading this book."

I took the book and set my satchel down on the counter. "I accept the position."

Chapter Two

The afternoon sun cast a brilliant glow over the city as I set out for my first day at MASHA with Administrator Hereswith, giddy as a foal on the first day of school—a school that taught magic! Mina guided us down the major thoroughfares that radiated through the city like spokes of a wheel, through the winding alleys stitching them together, past businesses that catered to Kami-Nihkia University. I peered curiously into the windows of shops selling herbs, potions, spell ingredients, meteor crystals, new books, used books, and glassware of all shapes and sizes.

Administrator Hereswith's composed stride beside my hoofsteps drew more than a few curious glances. It wasn't every day that a Sireliad woman of her stature strolled alongside a centaur. Rickshaws, mostly pulled by centaurs, glided through the slushy cobblestone streets, weaving between ox carts and a few riders on horseback. Mina, however, seemed oblivious to the stares, her eyes fixed ahead, hands stuffed deep into the pockets of her double-breasted wool coat. She had donned a neat cap and a red scarf that accented her dark golden skin and red lipstick perfectly. I wrapped my cloak tightly around me, as if it could shield me from both the chill wind and the awkward gazes.

The discomfort of the unwanted attention and the press of traffic melted away the moment we turned off the main thoroughfare. Just like that, the street noise fell away, as if we'd stepped through a magic portal into the parklike campus. Bare trees dotted the lawn, faded brown under the pale blue sky, waiting quietly to bloom into spring. Majestic stone buildings encircled the central open space like a henge of monoliths.

The university at Kami-Nihkia was the first of its kind, drawing the world's most talented wizards and aspiring alchemists to the city. Before the founding of the university, the secrets of powerful magic were largely inaccessible, taught exclusively from master to pupil. Excluding a few areas, these buildings of learning were all open to the public.

Mina described the university buildings arranged around the quadrangle, paths weaving between them to create a circular layout that mirrored that of the city itself. Dominating the scene was a palatial building with separate wings dedicated to the study of fire, air, and water magic. Nearby stood the grand library, and a glass-domed structure housed the study of plants and herbs. The magnificent Astronomy Tower reached skyward while the Arcane Archives building was home to a museum of invaluable exhibits in its basement. Our destination was the Alchemy Tower, connected to the gleaming Hall of Metals and New Elements.

"What about necromancy?" I asked. "There's quite a bit about necromancy in the *Rules and Regulations*. Where is that building?"

"Necromancy is . . . different. There are smaller schools devoted to that particular line of magic," Mina answered. "You'll find this city has a unique culture surrounding spirits. In fact, the name Kami-Nihkia translates to 'spirit river.' Some interpret this literally, believing the nearby river carries the souls of the dead to the Underworld. Others see it as meaning 'sacred confluence,' referring to the city's strategic position at the river's mouth, where waters flow between the mighty lakes and the ocean." Her tone left no doubt that she preferred the latter meaning.

As we approached the Alchemy Tower, a shadow fell across our path. I looked up, awed to see a woman on a broomstick soaring above us, bundled against the chill. Classes were not currently in session, but I imagined that once the semester started, witches would be zipping across the central lawn and between the grand buildings in the quest for arcane knowledge. What it must be like to be a student here!

"Remember, Simarron, it's not just about following the rules," Administrator Hereswith called my attention back to the present, her tone both stern and instructive. "It's about understanding why they exist—to prevent harm and encourage responsible magical practices."

I nodded, eager to demonstrate my knowledge of the material I had just read in the *Rules and Regulations*.

"What is the proper way to look into a potion bottle?" she asked.

"By peering through the side, never down into it," I recalled after a pause, my breath clouding the air before me.

"And how do we smell unknown potions?"

"Waft, not sniff." My correct answers were met with an approving nod, her chin dipping into her scarf.

Gargoyles peered down on us as we reached the Alchemy Tower and began our ascent to an upper floor. Spiraling staircases were really not my cup of tea, but I focused on placing each hoof carefully on the steps, one at a time.

"What is it with wizards and towers?" I mumbled through my gritted teeth.

"Whatever you do, do not call Professor Ashmin a wizard. She is to be referred to as 'Professor Ashmin' or 'Alchemist Ashmin.'" She paused on a landing and looked back with concern. "Can you manage the stairs?"

I nodded hesitantly. Carefully, I followed my supervisor to the brand new alchemy lab.

Windows set high into the turret ceiling let in the afternoon light and presumably vented out the fumes of transformation and discovery. Meteor crystals set in hanging candelabras added to the bright glow of the large open room. There was a blackboard at one end, its matte surface free from dust, ready for fresh ideas and new lessons to be inscribed upon it. Workspaces for students sat clean and empty, stools tucked beneath the wooden tables.

The clatter of my hooves on stone brought forth Professor Ashmin from behind a large still at the back of the room. "Administrator Hereswith," she intoned, her voice echoing slightly.

"Good day, Professor Ashmin," said my supervisor, bowing. I mimicked her.

The professor nodded in acknowledgment, her deep black eyes glittering in the light. "I was recently informed that the lab needed to clear an inspection before I could accept students. The winter break ends soon."

"Yes. Safety Inspector Simarron and I will take a look around, if you don't mind."

"I'm sure it's just a formality," Professor Ashmin muttered, a singed eyebrow raised. Her hands steepled, she tapped her long fingers together impatiently, reminding me of a spider.

I started at the smaller and closer of two stills, positioned in an old fireplace, and moved clockwise around the lab, finding shelves filled with glassware and ingredients stored in a large cabinet in clearly labeled jars. I paused when Administrator Hereswith asked if I observed anything.

"Flammable materials must be stored in secure cabinets, never on open shelves," I stated, noting the bottles labeled with fire runes secured behind the glass.

Administrator Hereswith nodded in approval. "And speaking of fire, can you find the quenchfire orb?"

I searched until I located the orb of swirling blue mist in its own little cabinet set into the stone wall. Shattered on impact, it would release a powerful mist, capable of extinguishing even the most stubborn of enchanted flames.

We proceeded around to the back of the lab, trailed by the professor. Upon the large desk by the blackboard, I noticed several unlabeled jars of ingredients.

"Shouldn't these be labeled?" I said.

"Very good, Simarron," said Administrator Hereswith. "Professor Ashmin, can you make sure all your bottles are clearly labeled?"

Professor Ashmin muttered something.

"Sorry, did you say something?" I asked.

"No . . . I'll take care of it right away," grumbled the professor, backing away.

I continued my inspection, pointing out various potential hazards or responding to Mina's guidance. Professor Ashmin clenched her fists, her annoyance simmering. We eventually made our way to the larger still that dominated the back of the room.

"This will not do. I'm afraid I can't sign the permit today," said Administrator Hereswith, after a mere glance at the equipment. Turning to me, she asked, "Can you tell me why?"

"Why indeed!" cried Professor Ashmin. She had been keeping her distance from me, but now stormed forward to demand an answer.

I circled the contraption of hammered copper. A smaller person than myself, such as the alchemy professor, would need to use the stepladder to see the top of it. The fires beneath it smoldered while the hood in the ceiling carried away the vapors. The working still, bubbling and dripping away, had an assortment of glassware arranged around it. This area, then, was already being used. It all seemed to be in order, and I checked the paperwork but came up with no immediate answer.

"It is much bigger than the initial permit allowed," my supervisor said impatiently.

"You surely aren't serious!" the alchemy professor protested. Her tan complexion flushed red, and I'm afraid mine did as well at overlooking such a simple thing.

"You must remove this still or apply for an industrial-scale workshop permit," Administrator Hereswith said firmly.

"This is the university!" Professor Ashmin exclaimed. Her frustration had reached such a boiling point that it seemed like she might erupt like a volatile chemical reaction. She did not argue further, but simply shook with silent rage as the inspection continued. I voiced my observations while Mina prodded, corrected, and evaluated.

After completing the inspection, Mina's rigid demeanor softened. "Ashmin will complain to Moosekind," she said with an air of resignation as we stood on the worn path outside the tower.

"I'm beginning to understand the difficulties he alluded to earlier," I said, thinking that Director Moosekind's responsibilities were like balancing the needs and demands of different parties on an apothecary's scale—or an alchemist's.

"You handled yourself well today." She then half-joked, "Your size certainly makes an impression."

I snorted, not fully comfortable being seen as intimidating.

"You're quick on the uptake—that's what matters."

"Thank you, Administrator Hereswith."

"You may call me Mina."

I hesitated. "You can keep calling me Simarron. You don't need to use my herd name." I wanted to leave my herd in the distant Wildlands. Seeking to shift the topic, I took out my pocket watch and glanced at the brass dials.

Mina nodded. "Simarron, it's getting late. Why don't you head home? I'll finish up at the office. We have a major inspection scheduled for tomorrow."

I snapped shut the cover of the watch, slipping it back into my pocket. "Thank you, Mina. I'll try to be ready for tomorrow." But as I thought back to everything I had learned so far, I couldn't help feeling a twinge of self-doubt.

Chapter Three

I didn't quite understand the rhythms of life with an office job yet, the way everything started and stopped at precise times, but with the aid of my pocket watch, I was trying. I headed back to the main thoroughfare and its cacophony of bustling activity, the clattering of hooves and the rumbling of wooden wheels on uneven stones. Reticent to return to The Docks, I picked up the latest edition of *The Kami-Nihkia Mercury* and leafed through the housing advertisements.

Mansion in Colorful Sunset Bank District
Seeking Quiet Souls for Cozy Residence
Furnished Chambers, Two Meals a Day
Ground floor available. Inquire for Rates.

It was the only listing that mentioned being at ground level. I headed for the address on Slant Row straight away, but before long found myself lost in the maze of streets and alleys. The chill deepened with the coming of evening and the streetlamps flickered on. Meteor crystals, once burning bright through the atmosphere as they fell to the earth, provided their smokeless light.

I found myself on the opposite side of the aqueduct that divided the city into rough halves. The grand structure brought in water from the mountains, less murky than the river water, piping it directly into public wells and the residences of the affluent.

The further I walked, the more weathered the grand houses that lined the avenue became. Dogs barked their warning calls as ragged-looking men loitered in the shadows, following me with suspicious glances. The women walking the street, by contrast, appeared very elegant in extravagant dresses and flamboyant hats. Maybe a bit too ostentatious, if I was honest.

I reached the listed address, hesitating before the front door, my hand raised to knock. Locating the place had proved an unexpectedly time-consuming challenge. It felt improper to stop by this late and, on the verge of turning back, I noticed something amiss.

The front door was slightly ajar, its hinges creaking as it swayed gently in the stiff breeze. A moment later, it burst fully open and I stumbled a few steps backward in surprise as a man clad in black clothing slammed into me. He squawked in pain; I grunted at the impact. His beady eyes flashed briefly behind a dark mask before he vaulted over the porch railing, his boots hitting the cobblestones with a sharp thud. Then he disappeared into the shadows of the rapidly darkening street, cloak billowing behind him.

My heart beat quickly, urging me to run. I forced myself to stay rooted, calming my breath as I tried to make sense of what had just happened. That man . . . It didn't seem like he was supposed to be here. A thief, surely. Just what kind of neighborhood had I stumbled into?

"You there! Who are you?"

I turned to face the speaker, a stooped man whose gray hair curled close to his scalp. "Safety Inspector Simarron," I said. "I apologize for the lateness of the hour."

"Thank you, officer! You stopped that man from robbing me," said the old man. His face, lined with age, broke into a relieved smile.

"Oh no, I . . . I'm not with the City Watch," I stammered, still tense from the encounter.

"Did you get a good look at him, by chance?" He squinted at me, and at my four legs, perhaps wondering if he was seeing correctly in the dim light.

"I'm sorry, it all happened so quickly," I replied, rubbing my chest. It still stung from the collision.

"I heard a strange sound, but before I could see what it was, he went running out the door. He didn't have time to take anything, I reckon. Lucky you were here—you must've spooked him."

A faint gleam on the porch caught my eye. Bending down, I picked up a black quill, its iridescent sheen reflecting the light spilling from the doorway. "He dropped this," I said, holding it up.

The man squinted again and shook his head. "Not mine. You keep it."

A chill ran down my spine as I turned it over absently. It wasn't a quill but a raw feather, sleek and cool in my hand. Its edges were unnervingly sharp, and it felt completely out of place.

"Actually, I'm here about the room to rent?" I had almost changed my mind about the endeavor, but I was already here.

"You'll want Daniella Lyness's place," the man said, gesturing across the street. Following his gaze, I spotted a weathered two-story house tucked back from the street, its turret piercing the sky. A twisted old tree stood sentinel, its skeletal branches swaying faintly in the wind. "Common mistake. Even the Witchy Whisk messengers get it wrong sometimes." He began to shut the door and paused, adding, "Lyness is a good woman from an old family."

Thanking the old man, I crossed the street, still jittery as the high of confronting the would-be robber began to cool. Seeing no need for it, I let the feather flutter away.

A silhouette in the front window watched me approach the mansion along the overgrown path. The entrance was tall and framed by impressive columns. I knocked firmly on the door, and a few moments later, it opened to reveal a round, middle-aged Sireliad woman wearing an apron and an uncertain smile. Her hair was a pale cloud piled atop her head, and the scents of tea and cooking herbs wafted from her.

"You're not a copper, are you?" she asked, inspecting me with keen gray eyes that shimmered with flecks of silver and blue in the low light.

"Ah, no. Safety Inspector Simarron." I bowed awkwardly. "I'm here about the room to let. Advertised in the paper?"

She hesitated, looking me up and down from head to hooves. "I saw how you handled that ruffian just now. Impressive, I must say."

"Thank you," I said, although I felt I hadn't really done anything.

"Well, I do have a room available," she said brightly, the corners of her eyes crinkling as her smile became genuine. "Would you like to see it? Here, let me take your cloak."

"Yes, please," I replied as she led me inside the vestibule, where a small household shrine stood.

The carved figure of a serene woman rested in a niche, her hands open as if shaping something unseen. Her skin resembled a slab of stone threaded with pinkish-gold flecks, each rimmed in silver. Scattered at her feet were smaller crystals of the same mineral, their surfaces oxidized into soft blues, muted violets, and tarnished greens.

"Prismuth draws creative minds," she mused, noting my glance. "You must be one yourself. But her crystals aren't just for beauty— they offer protection, too."

I nodded politely, not knowing how else to respond. The gods of the two-leggers were mysterious to me.

The entrance hall was a grand affair, with a red-carpeted staircase curving down from the second floor. We continued to the parlor, off the left side of the hall. It was a spacious room featuring a fireplace and large windows that overlooked the front drive and street. The ornate red-and-gold damask wallpaper was faded, and the plush furniture patched in many places. I couldn't help myself and smoothed a hand over the velvety arm of a deep cushioned chair.

Paintings adorned the walls in gilded frames, though the gold was flaking off in places. A framed piece of cross-stitching hung prominently on the wall above the mantel. Its precise lettering spelled out the house rules: *Books are to be read and returned, not borrowed indefinitely. No casting spells on others without consent.*

Books overflowed from the shelves, forming piles in every corner. On the various side tables, little personal belongings were scattered— signs of the people who called this house home. I loved it immediately.

"Women live upstairs, everyone else downstairs," said the landlady.

Through this magnificent high-ceilinged chamber, I glimpsed the dining room toward the center back of the house, with its large polished table and sideboard gleaming in the lamplight. There were four high-backed chairs, no two of which were exactly alike. The aroma of a warm meal lingered in the air.

"We've just had supper. I serve two meals a day," she informed me. "But the jewel of this estate is our indoor plumbing system. Constantly flowing hot and cold water, heated with an enchanted hypocaust system," she said proudly.

"Very nice. How many people live in this house?" I asked, my hooves creaking on the weathered floorboards as she led me back into the entrance hall and into a more narrow hall hung with paintings. I greatly appreciated that I didn't have to duck going through any of the entryways.

"Kai Anise would be your neighbor. Lilimari adAnsa, Tia Larose and I live on the second floor." She counted off on her fingers as she named each person. We continued to the room off the right side of the gallery.

The landlady unlocked the door and pushed it open. The room was simply furnished with an enormous four-poster bed, heavy oak wardrobe, dressing table, and chair. A tall curtained window faced the street, and an adjacent window looked over the side garden. It smelled like aged, polished wood and faded memories. And best of all, it wasn't a shared dormitory in The Docks.

"It's beautiful," I said.

"It's my life. I'm Daniella Lyness and this is my family home. As you can see, I manage on a modest budget. Times are tight and I employ no servants. I do what I can to keep up the old place, and everyone helps a little."

"That sounds perfectly acceptable," I assured her. "I'm not looking for luxury, just a quiet place to rest my head. I don't even need the bed. A straw mattress will do nicely."

"In that case, I'd take that beautiful four-poster, but I don't think I can move it," said a voice behind me.

Somewhat startled, I awkwardly turned to face a dark man with golden eyes. His long, pointed ears told of his Helvenkin heritage, and he carried the faint, smoky scent of sage. With a bow, he introduced himself as Kai Anise.

"You seem like you have an aesthetic sense," Kai continued, his gaze sweeping appreciatively over my outfit: a high-collared shirt and vest, from which the chain of my pocket watch looped. "Don't you just love the furnishings? I wish I was better at repairing it. Well, the bed curtains I can do. I'm still trying to spruce up the old evening room."

"This used to be the morning room," said the landlady. "It gets the most beautiful light early in the day."

"Wonderful." I had no idea what either a morning room or evening room was. "Oh, I can probably move the bed," I said, turning to Kai.

"That would be lovely. I'll trade you some throw pillows—my own creations." He wore a flowing cobalt robe with intricate silver embroidery, layered over loose, wide-legged trousers that made me wonder if they, too, were his own design. Richly colored sashes draped over his shoulders and wrapped around his waist, adding to the vivid ensemble. A long chain necklace with a single gemstone rested against the dark fabric of his robe.

Landlady Lyness turned to me with a thoughtful expression. "Very well. I'll give you a discount, considering the good deed you did by stopping that thief. You look like a strong young . . . man, and I could use help with fixing odds and ends around this old house."

"That's more than fair," I agreed.

"Welcome to your new home, Simarron," she said, offering me a slight bow and a small key. It felt like the world. The warm brass in my hand filled me with excitement, signifying a new beginning for me and a space I could call my own.

Chapter Four

The next night, I sat on my haunches at the table in the parlor, writing in my journal by candlelight. There were no newfangled meteor crystal lamps at Slant Row Boarding House. A fire crackled invitingly in the hearth behind me, lending its warmth to the cozy room and reviving my spirit. I was trying to recall what exactly had happened during the day, for it had passed in a mysterious whirlwind. Perhaps, in recording my reflections, I can form a clearer picture of what transpired.

* * *

That morning, Mina and I departed from the Magic and Alchemy Safety and Health Administration building, our destination being Château Gorget—or rather, the remnants of it. The journey to our destination, beyond the city of Kami-Nihkia in Misty Vale, was too distant to undertake on foot, burdened with the weight of our equipment.

Mina drove the borrowed ox cart, procured from a nearby stable, while I trotted beside her. A chilling mist cloaked the landscape, seeping into my bones. The hills, covered with evergreen trees, were nothing like the open plains I knew growing up. Still, the journey stirred memories of my days traversing the wilderness for the Centaur Post. She recounted the detailed case notes as we ascended, the cart creaking along the dirt road.

Eighty-five years ago, "The Alchemists' Inferno" occurred when unregulated alchemy experiments with meteor crystals caused devastating explosions, leveling portions of the city and leading to a city-wide ban on alchemy, Mina explained. Afterward, the uninhabited Château Gorget fell into the hands of Andreas Hippolyte, a powerful alchemist who moved his laboratory there. Five years later, another catastrophic explosion destroyed much of the castle, resulting in its permanent desertion.

Now Lysandros Garbor, a reclusive but well-known alchemist and wealthy investor, has taken ownership of the ruin with plans to restore it. Given the castle's reputation, however, the city wouldn't allow renovations to begin until MASHA tested it for unsafe levels of the alchemical aftermath. One of the primary goals of alchemists was to transform base metals, such as lead or copper, into more valuable metals like gold or silver. This process, called transmutation, used dangerous substances such as mercury.

The castle itself was proving as slippery as quicksilver. I kept expecting its towers to rise over the next ridge, but somehow we kept getting turned back the way we came. The shape of the hills and the forest canopy obscured our destination, and sometimes we found ourselves headed back down the slope somehow without realizing it.

When we finally arrived within sight of the rusty iron gates, the ox balked and refused to go any further. Mina tugged at the reins and coaxed it, but the beast wouldn't budge. Until now, it had been a slow but docile animal; a horse, however, would have been faster.

"I won't be offended if you take a horse next time," I said, my suspicions bubbling to the surface. "For the record, I don't think horses resemble centaurs any more than bears resemble your kind—and by that I mean two-leggers."

"Two-leggers?" Mina enunciated the word carefully, testing it. "Are we really said to look like bears?"

"Before my days with the post, bears were the only two-legged beings I ever encountered," I said with a shrug, patting the ox, which shot me a wary glance from one eye. "Well, Kin. You know what I mean," I added, the heat of embarrassment branding the words into my memory. Sireliads, Bloodborn, and Helvenkin were all Kin, but the ethereal dryads and naiads I'd met weren't.

I remember the strange hat that Mina handed me. It was bright coral in color, with a wide brim and a pointed cone encircled by a wide band inscribed with runes. A small meteor crystal lamp was affixed to the front.

"Put it on," she said as she adjusted the fit of her own by tugging the chin strap. "It's firm, providing protection from any falling debris. The conical shape may look funny, but it serves a purpose. It acts as a lightning rod, drawing stray magical energies away from the body."

Next, I recall the green metal gates, and shoving them open on protesting hinges. Beyond lay a landscape obscured by dense trees and thick vegetation. A black vignette crept around the edges of my vision. I picked my way carefully, hauling the equipment. I saw crumbling walls of stone covered in vines, silvery birch trees, and towering pines shrouded in mist. Amidst this natural reclaiming, bright green fiddle-head ferns and red toadstools glistened with morning dew—beautiful, yet conspicuously devoid of any castle.

Mina waved me over to a relatively flat area paved with wide flagstones. I slipped my arms out of the straps of the case for the Magical Energies Detector and set it up on the ground. Constructed of wood with brass fittings, the boxy device came up to my knee. It resembled a large timepiece, with various dials, a glass bell-shaped piece on top, and a spool of wire attached to a wand that fitted neatly into one side. I had never before seen any contraption quite like it.

"Simarron, pay close attention," Mina instructed. "The Magical Energies Detector, or MED, is a delicate instrument. It's designed to pick up echoes of powerful spells. Hold the wand like this, firmly but gently."

I nodded. The protective hat felt a little strange as I moved my head, but as I watched a small spark of magic travel down Mina's hat, I was suddenly glad for its protection.

Mina demonstrated the MED, unclipping the metal wand from the device and unspooling some of the fine wire. "The key is to sweep the area systematically. While I sweep, note down any changes in the readings. Our goal is to understand the magical residue left behind and assess potential risks."

She proceeded to sweep the area with the wand. I recall Mina in flashes, her arm outstretched, glimpsed between my studies of the dials on the MED. A sea of darkness ebbed and flowed around her, seemingly kept at bay by the wand in her hand.

Whenever she paused, I jotted down the position of the dials. The number "51" sticks in my mind, but I'm uncertain as to what it refers to. Wearing spelled gloves, I filled a dozen slender glass tubes full of earth to test in our lab and packed them into a compact leather case.

Something gave off an acrid odor that I couldn't identify. Strongest in the shadows, it slowly built in intensity until my eyes watered. It was so strong, it almost knocked me out of my senses. The only castle I saw was that one in that brief hallucination when I nearly passed out.

Time passed very strangely, and the next thing I can recall, we had packed it in and were on the road heading away from the castle. I was out of breath, like I'd been sprinting.

"Not much of a castle to speak of, is there?" I remarked, to break up the uncomfortable silence that had built up between us like a fog. "Did we find it?"

Mina grimaced, looking rather peaky. "Find what?"

"I'm worried that we might be forgetting something important. We did some precise scanning and gathered soil samples, but I can't remember what exactly we were looking for." I paused for a moment. "Are you well? I feel quite strange."

"I'm fine, of course. Don't worry. Once we take these samples to the lab, it will all make sense," she said firmly. "We encountered some kind of enchantment today, but the information doesn't lie."

I wasn't as concerned about the results of our safety inspection as what the Hecatonchires had just transpired. I walked beside the ox cart in silence for a while, my thoughts churning. It was strange: I remember the rattle of the cart on the dirt road, the mingled smells of ox and pine, and entire conversations on the journey, yet the job site itself slipped through my grasp like a dream upon waking.

"How could a castle simply vanish? Is it possible this is a lingering result of what Andreas Hippolyte had done?" I knew I was missing something, but I felt overcome with vertigo when I tried to turn my thoughts to the castle. I tried to push past the pain and probe the edges of my memories further, but they dissolved into mist.

Mina didn't answer immediately, focusing instead on the road ahead. The cart jostled as it hit a bump in the road, and she steadied the reins. "It's possible," she said at last, her voice measured. "Although it seems forgotten, Château Gorget wasn't just any old structure. It's a very old stronghold that's been standing for hundreds of years. If it vanished, it's more recent, and likely deliberate."

I frowned, glancing at the fading outlines of the hills behind us that hid the valley and everything in it. "People would notice if an important landmark went missing."

"Yes, although it's not so important anymore," Mina replied, her tone thoughtful. "Château Gorget was once a symbol of power—first under the Otselian Empire, and then during the War for Independence. It was abandoned as a governmental center shortly after the war, with the administration moved to Castle Ward in the heart of Kami-Nihkia. And after Andreas Hippolyte took Château Gorget over and nearly destroyed it, it was abandoned again."

"But you said that was eighty years ago or something, and this road is still used. Who else goes up to the castle besides Garbor and us?"

"Very observant, Simarron. I'm hesitant to speculate further until we test the samples and complete our report."

The next thing I remember, we were approaching the MASHA building as evening swept over the city. Lights winked out one by one in windows of storefronts, and meteor crystal streetlamps spilled their glow onto the cobblestone street. A sense of relief at the familiar sights flooded me.

"Good work today, Simarron," said Mina as I unloaded the equipment.

Despite her reassurances, my head throbbed behind my eyeballs, like I had a hangover—a disconcerting cocktail of fatigue and foreboding. Her words felt placating. I didn't feel like I'd done a good job. I felt guilty for not having done anything, or not being able to remember clearly what it was. And I was still plagued by the sense that I had overlooked something critical. A wave of nausea, paired with discontent, told me I was letting everyone down, including myself.

I took off the safety hat, shaking my head as I handed it to Mina. "Is this a normal day on a job site?"

"Well, not exactly," she admitted.

My voice trembled slightly. "I've never experienced anything like it before. The wrongness of it all, and yet a sense of some awesome force, a mystical power. Is this what magic is like?"

"I don't know what it was, yet." Her red lipstick had faded, her pale lips pressed into a thin line.

"You must have some ideas. Humor me," I insisted, taking a step forward. My tall frame towered over my superior.

Mina backed up a step. "I need to think about what I've just experienced. You should do the same. Sleep on it, and we'll work on the analysis and report tomorrow."

* * *

That evening, Slant Row Boarding House welcomed me home like an old grandmother, sagging with age. She gently corrected me when I nearly tripped over the threshold in exhaustion. Her scent of ancient wood soothed me, while the incense smoldering in the small house-hold shrine tickled my brain, momentarily cutting through the fog.

Fumbling around for a quill and ink, and struggling even more to find the right words, I resolved to record in my journal everything I remembered. For how was I supposed to protect anyone in my new job if I couldn't even trust my own memory?

I picked up the quill, but it snapped under my heavy grip. I stared at the broken halves in dismay. Then I trimmed the bottom half with a knife and began writing anyway, the flow of ink in the compromised tool as unsteady as my thoughts.

Chapter Five

A loud pop from the fireplace snapped me back to the current moment—which itself felt part of a dream. I could hardly believe I was sitting here, taking up space in this beautiful parlor with a real life Bloodborn—those sharp-fanged people of the mountains, metalworking, and mysterious magic! And sharing the same space, a Helvenkin. I found the elegant, pointy-eared forest folk to be the most enchanting of all two-leggers.

"Is it possible for an alchemist to make a castle disappear?" I paused mid-sentence to ask the room at large. "I thought alchemists were forever distilling ingredients to find some basic element that would render all other metals into gold, but it seems there's more to it than that." What would the readings from the Magical Energies Detector reveal?

"Umb, alchemists are driving the research on *meteor crystals*. They're producing magical effects for the common good, you know," came a nasally voice dripping with weary scorn.

I looked up at a skinny figure in an overstuffed armchair. Lilimari's long hair hung like a dark curtain, obscuring her face as she hunched over her university textbooks. She appeared drawn and fatigued, her tan complexion bearing the unsettling undertone of unhealthiness reminiscent of the alchemists she so admired. Her brooding appearance delighted me, however, tugging a corner of my mouth into a smile. She reminded me of my favorite cousin when he was a young colt. Beneath that same stormy expression, he had been the softest centaur I knew.

"How do we know that meteor crystals are safe?" asked Kai, absently scratching a long pointed ear. He was engaged in a game of solitaire, or perhaps reading the cards to divine the future, across the table from me.

"Well, that's where MASHA comes in. We make sure meteor crystals and other substances are handled properly," I replied, like some kind of expert. Before this week, I didn't even know the difference between alchemists and wizards, or the top of a retort from the bottom.

Lilimari's hair rippled with the impolite sigh she directed our way.

The sound of approaching hooves and the creaking of wheels outside reached my ears.

"Has anyone seen my hat?" asked a red-haired woman as she descended the grand staircase on loud, squeaking stairs.

"It's right here," said Lilimari, forcefully pointing to the hat decorated with a long feather resting on a side table.

"Are you working at the tavern tonight, Tia?" asked our landlady, entering from the kitchen. She carried a silver teapot and five mismatched teacups wobbling precariously on a tarnished tray. The swirling, multicolored patina caught the light in a mesmerizing pattern.

"No, but I'm going to see my beau, so I won't be back until after supper," Tia said, adjusting her curls in the hallway mirror.

"Which one?" asked Kai, glancing up from his cards, a sly smile playing on his lips.

"Kai, you know who," Tia replied, casting him a pointed glance. Her expression softened as she turned to me. "Simarron, you must tell me all about yourself when I get back." She waved, her red curls bouncing as she left, rose perfume lingering in the air behind her.

"Simarron, how was work today?" inquired Landlady Lyness, setting a cup down on the table and filling it with an easy tilt of her wrist. It smelled wonderful, like a perfect spring day remembered from one's childhood. But a touch bitter, too, like the realization that comes as life becomes ever more complicated with age.

"Do tell," chimed Kai. "So, what is Mina Hereswith like?" He leaned forward, regarding me with his round, amber-colored eyes.

Lilimari blurted out, "It must be a nightmare working for that alchemy-suppressing tyrant, right? I mean, does she think she's still an inquisitor for the Bureau of Magical Inquiries, or what?" Her nasally voice carried a mixture of disdain and genuine curiosity.

I was momentarily taken aback and looked down at my delicate porcelain cup, encircled with painted clusters of red buds with yellow centers. I smoothed my thumb over the crack in the handle.

"She's very dedicated," I answered cautiously, mindful of Kai's penchant for gossip. During our initial encounter, he had welcomed me warmly and graciously inducted me into what felt like a clandestine society of housemates, sharing intriguing morsels about each of our fellow residents.

Tia, an aspiring artist who worked at a tavern, had apparently become the muse of a wealthy admirer of her art. Lilimari, a student of alchemy at Kami-Nihkia University, was conducting some rather eccentric experiments in her room, judging by the hissing and bubbling coming from behind her door. Strange sounds had sometimes emanated from the room I was now occupying, as well.

"Simarron, I trust you slept well in that old room?" Landlady Lyness said, setting out the dishes of sugar and cream. Steam curled invitingly from the teapot.

Unperturbed by the landlady's attempt to shift the topic, Lilimari pressed on. "So, any chance you'll rub elbows with the big shots in alchemy, or is Hereswith too busy hunting down the last fun in the city?" She dumped an excessive amount of sugar into her cup decorated with tiny white bell-shaped flowers.

The room fell into an uneasy silence at Lilimari's outspoken comments. I stirred my tea, politely insisting that I had slept just fine and that I didn't know about meeting anyone famous, while Landlady Lyness fussed with the teapot. Kai merely sipped his tea from the cup with the star-shaped flower design, observing with a bemused expression.

I think this strange group of people was warming to me, as I was to them, but they were sometimes overwhelming. I wouldn't be able to get any studying done here. After tea, I picked up my book and politely excused myself to my room.

I loved my room at the old mansion. I didn't need the chair it came furnished with, but I kept it in case I made any friends among the two-leggers here. From home, I had Ma and Pa's hoofprints pressed into clay, decorated with dried flowers from the Wildlands. Arranged neatly on my dressing table next to a candle, it resembled a memorial to the dead, although they were both alive.

The rug on the floor also came from home, but it wasn't centaur-made. Rolled up, I had used it to transport my belongings to Kami-Nihkia. It was woven from plant fiber and dyed in beautiful shades of rich walnut and forest green. It was a package from the city of Tavlyn —and as it had never been claimed at the post, I'd gotten to keep it.

I lay curled up in my nest of blankets, trying to read *Rules and Regulations* by candlelight but feeling distracted by my thoughts. I obsessively recalled every conversation I'd had over the course of the day, convinced that my new supervisor thought I was a slow, clumsy centaur and worried that I'd given a rude impression to my housemates.

My eyes were scanning the pages without processing the information, and soon the book was slowly slipping from my limp hands.

I was walking through the halls of a castle's ruins while feeling an invisible presence following me. I caught a glimpse of phosphorous red when I looked behind me, but the elusive figure always managed to vanish behind a corner, curling away like smoke. Suddenly the shadow was upon me, while sleeved arms ending in bony fingers reached around me from behind.

I awoke with a start in a pitch-black room, not knowing how much time had passed. I listened intently, but if I had been alarmed by a noise, it was gone now. Rising to all fours, I crept to the window, my mind racing back to the robbery I had accidentally intervened in across the street.

Pulling aside the curtain, I peered out into the moonlit night. I saw nothing malign, only the dark outlines of buildings in various states of disrepair. Boarded-up windows and crumbling facades were black spots of decay among the more beautiful, kept-up homes with their ornamented gables and wrap-around porches.

It struck me that our landlady, Daniella Lyness, was a guardian of the fading grandeur of the district. Kai had informed me that Daniella grew up in a life of privilege and luxury, attending exclusive schools and traveling the world with her family. Her parents became wealthy by applying magical innovations to various industries. However, they were troubled with marital and financial problems.

After her parents split, they were forced to sell off many of their properties and business assets. Years later, after Daniella's father passed away, she inherited the old family mansion. By this time, the neighborhood had degraded, and the mansion was surrounded by rundown buildings on what came to be known as Slant Row. She could have sold the property and made a tidy profit, but she couldn't bear the thought of the family home being torn down.

Instead, she resolved to restore the mansion as best she could, and rent out the rooms to people who shared her appreciation for the beauty and history of the building. By welcoming a motley crew of occupants, she sought to breathe new life into her family's ancestral home, and I felt drawn to be a part of it.

After another few moments passed uneventfully, I sighed and sank back onto my bed. But I could not shake the feeling of being watched.

Chapter Six

Not every day at MASHA involved collecting data and evaluating cursed sites. We also had quiet days spent at the office, writing reports where we document our findings, reviewing other reports pulled from the massive oak file drawers, or issuing various permits. As it was all new to me, I found much to enjoy in these mundane tasks, even though I was anxious for the chance to test the samples from Château Gorget.

I delighted in the mechanical hole punch and the way a light press of the brass lever precisely perforated the paper with a powerful, satisfying crunch. I appreciated my solid wooden writing board, equipped with two large metal rings that securely held punched paper in place, such as a permit granting authorization to engage in specific magical and alchemical activities. I loved the way my fountain pen sounded as it scratched rhythmically across the paper, black ink flowing from the nib with the gentle glide of my hand, validation coursing through my veins as I signed my name and date.

I returned to Slant Row Boarding House after a busy day of what Mina called *paperwork*, a delicious smell greeting me. Landlady Lyness was in the kitchen, working on the evening's supper, the aroma of roasted garlic and fresh herbs wafting through the air. A large pot stirred itself, the spoon circling steadily as if guided by an unseen hand.

Kai was seated at the table in the parlor, surrounded by a chaos of sewing supplies and sartorial selections.

"Perfect timing! You're my new date for the gala tonight," Kai declared without looking up. His date to the art gala had apparently canceled at the last minute, and he was not one to let a ticket—or an evening—go to waste.

I dropped my satchel onto a chair. "What I need is a cup of tea and a good brushing. Besides, I can't, I have work tomorrow, unlike the wealthy folk that will be there."

"I'm not wealthy," Kai pointed out, his elegant hands guiding a needle and thread through an inside-out pair of trousers that he was mending. "Why are you all scratched up anyway?" he asked, finally glancing up from his work.

"It's just . . . It's been a long day," I said, desiring to brush off the chain of embarrassing missteps that had led me here with feathers in my mane. The animal permit for the cockatrice had been a bit harrowing and the scratches on my arms still smarted.

"Why are you going to the gala?" I asked, quickly changing the conversation.

"I trade in stories, so it's essential work for me to be there," he replied, tying off a knot. "And tonight promises some good ones among the city's elite. Everyone is talking about the haunted painting that will be on display, and I'll be observing the people gawking at the painting." His gaze fell on the bow tie and cravat laid out on the table.

"Why not take Tia with you?" An art gala seemed right up her alley.

"Tia is already going with her rich beau, her art *admirer*." Kai trimmed the end of the thread with a small pair of brass scissors shaped like a bird. He turned the trousers right-side-in and shook them gently. Setting them aside with a sigh, he returned his attention to the bow tie and cravat.

"Landlady Lyness?" I ventured, knowing she was likely to refuse.

She suddenly appeared at the doorway between the dining room and the parlor, wiping her hands on her apron. "I heard you two plotting from the kitchen. And no, there isn't enough illusion magic in the world to make these old clothes gala-ready," she declared with a chuckle.

She leaned against the doorframe, a nostalgic glint in her eyes. "There was a time," she began, her voice softening, "when I attended every gala, every opening."

"I imagine today's galas can hardly hold a candle to the grand balls of your time," said Kai.

"Well, there was one particular night," the landlady continued, "at the Governors' Ball, when a dispute over a magical artifact almost led to a duel right in the middle of the dance floor. The energy! Oh, but those days grow further behind me."

"What about Lilimari? I gather the university is on winter break until next week," I suggested in desperation.

"I happen to know that you own formal attire," Kai pointed out.

It was true, although I didn't know how he knew that. When I had first come to the city, I had made a conscious effort to dress like a gentleman. I didn't want people to think I was a day laborer like most of the other centaurs here.

Cornered by Kai's logic and my own vanity, I relented with a sigh. "Fine. And you should go with the bow tie."

Kai beamed, victorious. "Splendid!"

"Go on, you two, enjoy yourselves," said the landlady, pushing off the doorway and returning to the kitchen.

I picked up my satchel and headed to my room, slowly warming to the idea of an evening of art and intrigue. After all, what's the worst that could happen?

The ballroom was a grand space within the Kami-Nihkia Club, a prestigious social club for the city's elite and wealthy. It exuded opulence, from its high ceilings adorned with intricate moldings to its polished parquet floor. Meteor crystal chandeliers cast a dazzling glow across the room. I breathed in deeply, taking in the room's atmosphere.

Elaborate flower arrangements, created by the most talented nymphs, filled the room with the aroma of a spring garden. The walls were painted in a rich, deep blue, and hung with paintings in gilt frames. Some of the still lifes wouldn't stay put, their brushstrokes shifting and sometimes revealing completely different subjects.

The interior matched the blue hue of my tailcoat and back trousers, which I paired with a white wing collar shirt and white front kilt. *Good, maybe I won't stand out too much if I blend into the walls.* What was I thinking—I was probably the only centaur in formal wear. I definitely stood out.

"How did you get invited to the gala, Kai?" I asked, adjusting my collar nervously. I had been convinced that the doorman would sense my inferiority and refuse me entry, but he had only glanced at the pair of invitations Kai had presented.

He smiled. "I have connections." He wore a black tailcoat and trousers, a white shirt with a stiff collar and a black bowtie. Above his pointed ears rested a top hat. I caught our reflection in a high arched window and had to admit that we both looked impressively dapper.

Elegantly dressed guests mingled and chatted with each other, sipping on wine and nibbling on miniature foods—*canapes*, Kai said they were called—while enjoying the art, including sculptures that were scattered around the room. As we walked, Kai pointed out various pieces, describing the technique and meaning behind them. I listened in silence while I continued to absorb the sights, sounds, and smells around me.

In the center of the room, people danced in swirls of brightly colored silk to a tune that eluded my grasp, performed by a six-person ensemble. A siren played the flute, a faun played the aulos, a centaur played a mellow-sounding horn, two pointy-eared Helvenkin played stringed instruments of different pitches, and the lone Sireliad kept the beat on a drum.

"I don't dance," I warned Kai.

"It's more fun to people-watch anyway," he said.

He proceeded to point out some of the other guests, including well-known art collector Nikos Demetriou, whom Kai expected would be after works from the rising young artist called Xena. And there was Tae Blackwood, who was on the Council of Governors.

"Look, Simarron," Kai murmured, his golden eyes shining with awe. He nodded toward a striking figure across the room. "That's Margot Fairwind."

I followed his gaze. "Who is she?" I asked, my curiosity piqued.

"Margot Fairwind is a champion Paganika player. I just love her sense of fashion, don't you?" Kai replied in an awed tone. "She has such a unique style, equally at home on the course or at a formal event, although it shouldn't fit either."

I nodded politely, taking in the impeccably tailored jacket paired with knee-length trousers and diamond-patterned stockings. "She certainly knows how to make an impression."

Not wanting to be caught staring, I looked away and thought I saw Professor Ashmin—but it was just a glimpse before the figure vanished in the crowd.

"Over there," Kai said, tilting his chin toward a pair of Bloodborns. "That's The Incredible Spectra and Alchemist Lysandros Garbor."

I followed his direction to an elegant figure who seemed carved from the night sky. She wore a flowing gown of black and silver, its fabric shimmering with embroidered necromancy runes that caught the light and danced like living things. She was speaking animatedly to a thin man in black velvet robes, but her presence dominated the space.

"That's Lysandros Garbor? I've been to his castle," I said, noticing that he wore a heavy amount of makeup that accentuated his eyes but didn't completely hide the dark circles beneath them. He appeared frail for a man in his middle years, his drooping nose lending him an air of weariness.

"Have you? It seems our centaur has found his way from the Wild-lands and into Kami-Nihkia high society with surprising ease."

"Perk of being a MASHA safety inspector," I said lightly.

"Well, never mind *him*, look at *her*," Kai said. The crowd seemed to orbit The Incredible Spectra, acknowledging her with quick glances or murmured greetings. She responded with sharp-toothed smiles, drawing everyone into her sphere without ever losing focus on Garbor. It was as if she commanded the ballroom simply by existing.

"She's . . . impressive," I admitted, watching how effortlessly she held the room's attention.

Kai let out a quiet scoff. "Oh, absolutely. A genius in her own way. But it's all an illusion, Simarron. You should watch her perform sometime."

"I can't tell if you admire her or mock her," I said, giving him a sidelong glance.

"Why can't it be both?" Kai replied with a faint smirk. "I respect anyone who can hold a room in the palm of their hand. But The Incredible Spectra uses her brilliance to blind people to the truth. She's a performer, and behind all the glamour she's simply Anya Vedeva, the circus girl who learned how to make a spectacle. I, on the other hand, am a seeker and teller of *true* stories." He adjusted his bow tie and shifted his gaze to another direction. "Now, look away, and listen."

"We've put so much effort into this venture," Anya was saying. "You're still serious about this, aren't you? The spirits are whispering worrying things."

Lysandros's voice was measured. "My resources are not limitless."

"But Les, this is our dream, a place where magic and entertainment intertwine. I thought you believed in it as much as I do."

"I do, but certain . . . complications have been brought to light. If I show you the money, will that convince you?"

I risked a glance at the pair and saw Anya gesturing to a passing server. The man seemed startled as he approached, holding the tray awkwardly, perhaps overly awed by her presence. Anya plucked two goblets of wine with a dramatic gesture, accented by the flowing sleeves of her gown. "Then let's toast to our success," she said, holding a glass out to Lysandros.

"I'll toast to that," he said, raising his crystal goblet.

Anya paused, noticing my gaze on her, and my face grew warm with embarrassment. But Kai was already turning my attention to another set of guests.

"Over there, by that painting. There's Tia and Vanadar, her bad news beau." His golden eyes narrowed in disgust.

I followed Kai's gaze to find Tia. She was wearing her fiery hair in an intricate style and dressed in a beautiful gown. Phosphorous red skirts swirled out from her in luxurious layers when she moved, and beads of dark red beryl and translucent amber caught the light.

Next to her was a man who also stood out from the other guests—not because of his attire, which was baggy on his thin frame and dreadfully outdated—but because of the confidence that exuded from him. His chin was held high, and above it were strikingly bright green eyes that gleamed like a cat's as they discussed the painting before them.

"The brushstrokes lack direction," he said, loud enough for us to hear.

Tia said nothing, her jaw clenched.

"I have big plans for the Van Adair name, and for you, my love. But you must trust my guidance," he continued. "I understand the art world."

Tia, self-consciously playing with a loose curl, briefly glanced over her shoulder.

"Should we go talk to them?" I asked, but Tia immediately turned away and pulled the man elsewhere. I'd barely met her, yet I wondered if I had somehow upset her. "Kai, why is he bad news?"

"She thinks Vanadar is handsome and brooding, but he's just cold. He's old money and says his family has shaped the artists of this city, but he just likes to be in control. He tells Tia what to paint and even how to dress when . . . well, look at him. I've seen beggars with a better sense of style," Kai said softly. "And he clearly uses a cheap glamour spell to enhance his looks," he added with a sniff.

I approached the painting, a beautiful sunset over a lake in hues of red and orange that reminded me of Tia's hair. My eye was drawn to the signature in the corner—Tia Larose. A great gulf of incongruity opened between what I now observed and comments recalled from moments earlier.

How could Vanadar criticize her talents so harshly? I felt like I was on the banks of the lake, looking out of Tia's eyes as her hair engulfed me. The wind carried the faint scent of roses as it rippled the water. The depth of color and sense of movement drew me in like none of the other paintings on display.

It was with reluctance that I moved on, but I needed a break from the crowded environs. Leaving Kai to work the room, I headed outside to the balcony. The elevated terrace provided a breathtaking view of the river, and I lingered there, enjoying the reflections mirrored on its dark surface and the melodic applause of water cascading over rocks—a natural complement to the music emanating from the ballroom.

After a while, my ears perked up at the sound of Tia's voice, barely audible over the noise of the gala and the rushing river but clearly distressed. I waved her over to join me.

"Is something wrong?" I asked.

Tia wrung her gloved hands, muttering, "Why would someone do that?"

"Do what?" I was momentarily distracted by her perfume—the floral scent had a bitter edge that caught me off guard.

"The painting! I just went to check on it and I noticed the damage. Someone is trying to ruin my artistic debut," she wailed, tears in her eyes.

"It looked beautiful to me. I didn't notice any damage, but maybe it was an accident," I suggested calmly.

"Three regular scrapes along the edge. No, I don't think so." She tossed her head angrily, her cheeks flushed with emotion. "I can't deal with this. I'm going home," she announced, storming away before I could think of something else to say.

I gestured helplessly after her, watching her red curls disappear into the crowd.

Feeling I should rejoin the party, I found Kai in a newly formed queue to view a special painting. One work of art was hidden in an area that had been curtained off, and it had guests in a titter. I guessed it was probably a nude, although there were various paintings hung on the walls of two-leggers and wildfolk that demonstrated a profound understanding of anatomy in all its varied forms.

Outside the curtain, I spied Lysandros Garbor's scarecrow figure speaking with a Helvenkin woman who managed to look both delicate and healthily rotund, her luscious beauty stuffed in a peach gown.

"That's Benefactor Tae Bellwyn, a prominent socialite and philanthropist, married to Governor Tae Blackwood. She organized the gala, and all the proceeds will go to the local healing sanctuary," said Kai.

I nodded appreciatively. The music was in full swing, each note climbing toward a crescendo. As we approached the mysterious exhibit, I heard Bellwyn talking to a small crowd, including Lysandros.

"Enjoying the gala so far, Alchemist Garbor? Behind this curtain is a rare piece with a mysterious past. You've likely heard the rumors, tales of unexplained phenomena and a spectral presence. Some say that the brush of the unknown artist captured not only the subject's likeness, but that the spirit is trapped within the canvas."

Her gaze flicked toward the closed curtain. "Such tales may simply be the product of vivid imaginations and the mystique surrounding Château Gorget, but one never knows. We've kept it covered to protect it from modern lighting, of course, but also to spare the faint of heart."

After this pronouncement, Lysandros eagerly slipped through the curtain. Kai and I waited our turn outside, my curiosity piqued by the mention of Château Gorget.

In the peak moment of my impatience, there was a scream and the sound of a body falling hard to the floor. Surprised, I lunged forward and flung open the curtain to see Lysandros lying on the floor in a crumpled heap.

Anya rushed to his side, her gown swishing with her urgent stride. "Les, what's happening?" she exclaimed.

Lysandros, struggling for breath, managed a strained response. "I don't know. Something's . . . not right."

"He's having a seizure!" Anya cried, frantically gesturing for help. Gasps and shocked whispers rippled through the crowd.

"I know healing magic. Make room!" Bellwyn rushed forward and, begging the blessing of the gods, performed a spell while others sent for a sanctified physick. Most of the crowd stepped back, while others craned their necks to see what was happening.

Physicks quickly arrived on the scene and took over Lysandros's care. I watched in shock as two centaurs loaded him onto a stretcher and rushed him out of the ballroom. A siren began calling her piercing wail, clearing everyone from their path. The music stumbled to a halt.

As the ballroom began to empty, curiosity got the better of me—I had to see the haunted painting for myself. I ducked behind the curtain I had roughly shoved aside earlier. Lysandros's cup lay in glittering shards on the parquet floor. What I saw framed on the wall took my breath away.

My heart pounded and my muscles tensed, ready to bolt. Every instinct screamed that I was in danger, yet my hooves felt rooted to the spot. My vision began to tint red.

Then, a gentle hand touched my arm, cutting through the haze of panic.

"Let's go," said Kai.

Chapter Seven

The next day, I still couldn't shake the memory of the haunted painting from my mind. My housemates and I were having breakfast together in the dining room, as had become our morning routine. Sunlight filtered through the sheer curtains, casting a warm glow over the figures seated in the mismatched chairs arranged around the table.

Lilimari sat at one end of the table in silence, fiddling with her bread knife while reading from a book. I sat on my haunches on the floor on the opposite end, savoring my toast with preserves. Kai and Landlady Lyness were sipping their tea while conversing in soft tones. Tia was chewing loudly and reading the front page of the newspaper.

Despite the cozy scene, my thoughts kept returning to the haunted painting and its subject—a dark-haired woman looking down at her clasped hands. Disturbingly, the lines of her furrowed brow had also suggested a second pair of eyes. Moths fluttered around her head in the twilight, the sky expressed in energetic strokes of purple flowing into pink . . .

My nose twitched at the memory. There was also a peculiar smell: dark and musty, like decaying wood, tinged with the sharp metallic scent of blood, layered with red roses and garlic.

The smell had filled my senses and consumed me, until it felt like I was inside the painting itself, trapped behind her downcast eyes, my vision tinting red. I'd never felt anything like it before. But almost as soon as the fear had flooded me, it ebbed. Was this the power of the painting? Could it really cause people to seize in fear?

I was snapped back to the present by the rattling of a newspaper. Tia's hands were quivering.

"What is it?" I asked.

Tia looked up, her face pale as she turned the paper to face me. "BRUSH WITH DOOM: Man's Mysterious Death Linked to Exclusive Art Exhibition," written by someone named Manrik Skrift.

I glanced at Kai, his brow furrowed. The portrait depicted in the engraving could only be . . .

"Lysandros Garbor, alchemist and investor, age 56," Tia confirmed.

"Simarron and I were there when he suffered from a seizure," said Kai. "When the physicks arrived I thought, 'thank the Goddess.'"

"But it seems he didn't make it," I said, feeling ill.

Kai sighed, setting down his teacup with a soft clink. "How did I not hear about this until *The Mercury* printed it? What else does it say?" He reached across the table, but Tia sat further back in her chair, moving the paper out of his reach.

After a few moments of scanning the print, Tia continued reading aloud. "The article doesn't say much," she said. "Just that Alchemist Garbor, with ambitious plans to renovate Château Gorget, unfortunately met an untimely demise, ostensibly from fright after viewing a mysterious painting. Et cetera, et cetera . . . However, the City Watch has not ruled out foul play, and the writer is of the opinion that the possibility of a ghostly intervention is not to be dismissed either. His alleged final words as he collapsed were, 'If this is what awaits us in the afterlife, I want no part of it.'" She shook her head and tossed the paper behind her into a wicker wastebasket.

I opened my mouth, but no words would come out. That wasn't what Lysandros Garbor said! I was there, and he'd barely been able to gasp for breath.

The rest of the group seemed equally unable to speak, each contemplating the gravity of the news. The landlady was the first to break the silence, slowly lowering her teacup to the table. "This is terrible news, but why would the City Watch suspect foul play if he died from a seizure?"

"The poor old man might have simply died from fright. The painter couldn't possibly have known that would happen," said Tia, her own cup untouched.

"Nobody is suggesting that the painting is to blame, are they? Simarron saw it, too, and nothing happened to him." Kai paused. "What did it look like?"

I described the portrait of the raven-haired woman with an unsettling gaze. "It was beautiful, but there was also something about it that disturbed me. It wasn't just that the painting seemed to warp and shift subtly. Other paintings at the gala had combined art and illusion, but this was different." My hand went to my chest as I recalled the complex scent that had overwhelmed my senses and nearly given me a panic attack. It was too difficult to explain to my housemates. "I . . . I don't know what it was, but I have to admit that it almost spooked me."

"How horrible. If it *was* dark magic, the perpetrator of this sinister scheme was likely in the ballroom with us, waiting for the intended target to fall under the spell of the malicious masterpiece," Kai concluded with a shudder.

"Dark magic or not, the entire event seems to have fallen under a shadow," Landlady Lyness said thoughtfully, her gaze softening as she looked at Tia. "I'm sorry, I know this isn't how you wanted to debut your art." She reached across the table to gently clasp the other woman's hand in one of her own.

Tia stiffened. "What do you mean?"

"Your *Sunset Over Silver Lake* is truly beautiful, but unfortunately few will remember the art displayed at the gala now," the landlady replied with a rueful smile.

I rose from the table and retrieved the discarded newspaper. "Most of the article is actually about the haunted painting." Tia had skipped that part, not that it added anything of much worth.

"'Rumors suggest that the painting itself may be the culprit,'" I said, skimming the next line. "'One guest, visibly shaken, allegedly claimed to hear faint whispers emanating from the ancient artwork moments before Garbor fell.'" I paused. That didn't happen.

"Before this unfortunate news broke, I had already started hearing inquiries about the painting," said Kai. "Supposedly it survived the disaster at Château Gorget eighty years ago, but no one at the gala knew who the artist was, not even Tae Bellwyn."

"That poor old man," Tia muttered, shaking her head. She had slumped in her chair and her deep blue eyes were focused on her lap. "To be denied dignity in his passing, with everyone focused on a silly painting and spreading stories."

Lilimari had been silent through the meal so far and surprised us all with her casually insolent tone when she set her knife down and replied. "Garbor? Please." She rolled her eyes as she spoke in her pinched voice, which somehow always sounded like she had a slight cold.

"It's just, umb, Garbor was successful and all, but I can't help but feel that people like him are too obsessed with money. Actual progress comes from those who are true to the pursuit of alchemy and the wonders it can bring to the world, not just riches, you know."

"Lysandros Garbor did have quite the reputation for being fiercely competitive, even resorting to rather underhanded methods to achieve his goals," Kai commented, raising a single eyebrow.

"And look where that got him. Dead, possibly scared to death by an over-hyped painting. Or maybe by a ghost, if such a thing is possible," Lilimari said, her tone a mix of mockery and genuine curiosity. She leaned forward, her voice dropping to a conspiratorial whisper. "You know, I've noticed something about this house."

"Something unusual, Lilimari?" asked the landlady, her eyes narrowing slightly.

"Yeah, unexplained phenomena, especially at night," Lilimari replied, her lips curling into a sharp-toothed grin. "Strange sounds, flickering lights, and, umb . . . I think I've seen something, someone, in the hallways."

Kai's golden eyes gleamed with intrigue, and Tia looked up from her lap, her expression a mix of skepticism and fear.

"So I've been doing some research," Lilimari continued, launching into a discussion of alchemical residues and spectral activity, and their potential to redefine foundational theories.

Landlady Lyness interrupted, rising from her chair. "Spectral activity, what nonsense! But just in case there's a rogue necromancer going about, I shall be securing the doors nightly at ten o'clock and laying a stronger protection spell."

I snorted as I tried to imagine a black-robed magician of the dead sneaking into homes and enchanting paintings. There were many works of art adorning the walls at Slant Row Boarding House in dusty old frames, including portraits of the Lyness family ancestors and watercolors of flowers and fruit, but they were hardly the stuff to inflict terror. On second thought, the formal paintings of children were a bit unsettling.

"But I work late at the tavern sometimes," Tia protested with a grimace.

"I beg your landlady's pardon, but it hardly seems like a random act," I suggested in defense of our collective freedom.

"The curfew goes for all of you," said the landlady, looking at each of us in turn, her plump fists balled on her hips. "I won't risk the safety of my tenants."

"Great Goddess protect us all," said Kai wryly, his fingers brushing the amulet that hung around his neck. Whether he sought protection from our overzealous landlady or a rogue necromancer, his tone left it unclear.

I nodded absently, my mind racing. Most everyone seemed too quick to pick up the fantastical yarn spun out in *The Mercury*, but the reporting irritated me. I glanced at the byline. While Manrik Skrift knew how to craft a compelling story, I knew he was bending the truth. I dropped the newspaper back into the bin.

Yet the idea that Lysandros Garbor had simply dropped dead at the gala due to a seizure seemed equally implausible. The strange subject of the painting and its enigmatic scent refused to fade from my senses.

What truly gnawed at me, though, was the question of why anyone would resort to necromancy—or any other underhanded tactic—to harm someone, especially someone as frail as the alchemist. In the Wildlands, the weaker members of the herd were protected, not preyed upon. Disputes where violence became unavoidable were settled through fair contest, not treachery. The very thought of such behavior didn't sit right with me.

Deep in my bones, I knew I had to pursue what had really happened to the alchemist and former—albeit briefly—client, and set the record straight. Was it murder?

Chapter Eight

Was it murder? I repeated to myself once I'd reached my office. I revisited the chaotic events of the previous night again in my mind, and two figures stood out in the blur—Anya Vedeva and Tae Bellwyn. Both had been near Lysandros Garbor when he had collapsed.

I picked up my beautiful steel pen, so much superior to the quills I was used to, and pulled out my journal, flipping past the pages recalling the events at the castle site. I made a quick sketch of The Incredible Spectra on one side of the page and Benefactor Tae Bellwyn on the other. Inspired by the stack of forms on my desk, I made up a little outline beneath each portrait: *Name/Occupation/Connection to Lysandros Garbor*.

Based on her attire, Anya Vedeva wasn't just a performer, she was a necromancer too. She seemed to be doing some sort of business with Garbor, a venture connected to the castle he had purchased. If the haunted painting was possessed by a spirit, could she have controlled it?

Then there was Tae Bellwyn, a philanthropist. I wasn't sure what relationship she had to Garbor. Was it possible that the healing spell she had performed on him had done the opposite?

As someone from the Wildlands, where large feats of magic were rare and centaur wizards were unheard of, I was fascinated by the possibilities that the wizards here could conjure. They could manipulate the environment around them, bending the elements of fire, air, water, and metal to their will.

How their healing magic worked, I wasn't sure, other than it was normally performed at a temple called a healing sanctuary. I guessed they might have their own healing herbs and rituals, similar to those of my herd. But this death magic—necromancy—it was completely foreign to me.

For centaurs, magic involved making pacts with nature to bring about desired outcomes. The ability to communicate in this way was believed to be inherent in all centaurs to some degree, but I had never felt very skilled at it. And the magic of the two-leggers represented one of the most curious aspects about them.

The ink had just dried when Mina appeared in my office. I snapped my journal shut and stood up.

"Alchemist Garbor, he—" I began.

"I know." Mina cut me off, though her brusqueness didn't seem directed at me. "The City Watch has made it quite clear that they'll handle this case. However, Garbor's permit lists a business partner, and we still have a safety inspection report to complete. That is our duty."

Mina led me to the building's laboratory. The room was a smaller version of Professor Ashmin's lab, lined with shelves heavy with glass jars of compounds and various pieces of equipment. Charts and diagrams were framed on the walls, and the air was thick with the scent of herbs and chemicals.

A long polished table occupied the room's center. A shaft of light from the glass hatch above, operated by a pulley to ventilate the room, cast a soft glow on the table.

I lifted the wooden sample case onto the table and opened it with a sense of anticipation. The slightly musty smell of the earth collected at the castle site wafted up.

"Lab safety rule number one?" Mina prompted.

Abashed, I stepped back from the table and put on a pair of brass frames fitted with clear glass lenses. "Safety goggles must be worn at all times."

Mina nodded approvingly and set up what she called a "spirit lamp"—a small lamp with a polished brass base and a glass reservoir.

"Do spirits . . . tell us what's in the earth?" I asked.

"Spirits as in alcohol, for the fuel," she clarified. "The flames will tell us what's in the samples. As will the air, water, and the earth's own voice."

Mina turned to the shelves and began selecting ingredients. "Copper, the Reactor. Zinc, the Revealer. Aluminum, the Reflector. Magnesium, the Illuminator," she intoned, as if performing a ritual.

"Titanacala, protect us from any corruption in this soil, but do not shield us from the truth," said Mina, her demeanor as solemn as a priestess. Runes etched into the laboratory table— corresponding to the elements of fire, air, water and metal—began to glow.

With methodical grace, Mina combined the copper flakes with the soil in the first vial. She filled up the slender tube with water, then stirred the mixture and touched the vial to the flame. She repeated the process with the powdered zinc, aluminum, and magnesium.

As the flames kissed the final vial, a faint pink hue blossomed in the soil's solution. I watched as the mixture turned a delicate rose that slowly deepened. Mina's eyes narrowed behind her brass-framed goggles.

"Arsenic," she said softly, as if the word itself was dangerous.

I blinked. "Arsenic?" The word tasted unfamiliar on my tongue, like that of so many of the new elements.

"It's not a problem where it naturally slumbers in rocks beneath the earth. In small amounts, it is a popular ingredient in potions to cure everything from bone marrow blight to bad complexions. However, small amounts build up over time, and prolonged exposure can be fatal. It can seep into the water, into the air. People can waste away before they realize what is happening."

A poison lurking unseen in the very ground beneath my hooves. The thought made my stomach tighten. Where I came from, threats were tangible—a dire wolf's claw, a storm on the horizon. Although skilled healers could use poisonous plants to cure, too, so I supposed it made sense. These types of secrets were revealed through making pacts with the nature spirits and listening to the earth's wisdom.

But here, the wizards did not wait for the land to whisper. They reached out with their own hands and made it speak.

"These four metals you used," I said, "they bend matter to reveal things that are hidden?"

"We don't 'bend' anything, not in the way you're thinking. They say the elemental gods are silent, but each has its own language. We simply know how to listen."

The words sent an unexpected shiver through me. *Listening.* That was something I understood, but it seemed there was more than one way to listen.

By the time we finished, the case notes had begun to resemble an alchemical chart. We then returned to our desks, the air heavy with a metallic scent and the knowledge we'd uncovered, prepared to transcribe these findings. Yet my mind still swirled with uncertainties, lingering like the residue of a chemical reaction.

Mina periodically called me into her office to help clarify some detail or another. Trying to recall that day at the castle site felt inexplicably difficult. Why were our memories so slippery? Had it really only been two days ago? I was grateful for the journal entry I had made, and we relied on it heavily as we painstakingly put together our report.

Despite the space I occupied, I had felt small in the laboratory when faced with my limited view of the world. Was I capable of learning enough to perform my duties at MASHA, to protect people from unseen dangers as Mina did? But when my humble notebook proved invaluable in piecing together our findings, a quiet sense of pride swelled within me. However unfamiliar this world was, I had something to offer after all.

"The readings from the Magical Energies Detector suggest that a complex spell was performed recently," Mina noted, frowning. She had grown increasingly perturbed as we worked on the report.

"What kind of spell?" I asked curiously. "An invisibility spell?" My nose was telling me that there was more to the castle than we'd seen.

"The ability to hide something as large as a castle would require immense power, far beyond typical invisibility spells," she said. "During my time at the Bureau of Magical Inquiries, there was . . ." She shook her head. "Anyway, we aren't investigating a murder, merely doing our due diligence with a safety inspection." It sounded as if she were trying to convince herself as much as me.

I nervously shifted from hoof to hoof, the gravity of the situation settling in. "I was there last night when Lysandros Garbor collapsed, right after viewing the haunted painting. Some are saying it was a seizure, others a curse."

"Keep one eye open to wonder, the other to wisdom, and close your ears to the winds of deceit," she said. It sounded like the type of advice administered by priestesses, and I wondered where she'd learned that saying.

"I also smelled something strange when near the painting, like decaying wood mixed with iron . . . like blood."

"If we had the haunted painting, we could test that, but we don't. And this is about the safety inspection," she said firmly.

Mina began pulling some books from the shelf in her office. "I need to do some research. Simarron, contact Lysandros Garbor's business partner, Anya Vedeva, and ask her about any recent activities or spells that were performed there."

"All right. When does the Centaur Post arrive?" I said, taking the papers we'd been working on from her desk and returning them carefully to their envelope. I wound the string around the button on the outside flap, securing the envelope safely.

"Use the Witchy Whisk. That will be much faster," she advised, nodding her head toward the desk. "I keep some tokens on hand for payment."

It seemed that the eye on her pen stand watched me while I opened her desk drawer. Poking around, I pulled out a small metal disk engraved with arcane symbols surrounding a central eye.

Mina proceeded to teach me the incantation to summon the Witchy Whisk, a messenger service of witches on broomsticks:

"Through clouds and winds, they take to flight
Swift as a raven, day or night
On willow brooms, their journey brisk
I summon thee, now Witchy Whisk!"

Not even a quarter of an hour later, a young, pointy-eared witch entered the foyer, broomstick in hand. She wore a long swallowtail coat—no doubt allowing for comfort while seated—and pointed-toed boots. Her wide-brimmed hat was slightly peaked and adorned with an emblem bearing the same design as the token.

"You summoned Witchy Whisk, Safety Inspector?" she said, bowing slightly and holding out a gloved hand.

"Yes, I have a message for Necromancer Anya Vedeva," I said, handing her the token.

"Address, please? Or will you be needing a finding spell for an extra token?"

"I have the address, thank you."

Despite Mina's insistence on focusing on the safety inspection report, I was excited for the opportunity to conduct my own investigation into who I believed was a prime suspect.

Chapter Nine

A few Witchy Whisk messages later, I finally arranged to meet Anya Vedeva at a nearby tavern called The Angry Unicorn. She had declined to meet at MASHA, explaining that she feared being mobbed by fans and preferred the relative anonymity of the tavern.

I cut through a wooded park to find myself in Midtown, also called Mead Town, for the variety of breweries and taverns there. The narrow cobbled streets, still bearing traces of the melting snow, glistened under a pale, hazy sun as people hurried about their business. Steam puffed from hidden grates in the streets and the warm breath of passersby. I checked my pocket watch and hurried on, tucking it back into my vest pocket.

As I rounded the corner, my eyes were drawn to the bust of a single-horned beast protruding above the arched doorway of a brick building. Illusory flames sprang from its nostrils. Unconsciously ducking my head, I stepped through the door beneath its fierce gaze.

Inside, I was enveloped by the warm, inviting smells of the tavern: grilled meat, toasted bread, baked eel, roasted onions, and fermented grain mingled together, tantalizing my senses with their aromas, drawing me into the cozy place. The brick walls and exposed beam ceiling were lit cheerfully by a roaring hearth at the back, where a satyr piped a merry tune.

I spotted my housemate Tia Larose busy serving a group of men near the door. She glanced up at me and offered a friendly smile. The warmth melted the slushy snow from my hooves and I flicked the moisture from my tail. A cloth, moving as if by unseen hands, snaked over to the doorway and danced around my hooves as it soaked up the water.

From behind the bar—a long slab of polished wood—a wild-haired server wearing an animal skin top was pouring drinks and engaging animatedly with the patrons. The stools were all occupied by women, talking, laughing, and tapping feet along to the music. There was a brief dip in chatter as I passed by to curious glances.

I knocked into a table and cursed my clumsiness. Continuing around the corner, I pushed a chair out of the way and settled down on my haunches. Pulling off my satchel and cloak, I draped them on the chair. I wondered when Anya Vedeva would arrive, but I didn't have to wait long.

The tavern door burst open, and a Bloodborn woman swept inside as though she were stepping onto a stage. Her dark hair was pinned up with a golden comb and partially covered by a long veil. Golden hoops hung from her round ears and a matching pair encircled her slender wrists.

Anya paused dramatically in the doorway, striking a pose as if expecting a rapturous round of applause. Instead, the tavern patrons gave her little more than a passing glance before resuming their conversations, their tankards clinking and their laughter rumbling.

Undeterred, she slowly dropped her arms, as though lowering the curtain on a grand act. Her gaze swept the room until it landed on me. I gave her a small wave as she glided toward the back of the tavern where I sat.

"Ah, my dear fan!" she exclaimed upon her approach, voice carrying, ensuring that anyone who hadn't noticed her now would. "You are in the presence of The Incredible Spectra herself!" She smiled, revealing her pointed teeth, and gracefully sank into the seat across from me, positioning herself for maximum visibility.

I blinked, momentarily taken aback by the sheer force of her personality. "Well met. I'm Safety Inspector Simarron."

"Your message indicated you needed information for the permit." Her tone suddenly dropped, becoming serious. "However, with my partner's untimely demise, I have ceased all plans for our venture at Château Gorget." She dabbed at her eyes beneath the veil. "I was hoping you might enlighten me instead."

"My condolences on your loss. I'll help in any way I can," I assured her, though I wasn't sure what that might entail.

"What do you know about the haunted painting? Les was obsessed with it toward the end . . . believed it held some key to great power. Did it originate from Château Gorget and what role did it play in his death?"

"The Incredible Spectra—"

"Please, call me Anya."

"Anya, while I am a MASHA safety inspector, I can't confirm any supernatural properties of the painting based on my brief experience with it. I also don't know if it came from Château Gorget, so I'm afraid I can't help you there. As to what connections the painting or the castle might have to his death, perhaps we can figure that out. Why did Lysandros Garbor seek a MASHA inspection of a castle that apparently wasn't there?"

"There are many things that Les kept hidden from me. Initially, he was 'all-in'—to borrow one of his favorite phrases from the card games he so enjoyed—on our joint venture. Then, inexplicably, 'complications' began to arise. He explicitly forbade me from visiting the castle and refused to explain why."

"That's intriguing," I mused. "There might be something in the case notes. Recently, a powerful spell was cast there, something I intended to discuss with you."

Reaching into my satchel, I carefully extracted the envelope filled with case notes and handed them to her. I watched the necromancer's face as her eyes greedily devoured the words on the paper.

"Clearly someone has been trespassing," she hissed as she continued to read, her fingers trembling. Then her damp, kohl-rimmed eyes went wide as she looked up, her gaze fixed on a point behind me.

"What is it?"

Anya rose from her chair, dropping the papers back onto the table in one quick motion; she then turned in a swish of her skirts and walked away.

I looked behind me, but all I saw was our server coming to take our order.

"Anya?" I called.

I stood and followed her for a few steps, hesitating. If her entrance hadn't drawn much attention, her exit was certainly eliciting murmurs and stares. I watched as Lysandros Garbor's business partner fled the tavern and slipped out into the street. I clenched and released my fist, internally debating if I should follow her, frustrated by my uncertainty.

"So, what can I get for you, Simarron?" Tia asked.

I turned to face her, and for a moment, I swam in the Sireliad woman's stunning peacock blue eyes, which tapered gracefully toward the corners like the sweeping tail of that bird. I adjusted my collar and sat back down at the table, my troubles over Garbor's permit melting away like ice in water.

"Just a beer. Thanks, Tia." Though beer was quite bitter compared to the wine I was used to, I enjoyed its refreshing and less intoxicating qualities.

She left and returned shortly with a pewter mug brimming with beer. As she set it down on the table, I noticed a paintbrush pierced through her hair bun. A few loose curls of coppery red hair framed her oval-shaped face and faintly metallic freckles dotted her softly contoured nose.

"So you're an artist?" I asked. Mentally, I kicked myself for the stupid comment, but I was never good at small talk. Tia worked odd hours, and this was the first chance I'd really had to speak with her one-on-one.

She tucked a stray curl behind her ear and glanced down at the table. "Oh, I'm not very good, to be honest."

"I thought your painting at the art gala was outstanding," I said as I sipped my beer, inhaling the piney scent of the hops. The cool, golden liquid took me to an alpine meadow in the spring, dotted with blue and white wildflowers.

She gave me a half-smile and changed the subject. "What brings you here? Goddess, was that The Incredible Spectra who just left? I didn't even see her come in."

"Business meeting. MASHA," I responded, distracted. Taking another sip before setting down the mug, I suddenly imagined Tia painting a beautiful mountain landscape.

A loud whistle pierced the air, and we both turned to look toward the door. A group of rowdy customers had just entered, shouting and jostling their way to a table.

In my distraction, my elbow clipped the edge of my mug, tipping it over.

Tia reacted instantly, righting the overturned mug. I snatched up the case notes before the spreading liquid could reach them.

"Ah, sorry—" I said, momentarily setting the papers aside on a nearby chair while she grabbed a towel.

"Don't worry about it," she said, wiping the table as if she'd done it a thousand times.

"Thank you."

"Now I'd better get over there. Enjoy the rest of your beer!" she said over her shoulder, already headed toward the noisy new arrivals.

I slowly sank back into my troubled thoughts, eventually placing my empty beer mug on the table. I left a few bits of coin beside it for payment and headed back to work.

I was so lost in my thoughts as I made my way back through the park that I didn't notice the old woman until I collided with her. She stum-bled, then reached out flailing. She grabbed the strap of my satchel, then my arm, her grip surprisingly firm for someone so frail.

"Are you hurt?" I asked, alarmed, steadying her.

"Oh, my dear!" she exclaimed in a dry, creaking voice, her gnarled hands patting at my sleeve, then the front of my cloak, as if to check that I was real. "You gave me quite the start."

"I'm so sorry! I didn't see you," I said, my words tumbling out in a rush. The faint scent of pine needles and fresh earth surrounded her. Pale green hair, wiry and lacy like long chains of moss, spilled from beneath a floppy hat shaped like the cap of a mushroom.

"No harm done." Her skin, dark and weathered like tree bark, crinkled as she gave me a reassuring smile. She patted my shoulder one last time and tottered off down the path.

But when I returned to my office at MASHA, the harm done became glaringly clear. I opened my satchel and shuffled around with increas-ing panic. I felt the bottom drop out of my stomach. The envelope of case files was missing.

"It's not here," I mumbled, mortified. I took off my cloak and turned it inside out, refusing to believe my eyes. "The initial report, our case notes, they're gone." How could this have happened?

"What are you talking about?" demanded Mina, appearing in my office's doorway.

I patted myself down furiously. Anya had set them down on the table in the tavern. And I'd moved them briefly to the chair before returning them to my satchel, I was sure of it. "It must have been that old woman in the park!"

Mina beckoned me to her office and gestured for me to shut the door behind me.

"Explain, from the beginning. What exactly happened?" I felt the eye on her pen stand glaring at me.

Still patting down my pockets, I recounted my brief encounter in the park, describing the seemingly innocuous interaction with the elderly woman I now suspected of pickpocketing the case notes. I'd heard of such crimes happening in cities, but never imagined I would be targeted—and what reason could she possibly have had to steal them?

Mina listened intently, shaking her head. "It makes no sense. Regardless, we need to act quickly." She took the pen from its stand. "I'll initiate a finding spell. Meanwhile, you need to retrace your steps, Simarron. Think! Was there anything unusual about the woman? Anything that can help identify her?"

"She had a funny hat . . . I'll head back to the park immediately," I said. "She has likely disappeared by now, but there's a chance she could still be nearby. I'll talk to the locals—anyone who might have seen her—before she gets too far."

I hurried out of Mina's office, determined to repair my failure.

Chapter Ten

Late winter's daylight dwindled, tinting the sky pink, reminding me that time was slipping by as I raced to the park. The bare branches of the trees lining the stone walkways blurred past me and birds sang their evening songs in mocking tones against the thunder clop of my hooves. The air was thick with the scent of ancient trees and modern iron.

Near the park's center, by a cluster of wrought iron benches, I saw a woman in black clothing. Facing away from me, she was busy affixing a show bill to a nearby tree. It looked like Anya Vedeva, but it couldn't be her. Surely The Incredible Spectra was too important to put up her own billets.

"Good evening! Do you live around here?" I asked as I approached the cloaked figure, my breath rushing out in little clouds.

The woman finished pounding a tack into the trunk with a flourish. "Come see the awesome necromancy of The Incredible Spectra! She'll have you questioning what's real on this side of the river that divides our world and the Underworld. Watch as she calls upon the ancient spirits to make the Drakeus Kinrethys monument in the city square disappear!"

She smoothed the edges of the poster and turned to face me, striking a pose that mirrored her image on the poster. She was, indeed, Anya Vedeva. "Ah, dear fan, it's you again!"

"I don't mean to sound rude . . . Anya, but I'm in a bit of a hurry. I'm looking for a shabby-looking old lady who may live around here. Greenish hair, funny hat. Have you seen her? Please, it's important. I suspect she pilfered my belongings."

Her smile faded as her eyes narrowed. "Badly dressed, you say? Sounds like a wizard, and I suspect she may be the one tearing down my bills."

"Why would she do that?"

Anya sighed dramatically. "There's only one thing wizards hate more than alchemists, and that's necromancers. They say my magic isn't real, but what I do is an artform. Some wizards may be able to bend matter to their will, but I create a reality with my audience," she said, her sleeves trailing as she gestured expansively. "And what we create together can be even more real."

From the shadows of the trees, a voice rang out: "Anya Vedeva!"

We both spun to face the speaker, a disheveled old woman in a floppy hat shaped like a mushroom cap.

"You don't commune with the spirits, you fraud wizard. Leave my trees alone!"

"You there, thief!" cried Anya, which caused the other woman to bolt.

Then it dawned on me. The hair like moss, the bark-like skin, the voice like the rustle of dry leaves—she had to be a dryad. Trees were sparse on the open plains of my homeland, but I had encountered dryads before in the small, sacred groves that dotted the Wildlands.

"Wait, you're a dryad, aren't you? Please, I just want to talk to you!" I exclaimed, rearing up on my hind legs before leaping after the fleeing figure.

The dense foliage posed a challenge for my large body as I crashed through the tangled branches and thick shrubs. The dryad's form flickered in and out of view between the tree trunks before vanishing into the shadowy recesses of the urban grove.

I pawed the ground in frustration. "Curses!"

In answer, I heard a soft chuckle, seemingly echoing from all directions. "Catch me if you can!"

"Try to escape from this," said Anya, nearly out of breath from catching up. "By the power of Cythereus, master of transformation and shifting reflections, I weave your silvery threads . . ."

The park seemed to shift and warp, like a reflection in a pond disturbed by a ripple. Trees stretched and bent, their branches forming grotesque shapes and an almost impenetrable lattice overhead. The sun dipped lower in the sky, its vexing beams slicing through the tree trunks in eerie prismatic hues, creating a maze of shadows that played tricks on my eyes. I blinked, trying to make sense of the illusion.

"What the Hecatonchires?" I swore aloud. My voice bounced in strange directions—a whisper behind me, faint mocking laughter echoing. The air suddenly smelled warm and heavy, like a summer thunderstorm that rattled the plains—a specific stormy day from my foalhood I couldn't quite recall, as if the scent wafted in from a dream. A shadow darted across my path, and I sprinted after it, only to collide with a tree whose gnarly whorls resembled a face. Turning left twisted me to the right; moving forward only dragged me backward. Shadows became solid branches, while pale birch bark dissolved into shafts of light.

I had never been this lost and turned around before, not in all my time in the Centaur Post delivering parcels to strange places. The park was nearly unrecognizable as I knew it, but it reminded me rather of some misspent time in my youth. The other centaur foals had always made me play the monster, when we played "Minotaur in the maze."

The dryad maneuvered swiftly and effortlessly through the labyrinth of light and shadow that was shifting around me, her presence betrayed only by the faint rustling of leaves. Spotting her behind a large oak, I cautiously approached, but she vanished once more in a trail of laughter. Far from hindering her, Anya's spell seemed to conspire with the elusive dryad.

"Wait! I just want my envelope of notes back," I said, breathing heavily after an intense chase that had led me right back to the benches at the center of the park. My limbs were scratched; my mane was tangled with sticks and leaves.

"Cythereus, I release your silver threads!" Anya's voice cut through the illusion, instantly dissolving it.

Reality slid back into place with a gut-wrenching snap of branches and shaking of leaves.

The dryad reappeared briefly, glancing over her shoulder at me. Her face was shrouded in darkness, making it difficult for me to discern her expression as she spoke. "Sometimes, Safety Inspector, what's lost must remain so. Behind all things are reasons." Then, the green-haired dryad in the funny hat faded into the evening.

"Are you all right, my dear fan?" Anya's voice held genuine concern as she approached, her footsteps hurried on the stone path.

My head was bowed, my hands resting on my front knees. With a slight nod, I managed to assure her, "Yes, I'm fine, thank you. It's just. . . She got away."

"I'm afraid that hedge wizard has eluded us for now." She looked off into the trees, where the evening was deepening the shadows.

"You mean the dryad? I don't think she appreciated you nailing your show bills to her trees," I said, my tail lashing in frustration.

"Oh dear, is that so? I must apologize to her. And to you as well, for involving you in this mess. I didn't mean to ensnare you in my magic," Anya acknowledged with a sigh.

The park, no longer a twisted labyrinth, settled back into its tranquil routine. I brushed a few stray leaves from my mane, glancing around to make sure reality had fully returned.

"Well, that was . . . quite a performance," I said, still catching my breath.

"Magic is all about pushing boundaries. Though I admit, I may have gotten a bit carried away." She gave an apologetic smile.

"A bit?" I raised an eyebrow, but I found it was impossible to stay angry with her. Her charm was as polished as her tricks.

I walked with Anya partway to the inn where she was staying. She engaged me in conversation, not only regaling me with tales of her shows, but also asking me polite questions about my background and my hopes for my new life in Kami-Nihkia. As before, she was much better at drawing me out than I was at subtly steering the conversation to investigate her.

"If you make amends with the dryad," I ventured, "perhaps you can ask her to return my property."

"Yes, of course! Anything for a fan. You know, I performed in the Wildlands once, and the centaurs made me feel right at home. It was an amazing experience."

I smiled politely as I bid her a good evening, but I couldn't understand her at all, especially not her story about feeling welcome among the centaurs. And that spell she'd cast—based on what I'd read in MASHA's *Rules and Regulations* about the different branches of magic —it seemed to have more in common with illusion magic than necromancy.

My thoughts drifted back to our earlier conversation in The Angry Unicorn. Had Garbor really forbidden Anya from visiting the castle, as she claimed? If her expertise lay in illusion, could she have used it to conceal the castle itself? I recalled the faint magical signature the MED had picked up—a residue of something complex and deliberately woven. Could it have been her magic, cloaking secrets within the castle grounds?

And then there was her demeanor. She had switched so effortlessly into her showman persona, pushing aside any hint of grief for her business partner's death. Her earlier flash of emotion had vanished like a wisp of smoke. What was the act, and what was real? Anya seemed to revel in mystery and performance. Her lively manner almost felt too polished, too rehearsed. Had she secretly wanted Garbor out of the way of some ulterior goal?

There was also the question of her connection to the haunted painting—the one some claimed had taken his life. She had asked me about it at The Angry Unicorn, but could she know more than she was letting on? It was hard to shake the feeling that Anya was hiding more than just her trade secrets. She was an enigma, and my case notes might be missing, but I wasn't done investigating the connection between Château Gorget and Lysandros Garbor's death.

Chapter Eleven

"Good morning, Director. I was hoping to work on the Château Gorget case today," I announced as I walked into Director Moosekind's office the following morning, navigating around disheveled stacks of paperwork.

"Simarron, what's this about?" Moosekind looked up from his cluttered desk with a distracted expression. Scattered with papers and magical artifacts used as paperweights, it was a stark contrast to Mina's meticulous workspace.

I charged ahead. "Alchemist Garbor's death must be connected to his MASHA file."

"If it is, that's for the City Watch to decide. Anyway, you mustn't trouble yourself about these rumors, alarming as they seem. I'm not sure what passes for news reporting in the Wildlands—if anything— but you can't trust everything you read in *The Mercury*."

I flinched, the dismissive comment delivering an unexpected sting. "But Director, couldn't we possibly have information that may be useful to the City Watch in their investigation?"

Moosekind sighed. "Look, Simarron, I appreciate your enthusiasm, but we should leave it to the City Watch to do their jobs. We have our own cases to focus on. It's a confounded shame, it is. One mysterious death, and the entire city's in an uproar. Meanwhile, people die need-lessly every day from improper magic and alchemy safety, and no one bats an eye."

I opened my mouth to protest, but Moosekind held up a hand. "That's an order, Simarron. Leave it alone. I need you to organize the storage room today. Mina will show you how to get started." He then turned back to his paperwork, effectively ending the conversation.

Mina appeared in the doorway and cleared her throat.

As she stoically led me away to my task, or perhaps my punishment, my thoughts buzzed around my head like flies. They kept landing on Lysandros's strange death. Flicking my tail in frustration, I resolved to bury my disappointment for now and do some digging on my own time.

"I found the old woman . . . a dryad," I said softly, my earlier confidence dashed. "I believe she lives in the park. I don't think she'll give the case notes back. She simply laughed when I asked," I added, hanging my head.

Mina paused as we reached the storage room, her expression turning serious as she faced me. "Under normal circumstances, we should be notifying the City Watch about the theft," she began, her voice low. "However, Director Moosekind is concerned about how seriously they take us at MASHA. In any case, the finding spell didn't show a dryad's home but a unicorn's domain—any idea what that could mean?"

My ears pricked up. "The tavern where I interviewed Anya Vedeva is called The Angry Unicorn. Could that be it?"

"I'll follow up on this myself while you get the storage room sorted," said Mina. "We need to handle this discreetly but swiftly." She spun away, her steps echoing away down the corridor.

If my office was the old records storage, then the storage room was a cave where relics of the past languished, too old to die. I suspected MASHA had inherited the mess from the previous occupants, the defunct Bureau of Magical Inquiries. The lamplight dimly illuminated a dusty space, filled with shelves that sagged under the weight of the former organization's history. I sullenly mulled over my thoughts while gazing at the forgotten equipment, wooden boxes, and various paraphernalia.

A lot of the wooden boxes were filled with paperwork, labeled by a series of numbers and symbols. Many of the objects wore paper tags labeled in the same scheme. I opened the lid on one box to reveal a cloud of dust and a collection of papers dating back decades. One document was a list of evidence penned on parchment, stamped by the Bureau of Magical Inquiries. These must be old case files, then.

I started sorting through the boxes, making a pile for each case. Once I had everything sorted, I began to put the evidence away on the shelves, matching the tags to the case they belonged to. A lot of it consisted of confiscated alchemy equipment, from the days when alchemy was outlawed. There were illegal potions from witches too, and the wand of a wizard who had cast sections of the city into an enchanted slumber. Wands, as I understood, weren't required for the magic of the two-leggers, but they had been in fashion in the previous century. This one, with its arcane carvings, certainly made a statement.

Before now, I hadn't thought about the social impact of gathering this many powerful practitioners of magic in one place. There must have been a need for order, and the Bureau of Magical Inquiries had cracked down hard on those activities deemed too dangerous for society. But their methods were perhaps a bit too heavy-handed, I thought, eyeing a pile of silver chains and manacles piled in a corner.

A few of the boxes bore an ominous marking, a peculiar seal depicting what looked like the bones of a hand arranged in a snowflake pattern. These cases didn't have much evidence associated with them, if any. *Soul Anchor: Unsolved* read the notes of one such case. I shivered and dropped the lid back on the box.

In another pile, I set aside things that I was unsure of where else to place: evidence that had lost their tags and couldn't be identified any other way, as well as various jars with unidentified contents. One of the mystery jars contained an acrid smelling substance that reminded me of something just beyond the edge of recognition. I jerked away instinctively. I felt like I had crawled out of a dark river, my throat burning from coughing up fetid water.

"That's ectoplasm," Mina informed me of the white, wispy gauze-like substance when she came to check up on me some time later.

"Do we need it?" I asked. I had easily lifted even the heaviest boxes and crates, but the contents of this jar bothered me. I found I didn't want to touch it as I maneuvered my large body in the small room. I had pushed it into a corner, as far from myself as possible, with the edge of a hoof.

"No, but it's a very rare and expensive component used in powerful potions and spells. I'll put it in the lab for safekeeping." She picked up the jar without hesitation or concern. "How are things coming along here?"

I nodded toward the organized chaos. "It's sorted for the most part. But what about the case notes? Any luck at The Angry Unicorn?"

Mina's expression darkened slightly. "The case notes weren't there. It seems they've been moved." A sigh escaped her lips, frustration evident. "Then, the finding spell showed a lake shore at sunset. It's very possible the notes have been destroyed in water."

"Could Anya have taken them without me noticing?" I asked rhetorically, racking my brain. What had she seen in them that had apparently disturbed her so deeply? I distinctly remembered her dropping them on the table before she left—or had that been an illusion too?

"Well, if she's destroyed them, I guess we'll never know," I said.

Mina gave a small nod, but the downturned curve of her red lips painted a clear picture of her disappointment. I could feel her sharp eyes re-evaluating my reliability. "I'll keep an eye out for any traces of the notes or any indication that they might still be out there. But for now, we must focus on the work at hand. We have other pressing duties that require our attention."

She turned to leave the storage room. Guilt settled over me like the hush after a slammed door, although the door remained open. There was no way to recover what I'd lost, probably not even with magic. I breathed in sharply, my chest tight.

Then my nose twitched. Something was nagging my senses. I turned back to the jar of ectoplasm, feeling a chill creep up my spine. My instinct told me I had smelled it before—at Château Gorget! But that was impossible . . . or was it?

"Mina?" I said, then hesitated. What if I was wrong? Maybe it wasn't what I'd smelled at the castle site. Without reliable facts, I could be jumping to a conclusion based on a gut reaction. Maybe I just wanted to find a connection where there wasn't one. This was no time to look foolish in front of Mina, not when I was trying to prove I could do the job.

She poked her head back through the open doorway. "What is it?"

I cleared my throat and coaxed the words out, soft and uncertain. "Could ectoplasm be used in spells powerful enough to . . . say, obliterate a castle? Or . . . at least one's memories of it?"

Mina frowned. "Ectoplasm is typically a byproduct of spiritual manifestations. It's rare and highly potent. If someone is using it in spells, they're creating some dangerous magic."

"Should we check if there was any ectoplasm left at the castle site?" I asked, wincing at the eagerness in my tone.

"No," she said firmly, gripping the jar. "Director Moosekind has closed the Château Gorget file. Now that Lysandros Garbor is gone and his business partner doesn't wish to continue, there's no need for a permit. We have an appointment to inspect a potion atelier today."

Her words from yesterday echoed in my mind. "That is our duty," she had said, as if completing the safety inspection report would fulfill some greater purpose. But I was beginning to question whether simply following procedure could keep anyone safe.

"Simarron," she said, her tone softening just a touch, "your curiosity and instincts are valuable, but we can't get hung up on every detail, or we'll lose sight of the work at hand. File these observations away in that sharp brain of yours. Let's see what you pick up at the potion atelier. Your instincts might lead us to something important there."

I nodded in outward agreement, but I knew I wouldn't be putting my observations too far out of reach. What if Anya Vedeva had made Lysandros Garbor disappear in the most permanent way? A duty stirred within me to uncover the truth. I had ignored my sense of smell that day at the castle site, and now someone was dead. I was a safety inspector, and the city wasn't safe if there was a killer on the loose.

Chapter Twelve

The bell above the door chimed as Mina and I stepped into North Star Potions & Remedies, an atelier with an attractive storefront nestled on Gold Row. Despite its name, which conjured images of wealth and alchemical success, the street had yet to yield a single ounce of gold, earning a reputation instead for the wide variety of workshops and stores it had cultivated.

The air inside was thick with the mingled scents of dried herbs and the metallic tang of potions simmering in the back room. Tall windows inlaid with colored glass, skillfully created by alchemists, let in the light. Meteor crystal lamps hung from the ceiling, while smaller crystals lit the shelves of wares from behind. I carefully maneuvered between the displays, examining the bottles and jars filled with colorful liquids and mysterious powders, each promising relief or enhancement of some kind.

"Good afternoon," the woman behind the counter greeted us, her eyes darting nervously between my large form and her delicate wares. "How can I help you?" She had a bewitching smile and smooth dark skin—but her eyes, sparkling like those of Sireliad heritage, seemed old and wise.

"Good morning, Wiz. North," Mina replied, using the honorific for wizards and witches. "I'm Administrator Hereswith from MASHA and this is Safety Inspector Simarron. We're here to conduct an inspection."

Elodie North's smile faltered. "Oh . . . of course."

I searched the shop until I spotted a glass vial labeled "North Star Skin Restorative"—the one mentioned in the complaint—in the tall display behind the counter. "Can you tell me about this product?" I asked, pointing at it.

The wizard reached for the beautifully labeled blue vial and held it up. "This is one of our most popular potions. It's made with a blend of herbs, valued for their healing properties for centuries, combined with pure concentrations of the new elements. By the power of traditional and new potion-making combined, it will cure any skin condition."

"I noticed the symbol for arsenic is on the label. Can you tell me about your company's use of this substance?" I asked.

Elodie North's demeanor shifted. "I'm sorry, but I cannot divulge that information. Our exact formula is a closely guarded secret."

"Wiz. North, I'm afraid we must insist," said Mina, stepping in. "The use of arsenic in potions is highly regulated, and we need to ensure that your shop is adhering to proper safety protocols. Simarron, the MED?"

"I can assure you, we are following all necessary protocols," the wizard said firmly, casting a suspicious glance while I unpacked the Magical Energies Detector.

"Hold the wand firmly, like this, but handle it with care," Mina instructed. Her words echoed with an uncanny familiarity, as if I'd heard them before. A fleeting memory stirred—standing in a castle courtyard—but before I could grasp it, it slipped away.

She continued, "First, calibrate the MED by pointing to a neutral location."

I unclipped the wand from the wooden box and pointed it at the door, while Mina jotted down the base readings. I turned it toward the vial the shopkeeper held. The dials on the box quivered only slightly, and I worried that I was doing it wrong. I glanced sideways at Mina, but she indicated nothing as she recorded the readings in her notes.

I held the slender wand against several other vials of the same product, each receiving the same neutral result.

"Consistent, good. May we see the production area?" asked Mina.

The wizard's expression hardened, and she crossed her arms. "I'm sorry, but I cannot allow that."

Mina took a deep breath and tried a different approach. "Wiz. North, I understand that your shop has a valuable product, and I respect that. But I assure you that our inspection is not meant to harm your business. In fact, we can prove that the complaint about your skin restorative being a fraud is untrue."

The shop owner hesitated, but finally relented. "Very well. I can show you the workshop where Etienne makes our products."

Mina nodded, thanking her for her cooperation as the wizard led us to an area behind the counter.

The stone walls and high wooden beam ceiling of the workshop mirrored the storefront, but the space was utilitarian, feeling like a castle kitchen. An enormous stone fireplace with a wide hood dominated the spacious room. Shelves on the walls were filled with rows of herbs, roots, and other ingredients. Shafts of light shone through the small, high windows, illuminating a swirl of fine dust that never seemed to settle.

Alchemist Etienne Star was a middle-aged Sireliad man with dark hair, a graying beard and a stern expression working over a large cauldron in the fireplace.

"Excuse us," said Mina. "We're from MASHA, here to do a safety inspection. What are you doing?"

"Making potions," said Alchemist Star flatly, briefly glancing at us before turning his attention back to the gurgling cauldron. His tone made it evident that the answer to the question should be obvious.

"So, clearly white wax and . . . what's the plant?" Mina asked, peering over his shoulder.

"Alkanet."

"How much is in there?"

He turned back to us and gestured to the cauldron of simmering green liquid with the stirring spoon. "Well, that much."

"But how much?" Mina pressed.

He set down the spoon. "I don't know the exact amount."

"You've got to measure it. You can't just chuck it all in if you're going to sell the potions."

The flames beneath the cast-iron cauldron subsided and he took a step back from his work. With a sheepish air, he slid his hands into the pockets of his apron.

Mina persisted, her tone practical yet pressing. "What's the magical potency of this batch? Are there any toxic ingredients involved?"

He drew back slightly and frustration creeped into his voice. "What? Well, what if someone's pact prohibits alkanet?"

"That's why you need to make sure everything is listed on the label. Is it just wax and alkanet?"

"No, there's arsenic."

"Pure arsenic? Or does it contain traces of other minerals? Because you'll have to list those, too."

The potion maker sighed. "Well, we receive arsenic in bulk from the mines." He pointed to a large, plain ceramic jar on a top shelf.

Mina peered up at it. "May I see the container?"

Alchemist Star nodded. I carefully lifted it down, placing it on a sturdy wooden table between the scattered glass vials, mortars and pestles, and handwritten recipe scrolls. Examining the jar up close, I could see a very faint alchemical symbol for *arsenic*. Inside, an odorless white powder glittered under the bright light of the meteor crystal lamp hanging overhead. A regular teaspoon was immersed in it, up to the handle.

"This is highly dangerous. You should have labeled it clearly and put a warning on it," Mina said, turning to the alchemist. "The scoop also concerns me. A teaspoon is not a proper measuring implement."

Alchemist Star looked surprised. "We're very careful. I may be an alchemist, but we've both made a pact with Arsenicia to keep no salt in this space. We won't even take salt with anyone."

"We've been working with the new elements for years, and no one has ever gotten sick," Wiz. North interjected, sketching with her fingers what might have been the symbol for *arsenic* in the air. "I use the skin restorative on myself."

"Adhering to your pact with Arsenicia isn't the type of precaution I'm referring to," Mina replied firmly. "Arsenic is toxic in large quantities, and if it's not handled properly, with gloves, it can even be lethal. I suggest you clearly label the container and calibrate the scoop. You should also wear safety goggles while working with hazardous materials to prevent eye injury."

"I'll make sure to take care of it right away. Thank you for bringing this to our attention," said the alchemist sheepishly.

"Simarron, please check the cauldron for magical leaks," said Mina.

I made my way to the fireplace containing the cauldron and swept the wand of the detector around the cauldron's base with meticulous care. The MED's dials surged and waned in tandem with the wand's proximity to the cauldron, indicating the containment of magical energy. Tracing the edges of the fireplace and hood, I found no aberrations in the energy detected.

Mina nodded her approval, marking the readings down. "Well done, Simarron."

I hesitated. "Do you happen to use any ectoplasm in your potions and remedies?"

"Ectoplasm? No," replied the wizard. "Only a very advanced alchemist or wizard, like one of those university types, could use something like that."

We thanked Wiz. North and Alchemist Star for their time and left.

"That went well, didn't it?" I said as we stepped back onto the street, proud of our success in convincing the reluctant potion shop proprietors to handle their ingredients more safely.

"Better than most cases," Mina admitted. "You've seen firsthand how wary alchemists are about MASHA. And the wizards think we're a joke, nothing more than a token agency."

"How did you know the complaint about the skin restorative was unfounded?"

"Because the Magical Energies Detector picked up minimal magic on Wiz. North herself. She claimed to use her own product. If it were merely a facade, the MED would have detected a glamour spell enhancing her appearance," Mina explained. "The fact that they have a consistent product is a minor miracle, however."

I nodded, impressed by how she wielded logic.

After a brief silence, she asked, "Why did you bring up ectoplasm?"

"Oh, just thinking about the strange spell that the MED registered the last time we used it." I paused. We had tested soil samples and written a report, which was subsequently lost, but we never directly discussed our personal experience at the castle site. "What do you think happened to us . . . that day?"

Mina looked away. "Don't let your imagination run wild. We deal in facts at MASHA, not fantasies."

"It feels like a strange dream that haunts me in my waking hours, lurking behind my memories," I persisted. "We should go back."

"No, no," she said dismissively.

"Aren't most places in Kami-Nihkia closed on Goldday?" I asked, sensing an opportunity.

"That's tomorrow, the day of the Spring Equinox Fair. You should take a break, enjoy the festivities."

"The fair doesn't interest me. I need to understand what occurred at the castle site," I said, my tail swishing in agitation. "I think I smelled ectoplasm at the site. What was it used for?"

Mina's steps resumed, her heeled boots clicking in quick succession on the cobblestones. "Lysandros Garbor had ambitions beyond mere renovations. Whatever his intentions, they cost him dearly."

I frowned and dropped the subject, silently brooding over my thoughts as we headed back to the MASHA building. Why had Lysandros Garbor gone to such lengths to secure a MASHA inspection for a castle that seemed to have vanished? Was someone else now trying to conceal something at the site by eliminating Garbor? And what did it have to do with ectoplasm?

I had noticed the tension in Mina's voice as she dismissed the idea of revisiting the area. Her reluctance seemed unusual, but now that she'd determined that the case notes were beyond our retrieval, I supposed she didn't want to be reminded of our failure.

There remained, however, one more expert—possibly even a suspect—who could shed light on the use of ectoplasm in potent potions and spells. Checking the time on my pocket watch, I realized I would need to act quickly. I decided to make the most of the upcoming lunch hour to seek out Professor Ashmin at her university lab.

Chapter Thirteen

I entered the university alchemy laboratory, my hoofsteps echoing in the large round room. It looked a little different from when I'd been here before. The large still was gone, although the black mark remained on the ceiling like a shadow of past experiments. The lab smelled different too, a nutty aroma mingling with the scent of chemicals hanging in the air, prompting me to slip on my safety goggles.

Professor Ashmin stood hunched over one of the lab tables, engrossed in her work. Various papers were strewn across the surface amid the specially-purposed glassware and jars of ingredients. She glanced up at me from the center of this web of intricate notes, spiraling tubes, and bubbling flasks as I approached, her expression masked by her goggles.

"Ah, the new safety inspector. To what do I owe this visit?" she said, not bothering to hide her annoyance.

"Sorry to intrude on your work, Professor." I clutched my clipboard before me in what I hoped was an official manner. "May I please take a look around?"

"Go right ahead," she said, turning to the papers and scratching some notes.

To my relief, Professor Ashmin seemed too preoccupied to follow me around. As I navigated the workshop once more, my eyes skimmed over the neatly labeled jars lining the shelves. Aconite, bismuth, carbolic acid, and dragon's blood were followed by various other ingredients, but no ectoplasm. I compared the contents to their labels, but found nothing that looked or smelled like it.

"Coffee?" Professor Ashmin asked after I had completed a full circuit around the room. She appeared to be percolating a brown liquid from an alembic through a spiraling glass tube into a boiling flask. I couldn't tell if she was being sarcastic or simply too engrossed in her work to pay me any mind.

"No, thank you," I replied, casting a suspicious glance at the strange beverage. "Is your exhaust hood in working order?" The steam carried a strong odor, although not unpleasant.

"Check it yourself." Taking a sip of coffee, the Sireliad reached up with a gloved hand to touch a chain hanging from the ceiling. Faint scars from minor chemical burns marked her skin where it was ex-posed, and as she moved, subtle dark streaks—like mineral inclusions beneath the surface of her skin—shifted along her forearms.

At first glance, the exhaust system appeared to be a basic system of pulleys and brass gears. Without looking at it, she gave the chain a casual tug and the gears sprang to life, setting the entire apparatus into glorious motion. The bellows expanded and contracted, a crystal glowed faintly, and a soft whooshing sound filled the air as the wind spell activated, drawing the steam and fumes up and away.

I marveled at the seamless integration of magic and machinery. The spell's gentle hum, the clinking gears, and the rhythmic pump of the bellows were like music. But a working exhaust hood wasn't the reason for my visit.

"Professor Ashmin, I truly appreciate your time," I said, trying to sound polite but casual. "I wanted to discuss something I've come across during my safety inspections."

With a frown, the alchemist set down her flask of coffee near a rack holding an array of slender, neatly labeled tubes. They were labeled with a symbol that seemed oddly familiar, a sort of elaborate X. It wasn't any alchemical symbol I was aware of. It was right there, on the edge of recall, but I couldn't quite bring the memory into focus.

"Well, what is it?" She absently tugged at the glass stirring rod holding her hair bun in place.

"What does this symbol mean?" I asked.

Professor Ashmin barely glanced up from her work. "As long as my ingredients are clearly marked, Safety Inspector, why should it matter to you?"

I hesitated. The symbol continued to nag at me, but I let it go—for now. "I actually wanted to ask you about ectoplasm, Professor. It's not something I'm too familiar with, but I've heard it can be quite potent in the hands of a skilled alchemist. Is that true?"

"Ectoplasm is a very rare form of phosphorus," she said, her tone professorial as she selected a series of reagents. With methodical precision, she added measured drops into the tubes held in the rack. The colors of the solutions were vibrant under the glow of the meteor crystal lamps.

She transferred one of the tubes into a distillation column, adjusting brass knobs to regulate the intensity of the heat coming from the reboiler. I frowned, noting the distinct lack of a traditional flame source. While I knew meteor crystal lamps didn't generate heat, these crystals seemed to be activating a heat spell woven into the apparatus. Thin coils of vapor curled through the glass spirals, condensing into clear droplets at the receiving end.

"It can be a very powerful substance, used in various alchemical processes," she continued after a moment. "But its properties can vary greatly depending on how it's used."

I watched her work, struck by how different it was from the testing I had witnessed Mina perform in the MASHA lab. Mina had invoked the goddess Titanacala and coaxed the elements to tell their story, while Ashmin took apart the tale piece by piece, analyzing each fragment. Both were searching for answers, but in very different ways.

I nodded. "Could it be used to create a significant explosion or some other powerful effect?"

"In theory, yes," she said, still in teacher mode. "Ectoplasm can release a tremendous amount of energy when properly harnessed. But it's a complex and delicate substance. Controlling it to create such an effect would require an alchemist of considerable skill and knowledge."

"An alchemist like . . . Lysandros Garbor?"

She snorted derisively. "Although it's a shame what happened to him, the arrogant fool had more business acumen than real talent with alchemy." She set down a bottle and pointed a gloved finger at me. "But you didn't come here to gossip, did you?"

Instinctively, I took a step back from the accusing gesture, my hooves clattering on the smooth floor. I stammered, "No, I . . ."

She studied me intently through her safety goggles, her singed eyebrows slanting sharply. "So, Director Moosekind sends his latest hound after me, does he?" Her voice took on an edge sharp enough to cut glass.

"It's not like that at all." I had the distinct feeling that class was now over.

"Well, I have every right to know what Lysandros Garbor was doing at Château Gorget, considering he stole some of my research. In light of his untimely demise, I'm more than entitled to reclaim my work—that's all."

I gripped my clipboard like a flimsy shield against the force of her glare. "I didn't mean to suggest anything about your work, Professor. I'm merely trying to piece together what happened at the castle."

Professor Ashmin gave an exasperated sigh and returned to her experiment.

I shifted from hoof to hoof. Maybe I was on the wrong track with the ectoplasm. When I had found the jar in the storage room and recalled the smell from my visit to Château Gorget, I'd felt it had something to do with the vanishing castle. Yet Professor Ashmin didn't have any samples of this rare ingredient in her lab. Still, another mystery tangled up in all this, was the question of who or what had killed Lysandros

Garbor. She had openly admitted to holding a grudge against him. However, he hadn't died at his newly acquired property, but after viewing a painting purported to have originated from there.

Lost in thought, my gaze traveled to the uneven scorch mark on the ceiling of her lab. It resembled a ghastly face, giving the unsettling impression that the laboratory was watching me. This reminded me of another disturbing sight.

"Mind if I ask something on an unrelated topic?" I ventured after a pause.

"You're still here?"

"Do you think Alchemist Garbor's death could be connected to that mysterious painting at the art gala?"

"Perhaps he was unique among the guests at the gala in that he licked it," she suggested, her tone scornful.

True, paint pigments sometimes contained toxic substances. However, I knew she was being facetious.

"You say that, yet you should know better than to misuse lab equipment in violation of MASHA safety protocols," I said, irked, gesturing between the two setups: one for her experiment, the other serving as a coffee brewing station.

Her eyes, dark as magnetite, flashed in anger, glittering with hematite-like flecks. "I see what you mean, but coffee helps me focus during my experiments."

"Lab equipment should be used exclusively for their designated purpose. Cross-purposing them for culinary tasks can pose risks. What if you ingested something toxic by mistake?" I knew I had rekindled her ire, but as a safety inspector, I felt obligated to mention it. Besides, her attitude was starting to wear on me, too.

"Well, are you going to write me up?" she demanded.

"No, but please be more careful in the future. Thank you for your cooperation, Professor Ashmin," I said. Bowing my head slightly, I turned to leave.

I headed down the spiraling staircase one dreadful step at a time, my tail held stiff, my knuckles white. I felt that I'd successfully gleaned information in Professor Ashmin's lab, but I wasn't sure how it all fit together. The peculiar symbol on the samples she was testing, her evasive responses, her defensiveness of her work—I sensed keenly that she was involved in the events surrounding the death of her academic rival. Yet none of the fragments aligned with any clarity.

At the bottom of the staircase, I steadied myself, slightly dizzy, my mind awhirl with more uncertainties than I'd had before. The original spark of my suspicions against Professor Ashmin—the ectoplasm— appeared to have fizzled out, but new questions had arisen. I opened my notebook and recorded a sketch of the symbol—the elaborate X— but its meaning remained elusive. Maybe I needed to let the matter rest, like a fine sediment settling in an alchemical solution, and allow the answer to precipitate out.

Chapter Fourteen

On the morning of the spring equinox, I tried to focus on the work the landlady had left for me. Simple tasks around the mansion—a sagging shutter, a creaky door hinge. It kept my hands busy, but I found my thoughts wandering to Château Gorget.

Finally, the afternoon light slanted in just so, illuminating the distant forested hills where the secrets of the vanishing castle lay. Surely the landlady wouldn't miss me for a few hours, I reasoned. As I finished tightening the hinge on one of the many creaky doors of the mansion, Landlady Lyness approached me with a suggestion that caught me off guard.

"Why don't you take the afternoon off and visit the Spring Equinox Fair?" she said, her tone friendly but insistent.

"Well, The Incredible Spectra is performing, and that could be just the thing to see—or not see," I replied. My attempt at a joke fell flat, however, and the landlady simply nodded, taking me quite seriously.

"Take Lilimari with you. The girl's been cooped up all winter, and university classes resume the day after tomorrow. A bit of fresh air would do her good."

I opened my mouth to reply, but in my consternation, I couldn't find the words to argue.

"Go on, then."

Upstairs, I found Lilimari in her room, practically bricked in by a pile of books. Other than the precarious towers of texts and heavy black curtains, the room seemed fairly ordinary—no trace of the strange experiments Kai had warned me about.

I cleared my throat, trying not to disturb her concentration too abruptly. "Lilimari, Lyness thinks we should go to the fair," I said, shifting slightly. "If you'd like to, of course."

Lilimari looked up, her expression incredulous. "The fair? Umb, I have important research to do."

"It could be a practical study, seeing magic in use outside the academic world," I suggested. "The Incredible Spectra is conducting a mass spectacle of necromancy, using the spirits to make the monument in the city square disappear."

She considered this for a moment, then slowly closed her book. "You know, they don't actually teach necromancy at the university. Let's go see this 'Incredible Spectra' then."

Despite the chilly wind that tousled the colorful tents, the fair was a spirited celebration of spring's arrival, turning the city square into a lively patchwork of booths and pavilions. Banners snapped across the bright blue sky brushed with streaky clouds. And rising above the fairgoers, performers and vendors, stretched the long bronze-green serpentine neck of Drakeus Kinrethys.

"How will Anya—The Incredible Spectra—make such a large, prominent monument disappear, I wonder?" I asked, trying to make conversation with Lilimari.

She shrugged, but I noticed her gaze had caught on one of the stalls. Was it the firecracker stand?

"Alchemists are certainly good at blowing things up," I commented, thinking again of the scorch marks on Professor Ashmin's workshop ceiling.

Lilimari shuddered. "I abhor the noise of firecrackers." She wore only black, from the ribbon on her hat to the hem of her flared skirt, the festive occasion notwithstanding.

"Sing Corn! Taste the music!" called a vendor as we passed.

"What is that melody?" Lilimari asked, coming to a halt. Soft chords of airy notes drifted from the stall, like a harmonica being played by the breeze. It felt familiar, like a song I'd heard before but couldn't quite recall.

"Did you say 'spring corn?'" I asked, stepping closer to the source. Above the stall, a colorful banner bore a whimsical illustration of a unicorn with a corncob for its horn. As the music grew louder, weaving playful, ethereal harmonies around us, the sweet and buttery aroma grew stronger.

The music stopped. "No, no—Sing Corn!" said the vendor, a Helvenkin man whose tasseled hat and wispy golden hair reminded me of corn silk. He raised a bright yellow ear of roasted corn to his lips. As he took a bite, a soft, harmonious tune poured forth once more.

"It's . . . unusual," I said, scanning the stall. My training surfaced unbidden—*MASHA: Rules and Regulations* had an entire section on magical food safety. My gaze darted behind the counter, where the Enchanted Culinary Compliance Certificate was displayed. Satisfied, I fished a few bits from my satchel. "I'll take one. Actually, make it two."

"It's ridiculous, is what it is," Lilimari muttered.

The vendor ignored her protests and beamed, handing me two steaming ears of corn skewered on sticks. "I guarantee you've never had anything like it," he promised. I offered one ear to Lilimari.

She accepted it with a skeptical glance, turning it over in her hands as though expecting it to bite her instead. "Thank you," she said with reluctant politeness before sinking her sharp teeth into it like a wolf tearing into its prey.

The resulting sound was a chaotic fanfare. The burst of music startled a passing group of girls, who turned to stare before laughing. Lilimari's cheeks flushed as she muttered, "Ridiculous," again, though softer this time.

I bit into mine more cautiously, rotating the ear in small movements. The notes were clearer; a delightfully simple scale that changed with each careful bite. The sensation was unlike anything I'd experienced—I didn't just hear the music, I felt it vibrating lightly through my teeth and resonating up into my jaw. It was strange and exhilarating all at once.

We continued in companionable silence until suddenly, Lilimari paused at a display of miniatures at a stall by a fountain. A ribbon proudly declared the exhibitor the fair's winner of a prize in craftsmanship, and it was well-earned. Arranged on tiered wooden shelves, each tiny scene was a masterpiece. There was a banquet hall featuring minuscule meals made of wax, plated on diminutive dishes. A museum of art displayed little landscapes and petite portraits, each no bigger than the bits used for currency in this land. But the most intricate piece was a perfect recreation of the city square, complete with Drakeus Kinrethys rising above the tiny fairgoers.

The level of detail drew me in, and I leaned down to study the scene. Every scale on Drakeus Kinrethys was rendered with its own subtle variation of color, and its eyes were set with gemstones. The model of Castle Ward where the Council of Governors met was built with such care that I felt as if I could reach inside and walk its miniature halls.

"I see you admiring the palace. I adore castles," said the artisan in a gentle voice like the babbling of a brook. Her ethereal beauty, the water lily in her golden hair . . . She must be a naiad!

"The city square, the palace, it's like a fairyland!" said Lilimari. I smiled, amused to see the university student so excited about something so frivolous. As a prodigy, or so I gathered, she was deeply devoted to her studies, and I had never seen this side of her before.

"Then you'll enjoy this," said the naiad, directing Lilimari's attention to a miniature castle covered in vines. She handed the Bloodborn a golden magnifying glass, through which Lilimari stared with rapt interest. While I waited my turn, I perused the tiny art museum.

A sudden chill prickled my skin. A familiar dark-haired woman stared back at me with hollow, distant eyes. Even in miniature form, I recognized its caricature immediately—the haunted painting!

"Are these all copies of real paintings?" I asked.

"Ah, yes, the legendary soul painting," said the naiad, following my gaze.

"What's a soul painting?" I asked, my memories stirring until the dust cleared and settled on a certain file in the MASHA storage room. "Is that like the Soul Anchor?"

"It's just a legend," she replied, playfully shrugging a single shoulder, just as Lilimari handed me the magnifying glass.

Accepting the glass, I turned my attention to the castle she had been examining. Beneath the twisted vines that crept over its walls, I spotted something familiar: the smallest marking of that strange, elaborate X.

The detail was hauntingly real, as if the artisan had somehow transferred the true essence of the castle into her work. I almost dropped the magnifying glass as a pulse of pain throbbed behind my eyes.

"Simarron, are you well?" asked Lilimari.

"It's Château Gorget," I gasped at the sudden, jarring recognition, turning to the naiad. "How did you do that?"

"Trade secret," the artisan informed me with a coy smile.

"No, really, I must know," I pressed.

The naiad thought for a moment. "I adore games. Maybe if you can beat me at one of the games here at the fair, I'll tell you."

"All right, let's go find a game," I agreed.

"Lore! Watch my booth for a moment?" the naiad called out to the neighboring stall.

A faun looked up from where he was working on a wood carving. He flicked an ear in her direction. "Of course, Aurelia."

"Thank you!" The naiad swept out from behind her stall, water droplets trailing in her wake as she joined us in front of her display. "I'm Aurelia, by the way."

"I'm Simarron and this is Lilimari," I said, but the alchemy student was already heading down the thoroughfare.

Lilimari pulled me toward a milk bottle game. "You can win this one, easy," she informed me.

The carnie handed me and the miniatures enthusiast each three wooden rings as a group of people looked on. Lilimari made an encouraging sound and then, glancing around, collected herself.

"I'm not as dexterous as you, Aurelia, surely must be." I took aim at the middle of the pyramid of glass bottles. "Your miniatures are so detailed—they look like real objects that have been magically miniaturized." My first ring bounced right off the glass.

"Oh, so close, Simarron. You have two more chances," Lilimari called out.

"Thank you for the compliment. My grandfather used to build ships in bottles, and I always thought the same." Aurelia flicked her wrist, aiming for a bottle near the edge of the grouping, and the ring landed around the neck perfectly.

"Was your grandfather a wizard?" I asked, adjusting my grip on the next ring. There had to be a trick to it, but I had never learned how it was done. Maybe a shrinking spell was possible, after all. I took aim near the edge, but my second ring struck two bottles and settled on neither.

"He was a fisherman, with more artistic talent than magic," Aurelia said, laughing, the sound like a stream clattering across stones. It felt like she was laughing with me, not at me for being naive. Her ring again found its mark near the edge of the pyramid. "Cleverly, he made the hull look smaller than the neck of the bottle and pulled the sails and spars into place using tiny threads."

I took aim again.

"You've got this!" Lilimari shouted with an intensity that surprised even herself, judging by her startled expression.

I hurled my final ring at the stack of bottles, which unfortunately carried a bit too much force and knocked several over in an embarrassing crash.

"Whoa there, centaur," mocked the carnie.

"Sorry about that," I said, rubbing the back of my neck as everyone stared at the clumsy centaur.

Aurelia smiled. "I adore games—and castles. If I had that kind of power, I would shrink myself down so that I could walk around in my tiny worlds."

"They are beautiful," said Lilimari.

"Thank you. I didn't steal the castle, I promise," Aurelia said with a giggle. "Although . . . if I could miniaturize it for real, that would be one way to protect the area from further harm. If you want to see how I create my miniature worlds, visit me at Silver Lake in Misty Vale anytime. I have a wonderful view of the castle."

We bid goodbye to Aurelia and continued on. I was still shaken at seeing Château Gorget, but I was mostly convinced by her story. Disturbingly, if I had seen the castle after all, then why couldn't I remember it?

Something jogged loose in my memory. I remembered where I had seen that strange symbol before! It was at Château Gorget, and had even been depicted as the tiniest scratch in its miniature version. It resembled the elaborate X I'd seen at the university lab.

"Is something wrong?" asked Lilimari.

I opened my satchel and furiously flipped open my notebook to the sketch I had recently made in Professor Ashmin's lab. I refused to believe it was a mere coincidence.

"What is it?"

"I don't know yet, but whatever Alchemist Garbor was doing at the castle, Professor Ashmin has taken a keen interest in his work."

Chapter Fifteen

The afternoon sunlight was now burning out in a golden blaze, stretching shadows across the fair. Throngs of people milled about a tangled landscape of bright tents and the black shadows of structures that weren't normally there. The air was thick with the smell of food and excitement, voices and music growing more intense as evening approached.

Nestled between two stalls, one selling spiced cider and the other offering hand-painted masks, I spotted a familiar face draped in blue silk. The lanterns hanging from the booth's frame bathed the figure in a soft otherworldly glow. I did a double-take. "Is that . . . ?"

"Kai, what are you doing here?" asked Lilimari as we angled toward the booth.

Kai's golden eyes twinkled. "Why, inviting those with a story to tell to unburden their secrets in exchange for fortunes told and greater mysteries revealed." He shuffled his cards and fanned them out facedown on the velvet-covered table. "Sit down, Lilimari, and let's see what the cards have to say about your heart's queries. And in return, perhaps you can share a tale or two from your independent studies?"

Lilimari scoffed. "Umb, no thanks."

Kai flipped over a card, seemingly at random. "Ah, the Eight of Coins. I see obstacles in your path, dear, possibly due to academic or . . . parental pressure?"

"How does he do that? I hate it when he does that!" said Lilimari, stomping away.

"How about you, my centaur friend? My fortunes are known for their frightening accuracy, as you can see." The two halves of the card deck flowed into each other; he neatened the stack by tapping it on the table.

"Ah, maybe some other time," I said, glancing at Lilimari, where she stood slightly apart from us. She was fuming, although possibly for dramatic effect. "We're going to see The Incredible Spectra. Care to join us?"

Kai smiled. "I have much more fun with my own audience. Be off, enjoy yourselves!"

Lilimari and I slowly made our way to the main stage where Anya Vedeva would be performing. I walked at a steady, deliberate pace, my eyes scanning above the crowd, while my companion followed with her arms folded tightly across her body. Her long dark hair hung around her face like a protective curtain.

"I don't really like crowds," she admitted. "I'm used to walking around the city alone."

"We can return to the mansion whenever you'd like," I said. I wasn't overly fond of crowds, either. "We'll miss supper if we stay for the show."

Lilimari shrugged. A pair of stilt-walkers wove around us on their spindle legs. "I like how people move out of your way. Besides, I haven't found a stall selling roasted blood sausage yet. There's not a lot I miss from back home, except the food. What I wouldn't give for a good blood sausage right now, or maybe a hammer cake."

"You're from the Commonwealth, right?" I asked. I knew it was a clan-based society, like my own, but their lands were mountainous and rich in hidden gems and ore, unlike the vast tundra and open plains of the Wildlands.

She shrugged, but I was beginning to pick up, over the course of our meanderings through the fair, that this was an *affirmative* shrug. Lilimari's *negative* shrug was more closed at the shoulders.

"Why didn't you want to live on campus with most of the other university students?" I asked.

She scowled, showing her pointed teeth. "I don't really fit in with the other students. I find them cliquish and superficial."

"Fair enough. I don't really fit in with other centaurs," I said.

"Is that why you moved here?" she asked, her tone brightening with pleasant surprise.

I nodded. We continued on in pleasant silence, eventually finding grilled sausages and hammer cakes for sale, and a spot at the back of the crowd from where to watch the necromancer perform.

Anya Vedeva began by telling the audience a story about Drakeus Kinrethys.

"I invoke the spirits of our ancestors to join with us now in bringing my words to life. In the beginning, there was Chaos. It was not nothingness, but rather a lack of order of any kind. Then the first dragon, the Great Goddess, emerged from Chaos and, finding nothing substantial to rest her feet upon, divided the sea from the sky. She stretched her wings as she soared across the sky and then, coming to rest in the calm waters, laid the Universal Egg. When it hatched, the bottom half of the shell formed the earth, the top half formed the sky, and everything that exists tumbled out of the Egg in primitive form."

As she spoke, her words were accompanied by mysterious strains of music from unseen musicians. A shimmering dome of light formed over the audience and an enormous curtain, hung between the two towers lit with braziers, began to close and block the view of the monument.

"From the Universal Egg hatched seven dragons, who created a race of beings in their image and ruled over them as gods. These beings resembled dragons with their giant reptilian bodies, but they lacked the light of wisdom.

After many millennia, the gods became bored with their creations and destroyed them with fire in order to make room for a new intelligent lifeform."

People gasped as the sky deepened into darkness. Stars appeared— more numerous and brilliant than I had seen since leaving the Wildlands. As the music swelled, they pulsed with a fiery glow, shifting from silver to molten orange. Then, one by one, they began to fall; embers drifted down over the crowd, vanishing just before they could be touched.

"The new creation physically did not much resemble a dragon. These giant beings walked on two legs and had hair instead of scales, fingers instead of claws. However, they had the long ears and pointed teeth of dragons, and their large, intelligent eyes contained their wisdom. The gods were pleased—until they began to fear their creations were becoming too powerful. Whether the gods or the giants struck first, nobody knows, but the battle ended with the gods smiting the last titan with lightning."

Sudden flashes of light split the darkness, illuminating the stage and the sea of upturned faces. The music surged, each note crackling with intensity. The air itself felt alive, charged with an electric energy that made the hairs on my arms rise. Thunder rumbled—a deep, rolling sound that vibrated in my chest.

"As the last titan was struck, he was split into pieces that were scattered across the earth, each becoming a new race of two-legged beings. The Helvenkin of the forests got the pointed ears; the Sireliads of the islands kept the clever eyes; to the Bloodborn of the mountains went the sharp teeth. All three peoples were much smaller and weaker than their predecessors."

Anya told the tale of the creation of the world and of two-leggers— Kin—beautifully. I was surprised by how stirred I felt by a story that didn't even include my kind.

"What about centaurs?" I mumbled. But then again, centaurs didn't worship Drakeus Kinrethys.

"Don't worry about it. Although my people venerate the god of metal and his many offspring, alchemists don't put much stock in such tales," my Bloodborn friend whispered back. As the music quieted, the magical dome faded and the true sky—sunset now—shone above.

"Drakeus Kinrethys took pity on the pathetic creatures and gave them dragonfire. This was not only the art of making fire to create heat and keep darkness at bay, but also the gift of divine spark, or inner fire. And so at the beginning of each spring, when the light overcomes the dark, the people of Kami-Nihkia give thanks to the dragon god."

The giant curtain opened and the braziers flared, sending their flames high into the sky, revealing an empty space where the monument had stood only moments before. I could clearly see the sun setting through the space where it had been.

"We give thanks, because we must never take that light for granted."

The curtain closed once more and the flames died down.

"I thank the spirits for their power and I now command everything to return as it was."

When the curtain opened again, the Drakeus Kinrethys monument had reappeared. The crowd went wild, clapping and cheering and exclaiming their wonderment.

Anya bowed, basking in the audience's applause, but the City Watch suddenly marched onto the stage. Gasps and murmurs rippled through the crowd as the stern-faced captain led his officers—officially called *coppers* after the sacred metal—forward, closing in around her.

"What is the meaning of this?" Anya's voice, laced with shock and indignation, resonated through the stunned audience. The remnants of her act, now overshadowed by the grim reality of her arrest, lingered in the air like a fading dream.

"Necromancer Anya Vedeva, you are under arrest for unlawful invocation of spirits, fraud, and the murder of Alchemist Lysandros Garbor. Surrender peacefully," said the watch captain.

Silver handcuffs flashed in the stage lighting as he closed them around her wrists. Lilimari and I looked at each other in surprise, then a flicker of something—Confusion? Annoyance?—crossed her face.

"This is absurd!" Lilimari declared loudly, drawing the attention of those nearby. "This performance is a fraud, or, you know, showmanship, but that's hardly a crime. The visual effects, the energy of the crowd, it was stirring. I'll admit that. But I didn't feel any contact with the spirits, did you?"

"I'm not sure," I said, my mind racing as I tried to comprehend what I had just heard and seen. I didn't know what contact with the spirits was supposed to be like. But after watching Anya Vedeva's performance, and in light of what I had experienced in the park, I had to agree with Lilimari that she was no necromancer at all.

As the crowd's murmurs grew louder, their unease shifting into something restless, Lilimari dropped her sarcastic tone. "Let's get out of here," she urged. "Before this crowd gets too antsy and they start arresting people for disorderly conduct."

Chapter Sixteen

When we returned home that evening, I was in store for another surprise. There was a carriage waiting beneath the barren tree out front, the jet black horse foraging for brown grass between the cracks in the paving stones. The elegant vehicle might have belonged in a bygone era, but now it was a sore reminder of the current state of the mansion. With its rusty railings and broken gable ornaments, the boarding house on Slant Row was no place for such a posh visitor.

Inside the parlor, the fire crackled in the hearth, casting dancing shadows across the room. Tia, our landlady, and the visitor were arrayed around it, sipping tea. The visitor's gaunt figure wasn't so posh after all, but seemed to echo the faded elegance of the room.

It was Vanadar, Tia's bad news beau. He was ensconced in a patched armchair across from Tia. Landlady Lyness sat on the settee, her presence almost protective as she hovered near Tia. A palpable tension filled the air, punctuated by the occasional pop from the fire.

"Now my great-great-granduncle, Thaddeus, was a gifted illusion wizard with a penchant for orchestrating magical pranks, especially on necromancers . . ." the wizard said, his voice brimming with pride. Tia leaned toward him in interest while the landlady seemed preoccupied with studying her fingernails.

Suddenly, Landlady Lyness set her teacup down with a clatter and approached, waving frantically for Lilimari and me to join her. She never walked or strolled, ambled or shuffled; the only way to describe her movement was "bustled."

"Did you two enjoy the fair?" she asked in an aggressively cheerful tone.

"It was interesting. Is everything all right here?" I responded, taken aback by her unusual behavior.

She leaned close and whispered, "Well, it's a bit embarrassing, really. I couldn't let Tia's beau take her out late, so he's joined us for supper tonight, which he didn't even eat, complaining about salt. And he's such a bore—please, you have to save me."

"Umb, sorry, I have studying to do," said Lilimari. She excused herself to her room, no doubt feeling that she had satisfied her social obligation for the day—or year.

I regarded Daniella Lyness quizzically. She and Tia were only about a dozen years apart in age, and the younger woman was certainly capable of looking after herself. What intricate social nets these city dwellers weave, I thought, catching each other in a mesh of support and sometimes control. It was far different from my herd, where the vast plains offered more independence.

She straightened and said, "Simarron, please join us for tea!"

"I . . . I suppose I can," I replied with uncertainty, allowing her to lead me to the group.

Landlady Lyness lit an oil lamp in the corner and sat her plump figure back down on the settee. I awkwardly settled down on the floor across from her. Mid-way through introducing me and Vanadar, she suddenly peered at him with a thoughtful expression.

"Vanadar? Your first name wouldn't happen to be Horace, would it?"

Vanadar blinked in surprise. "Yes, indeed. But how did you—"

Landlady Lyness interrupted with a hearty chuckle. "Old Hoho! Now I recognize you, but why didn't you say anything before? Gods, the years have been kind to you, although you look different somehow. I'm Daniella Lyness. We attended the same art school for a time, you know, back when our families were some of the wealthiest in Kami-Nihkia."

Vanadar winced at the nickname. "Ah, yes, now I remember. Those were different times. Many wizard families, once prosperous, are now . . . well, not quite as much. But, as my ancestors engraved on our family crest, 'actions bring results.' What are we doing to improve our situation?"

"Vanadar was just telling us about the glory days," said Tia as she reached for the sugar dish.

Vanadar gently swatted her hand. "Too much sugar in your tea makes you too jittery to paint, dearest," he admonished. Tia smiled apologetically. Her eyes struck me as unusually blue today, much like Vanadar's otherworldly green eyes. I didn't understand why Sireliads, of all people, would need to use glamour magic on their eyes.

"Anyhow, lately these upstart alchemists have been gaining all the glory, especially with their discoveries of new elements," Vanadar continued, waving a hand dismissively and punctuating the word "new" with a dubious tone.

"You seem to have strong opinions on the matter," I observed. "Do you believe that the recognition these 'upstart alchemists' receive is underserved?" The tea tasted unusually bitter, though perhaps it was simply my tongue, unaccustomed to such sharp banter.

Vanadar leaned back in his chair, frustration creeping into his voice. "Oh, it's not that their work isn't valuable. It's just that some of us believe that the true pioneers, the great families of wizards, deserve their fair share of the credit. After all, we've been exploring the elements for much longer."

"Progress doesn't wait for titles or social class," I said, snorting in disdain. I quickly finished my tea, setting my cup down a bit more firmly than I intended. Landlady Lyness was right, he was a bore. And his dark robes, while of fine cloth, had a damp and musty odor.

Vanadar shook his head. "Alchemists are pushing the boundaries of knowledge too quickly. They take from nature without discretion, foregoing the traditional pacts with the elements and using their ill-gotten gains to buy up everything. Only wizards have the wisdom and experience to guide these discoveries safely, and in the proper direction." The iridescent blue and green veins on his neck stood out sharply as he clenched his jaw.

Landlady Lyness glanced at my empty cup and interjected, her tone diplomatic, "Well, this is certainly a lively topic. How about another cup of tea?"

As she bustled off to the kitchen, I groaned inwardly, feeling out-of-place amid the evening's polite but pointed discourse. Cautiously, I touched the roof of my mouth with my tongue, wincing at the tenderness from the scalding sip I had taken.

Vanadar smirked, as if sensing my thoughts, sipping his tea as he gazed out the window. Or rather, at the dim reflection of the room upon the darkened pane.

Tia spoke up, breaking the awkward silence. "Simarron is a safety inspector for MASHA, remember? He is helping to make sure that magic and alchemy is conducted safely in the city."

"Of course." Vanadar couldn't hide the contempt in his voice. "Well, I certainly hope you manage to find this supposed necromancer behind the soul painting and revoke their license, or whatever it is you do. It would be quite the accomplishment if MASHA could crack the case before the City Watch does, wouldn't it?" His tone suggested that he severely doubted my chances of success.

I shifted uncomfortably on my haunches. "It seems the case has already been solved. The City Watch just arrested The Incredible Spectra at the fair today."

Vanadar jerked his head back in surprise. "The Incredible Spectra? That charlatan? Arrested, you say? Well, I suppose even the City Watch must get it right sometimes."

I recounted the shocking finale of The Incredible Spectra's performance. Vanadar slowly sipped his tea, his eyes narrowing slightly as he regarded me over the rim of his overly ornate cup—a gaudy piece with excessive gold trim. Tia set her cup down, the one encircled with a delicate rose pattern that she always used.

She let out a polite laugh, her gaze flickering between Vanadar and me. "Well, that's a relief, isn't it?" she said tentatively. "To find the person responsible, I mean. But it's terrible to think that it was a murder, and not merely an accident."

"And to think it was a street performer," said Vanadar with a lopsided smile, shaking his head.

"Back where I come from, arresting someone is a serious matter," I said, frowning. "If the council agrees that you have committed a crime, they deliver swift and decisive justice."

Vanadar's laughter cut through the tension, his amusement clear. "Ah, the simplicity of tribal justice! Here in the city, we must navigate through layers of law and politics."

The veiled insinuations and polite facade of the conversation were incredibly unsettling. In my herd, conflicts were resolved openly, with clear declarations and often a test of strength or speed. Here, words could be as sharp as knives, hidden behind smiles and casual sips of tea.

"But what about the painting? What did they do with it after its debut at the art gala?" asked Tia, tilting her head. It was an exceedingly endearing pose.

I shook my head to indicate that I didn't have any news of the haunted painting.

"Indeed, although, wasn't it created many years ago, dearest? It's probably for the best that such an ancient and powerful artifact fades back into history," said Vanadar. "However, if the City Watch managed to nab the perpetrator of this crime, one would think recovering a missing painting would be simple enough for them."

He glanced out the darkened window for about the tenth time, where rain was beginning to drum against the glass.

Landlady Lyness returned with a fresh pot of tea, her timing impeccable. As she poured, Vanadar rose to leave, excusing himself with a cursory nod. His departure lifted a weight from the room, although my disquiet lingered. Something felt wrong about Anya's arrest, and this evening's conversation had only deepened my concerns. I resolved to continue my investigation, driven by a growing suspicion that there was more to uncover.

Chapter Seventeen

The rain continued all night, and when the small sun Hyperion was eclipsed by the moon Phoebe, the week officially came to a close. Eclipseday turned stormy, ruining my plans to return to the castle.

Outside, the storm screamed with a thousand forked tongues and the wind lashed thick drops of rain against the windows. I sat by the hearth in the parlor, where the fire provided pleasant warmth, writing in my journal.

I flipped to my profiles of Anya Vedeva and Tae Bellwyn, then turned the page and started a new spread. Copying the layout, I penned a sketch of Kari Ashmin on one side and, after a moment's thought, the naiad Aurelia on the other.

Professor Kari Ashmin was an alchemist who admitted her bitter rivalry with Lysandros Garbor. She was testing samples marked with an elaborate X, a symbol connected to Château Gorget. Had she done something to the castle—or to Garbor?

Aurelia—even my rough sketch of her—was too charming to truly inspire suspicion in me. But she did live in the lake near the castle, and she had recreated the haunted painting in miniature detail. Could she be involved somehow?

"What are you writing?" I looked up to see the speaker, Kai, paused in his game at the table. The gentle ruffling of the cards, along with the sound of Lilimari turning the pages in her book, created a calming rhythm accentuated by the crackle and pop of the fire.

"Just musings. What are you playing?" I asked.

Kai chuckled. "The gods may play games with us, but these cards, they tell us truths, revealing mysteries about ourselves and the unseen world around us. Let's see what they reveal tonight."

He flipped over a card. "Ah, the piper at the gates of dawn. A keeper of hidden knowledge and secrets, straddling the division between night and day. Part of two worlds, he senses the invisible threads that connect our world and the Underworld. Could it be someone we know? Someone who senses more than meets the eye?"

He glanced at me mischievously and I shifted uncomfortably on my haunches. Relief washed over me as Tia entered the room then, drawing everyone's attention with her arrival.

"Hello, Tia," Kai greeted her, glancing up from his cards. "You won't believe the tantalizing bits of news that have fluttered into my ears." He held a cupped hand to one of his long, pointed ears.

Tia took a seat next to Kai. "Do tell."

"I've been hearing stories lately of mysterious lights swirling about at the old castle in Misty Vale. Some say that it's the spirit of Lysandros Garbor, and others claim that it's the previous owner, Andreas Hippolyte. Garbor never resided at Château Gorget, after all. The place was in a state of ruin after Hippolyte destroyed it, along with himself, in his mad experiments. Ironic, really, when Hippolyte's goal was only ever the preservation of life. He had a daughter, you see, a sickly child whom he dedicated all his knowledge toward saving."

Intrigued by the mention of the castle, I leaned forward to listen. A flash of lightning illuminated the window behind the closed curtains.

Kai continued. "He was struck by inspiration when he found a unique ore on the castle grounds, by the shore of Silver Lake. From it, he isolated a beautiful metal that wouldn't tarnish—like gold, titanium or aluminum—and shone with all the colors of a phoenix's tail. He spent years developing potions, tonics, and tinctures from the metal, testing them on himself and any rats who found their way into the castle."

"What happened?" asked Lilimari in a bored voice, but her dark eyes gleamed with interest as she stared at Kai over the top of her book.

"Nothing happened to the rats, at least not right away." He paused for dramatic effect. "It wasn't until years later that the castle residents began to notice unusual behavior in the cats. Without any apparent cause, the felines would go from a state of calm to abrupt alertness, tensing up and fur bristling. They would sometimes stare for long moments at seemingly empty space."

Lilimari sighed, her book resting in her lap. "I would love to read the details of Hippolyte's experiments."

"The alchemist realized that the spirits of the laboratory rats, once their bodies expired, were unable to pass on and they were tormenting their former hunters! He gave up on his miracle metal. His daughter ended up living a normal life span despite her fragile health, but what happened to Andreas Hippolyte after the disaster? I'll let you decide," Kai concluded with a wink.

Thunder boomed, causing Tia to startle.

"Don't try to scare me with ghost stories, you goof," she admonished, lightly pushing his shoulder. "You know they prevent me from sleeping."

Kai's graceful hands briefly faltered over his cards at the playful shove.

"Now, now," Landlady Lyness interjected, turning from where she was meticulously arranging books on an overflowing shelf. "Let's not trouble anyone by spreading these spooky tales. Nonsense, they are."

Nature, of course, was filled with spirits. As a foal, I had been taught that our magic relied on cooperation between centaurs and nature spirits. But the spirits of the dead were not a subject for concern, and death by spiritual attack was completely unheard of—even, as I understood, in this foreign city.

"Simarron, you went to the castle, and you didn't see any . . . ghosts, did you?" Tia spoke up in an uncertain tone, as if trying to convince herself.

"I didn't see any ghosts at the castle," I confirmed. However, I didn't remember telling my housemates about the safety inspection at Château Gorget.

"But, my dears," Kai continued, "there's a more enthralling piece of gossip. Whether or not you believe in The Incredible Spectra's powers, Anya Vedeva managed to vanish a part of Lysandros Garbor's fortune into thin air."

"What, how?" I asked. I vaguely recalled the pair discussing a business deal at the art gala, but I thought those plans had died along with Lysandros Garbor.

"Apparently . . ." Kai placed another card down with deliberate emphasis, like an exclamation point punctuating his words. "Anya convinced Lysandros to invest a substantial amount of money in a project to convert Château Gorget and healing springs at the nearby Silver Lake into a luxury hotel and theater," he continued. "Just imagine: plays, musical performances, magic shows, and rooms for card games and roulette! There were plans to develop Silver Lake, too."

I frowned. "It's just . . . Château Gorget is so far from the city. It takes hours to get there. I'm not sure how many wealthy patrons would make the trip often enough to make it a viable business."

Landlady Lyness sighed. "Are you saying my family mansion isn't rich enough for your tastes? How I would love for someone to invest in this place."

"Dani, we love this place!" Tia assured her.

As she spoke, a loud bang echoed throughout the room, causing us all to jump. The icy wind gusted in, extinguishing the oil lamps. In the hearth, the fire sputtered.

"What was that?" I exclaimed, my hooves clattering on the wood floor as I rose to all four feet.

"That wind!" The dark form of the landlady, silhouetted by the fire, rushed to close the window that was flapping open on creaking hinges. "Oh, what are they *doing* in the Weather Tower today?"

The room was quiet and still once more. As my eyes adjusted, I noticed an eerie green light, pulsing and flickering in the darkness of the hallway.

Tia's voice trembled as she spoke, "Is that . . . is that a ghostly app—apparition?"

"Not necessarily," I said, sniffing the air for ectoplasm, but all I smelled was the fireplace and smoke from the extinguished lamps, mixed with the sharp, crackling scent of fear and the lightning outside. "Lilimari, are you using a luminescent potion?"

"It's not me." The alchemy student was approaching the ball of light cautiously, its green glow faintly illuminating her face and outstretched hand.

I followed her into the hallway, the landlady trailing behind us. Just as we reached the glowing orb, a deafening crash of thunder rattled the mansion. The green light flared momentarily before vanishing.

"What is this?" My hand touched something solid where the light had been—a brass wall fixture. A meteor crystal had been set in the old wall sconce in place of a candle, draped with a piece of cloth. The octagonal glass housing the crystal was not the same shape as a taper, and so it sat very loosely in the antique fixture. Any slight vibration caused the ethereal light to waver as it shone through the cloth.

"Landlady Lyness, did you install a meteor crystal light?"

"Well, I can afford some improvements after all," she said with an air of indifference. "I've been told this hallway is too dark at night. But I find myself wondering, how does one go about snuffing out its glow when it's no longer needed?"

"Umb, you don't need to worry about burning it out like a candle or fading like phosphorus, you know," said Lilimari with a nasal twang as she launched into an explanation. "You see, the crystals contain a sort of elemental composition that's unknown here on Mirtoklas.

When they fall from the sky in those meteors onto the ice sheet, they bring with them a power unlike anything else."

She paused thoughtfully. "Now, this power, it's like a fire that never goes out. Inside those crystals, there's a constant energy at work, like tiny elemental spirits dancing around, always moving, always glowing. And when you want to put out the light, you have to find a way to quiet those spirits. You do this by covering it, like a birdcage. You know, you had the right idea, but a lead-lined cloth or a lead shutter works best."

"And they are quite dangerous if not handled properly. You should let Lilimari or myself install it," I added. As ubiquitous as meteor crystals were now, it wasn't so long ago that the Bureau of Magical Inquiries actively cracked down on alchemists who experimented with them, and for good reason.

Landlady Lyness nodded. "Good thing I got myself an alchemist and a magical safety inspector."

As we made our way back into the parlor, Tia gasped. She was pointing to something with one hand; Kai gripped her other arm.

"Whatever is the matter?" asked Landlady Lyness, then she immediately sucked in her breath.

There, on a side table, where it clearly hadn't been before, a yellowed piece of paper sat in the light of the oil lamp.

Kai picked it up. "It's . . . a note. 'Dear friend, are you fatigued by the relentless march of time? Do you wish to avoid the journey to the Underworld and hereafter? What if I told you that I could anchor your soul to the here and now?' . . . What's this doing here?"

He handed it to our landlady, who took it with shaking fingers. Her breath caught in her throat as her eyes scanned the faded words.

"Dani, are you quite well?" Kai asked, concern etched on his dark features.

Landlady Lyness hesitated. Finally, she swallowed hard and replied, "It can't be."

Tia placed a gentle hand on her shoulder. "You can talk to us, Dani."

"About how my alchemist mother was involved with the Soul Anchor? The constant arguments with my father about its dangers?" Her fingers clenched the aged paper, creasing it.

"Soul Anchor? I saw something about this in the MASHA storage room," I said. I wondered if Vanadar could have somehow left it yesterday. He had called the haunted painting the "soul painting." What did he know about it? Of course, there had to be a connection! "The haunted painting—it's a Soul Anchor."

"Wait, a Soul Anchor?" asked Lilimari, my excitement mirrored in her eyes. "It makes total sense that the haunted painting is really a Soul Anchor, if it came from Château Gorget. Andreas Hippolyte wanted to save his daughter, and a Soul Anchor is meant to grant immortality of a sort to the subject, right? It's ingenious! You know, there's theories on using alchemy to bind souls to objects. I wish I had been able to examine the painting at the art gala . . ." Her voice trailed off as she caught sight of Daniella's stricken expression. "Oh," she added awkwardly, as Tia pulled the older woman into a warm hug.

"Perhaps this isn't the time," Tia murmured as Daniella gazed over Tia's shoulder into the fire.

I burned with shame. Daniella Lyness had been nothing but kind to me, and here Lilimari and I were coldly examining the source of her family's drama. But if the haunted painting was really a Soul Anchor, it couldn't have killed Lysandros Garbor. A Soul Anchor didn't take life—it preserved it. I opened my mouth to ask something, but the weight of the moment held me back.

Outside, the storm raged on.

Chapter Eighteen

I arrived at work early the following day—perhaps a bit too early, as the sky was still tinged with pre-dawn darkness. Excitement over last night's revelation—that the haunted painting was a Soul Anchor—kept me restless. Eager to check the files in the old storage room, I found that once I woke early, sleep refused to return.

The MASHA building looked strange at this hour. Light from the meteor crystal streetlamps cast an eerie glow on the ground floor of the brick building, while the upper floors remained shadowed, their outlines only beginning to emerge from the night. The air was chilly, but the rain had washed away the stubborn remains of packed snow.

I didn't have a key, I realized, mentally kicking myself at my lack of forethought. In the city, buildings were locked overnight, of course. I placed my hand on the door anyway, and it moved slightly. I paused, then continued inside, feeling a tingle in my spine as I crossed the threshold. Shadowy lumps of furniture lurked against the dark wood background in the lobby. Wan light filtered in through the slats in the tall shuttered windows. I caught a flicker of movement where the secretary's desk should be.

"Hello?" I called softly, my voice echoing through the empty building, feeling somewhat foolish.

With a rhythmic clap, I activated the spell that opened the shutters over the meteor crystal lamps. Despite the sudden blaze of brightness, the chill lingering in the air made me shiver.

"Is anyone here?" As my eyes adjusted to the brightness, I noticed nothing amiss. I went deeper into the building.

I didn't notice my supervisor's arrival until her voice startled me.

"Simarron! What are you doing here so early?" asked Administrator Hereswith. "I suppose I should have made it clear: your work hours are from nine in the morning to five in the evening."

"But Mina, the door was unlocked when I got here," I said cautiously.

"The secretary has a key." She paused. "You have met Secretary Ami sanMaelthara, haven't you?"

I shook my head. "I was beginning to think they were a ghost."

"She is of a frail constitution and often works odd hours." Mina called down the hall, "Ami?"

"With the lights out?" I voiced doubtfully, following her. The corridor lamps were dark, and there was movement close to the floor. Something was crawling in jerky movements, setting off a wave of fear in me. I felt the need to run and simultaneously the inexplicable urge to stomp it with my hooves.

The thing moaned, lifting its pale face from the floor. Two-leggers just shouldn't crawl on the floor like that!

"Ami, are you well?" Mina rushed forward as I scrambled back, my nostrils flaring. The secretary smelled strange, an aroma I could only describe as *gray*.

"So loud," Ami complained in a brittle voice, slumping forward again and covering her head with her frail arms.

"I have a headache charm in my office, I'll fetch it for you," said Mina soothingly, dropping her voice.

Ami wailed again and followed Mina into her office, dragging herself along the floor.

I rubbed the back of my neck. "Nice to meet you—sorry to be a bother—I need to go now." The hallway now clear, I turned to bolt into my office, but was halted by Director Moosekind's stern voice.

"Simarron, my office, please."

Swallowing hard, I stepped in and he closed the frosted glass door, sitting down at his desk.

His mustache twitched as he spoke. "What's this about you bothering Kari Ashmin, coming to her workshop unannounced and pestering her with inquiries? You do know that the professor is on the board that oversees MASHA, don't you?"

I shifted from hoof to hoof. "Well, Director, I did inquire about a particular substance. Don't you think the City Watch's arrest was a bit hasty?"

Director Moosekind's eyes narrowed, disappearing almost completely into his bushy eyebrows. "And now you're questioning the City Watch, too? Would this substance be related to the Château Gorget safety inspection and Lysandros Garbor?"

I nodded, and the director let out an exasperated sigh. "Mina told me that the case notes have gone missing. For one thing, such carelessness reflects poorly upon the entire organization."

I winced. "Apologies, Director."

"For another thing, we cannot be seen to be criticizing the City Watch, especially when our own methods can be found lacking. And finally, I don't want to hear about you bothering Kari Ashmin without reason, am I clear?"

"Yes, Director Moosekind."

"The secretary has booked a number of appointments for today, with folks seeking licenses, permits, and whatnot. The first one will be arriving soon. Since you're here so early and she is unwell, you can take it."

"But why are we taking appointments before nine o'clock in the morning? When did the secretary get here?"

Director Moosekind answered patiently, "We have certain clientele who, like Ami, prefer to work outside of normal daylight hours. Now, I know everyone's captivated by the intrigue surrounding Lysandros Garbor, but we've got to keep things running smoothly. You're a good worker, Simarron, but it's no good to MASHA to go galloping off on your own and losing files. Focus on your duties today or your position here is at stake—am I clear?"

"Yes, Director."

He handed me the list of appointments Ami had scheduled.

"Thank you, Director," I said, my tail low, taking the list as I left his office.

I closed the door behind me, took a calming breath, and glanced over the vacant secretary's desk to a figure seated in the lobby, an unassuming woman with chestnut hair pulled back into a neat bun. She was holding a small child in her lap. I glanced at the appointment sheet again to be sure of what I read.

"Helena Thanamara?" I asked.

"Yes, I'm here about a necromancy license?" Her child shook its wooden rattle, shaped like the two-pronged staff of the goddess of the Underworld, topped with a globe.

"I'm Safety Inspector Simarron. Right this way please."

Helena nodded, moving her little one to her hip as she stood. The child hadn't taken its eyes off me, and as I moved away down the hall, I could feel its eyes boring into my back. When we passed by Mina's office, I was relieved that her door was now closed. I didn't know what to think of the secretary or the clients she normally saw.

In my office, the child lunged toward the armillary sphere, but the mother deftly shifted position so it was out of reach. All would be fine as long as the miniature two-legger stayed off the floor, I reassured myself. Inexplicably, even more so than stairs, nothing distressed me more than crawling things.

"Helena, I'll need to verify the authenticity of your necromancy abilities and ensure you understand our regulations," I began once she was seated. "First, may I see your necromancy certificate?"

Helena undid the drawstrings on her reticule with one hand and pulled out a scroll, handing it to me. I pulled a blank necromancy permit and affixed it to my clipboard.

Unfurling the scroll from Vivian's Academy of Eternal Arts, I scrutinized the runes, symbols, and the signature of Vivian Van Adair. "Very well. Now, let's discuss a few important safety measures. First, are you residing within a quarter mile of any cemetery or graveyard?"

Helena shook her head. "No, my home is quite far from any burial grounds."

I took her address, printed it on the form, then checked my map of the city's cemeteries and graveyards to verify the accuracy of her statement.

"Good," I acknowledged with a nod. "Next, our regulations stipulate that necromancers must adhere to time limits when summoning the deceased. No more than thirty minutes of interaction with a spirit is allowed at a time, to avoid anyone becoming lost in the Underworld or any spirits set loose in the world of the living."

Helena's bun bobbed as she retrieved an hourglass from her reticule, its frame shaped like skeletal hands. "I always use this."

Suddenly anxious about what else was in that drawstring bag, I hurried on, "Lastly, it's important to obtain consent from the family or next of kin when attempting to communicate with a spirit. This ensures both ethical practice and the well-being of all parties involved."

"Oh, I would never attempt contact without the family's consent," she responded in a sincere tone. "It's about offering closure and comfort—or finding out where Grandpa buried the money, not causing distress. I'm very attuned to the sensitivity toward necromancers right now, what with Necromancer Anya Vedeva's arrest for murder, and the haunted painting and all."

"Yes, very wise to be aware of these things." She was the image of a perfect mother with kind eyes and an attentive manner. The child smiled to reveal a single pointed tooth in the middle of its maw, and I stifled a shudder.

"If you stick to these rules, I have no doubt that you'll be an asset to our community, Necromancer Helena Thanamara," I said, inscribing her name, the date and my signature to the form. I waved my clipboard for a moment to speed the ink drying.

Helena smiled warmly. "Thank you very much, Safety Inspector Simarron."

She checked that everything was written correctly on the form, and then I made another copy for MASHA records using a sheet of duplication paper. I smoothed a sheet of the enchanted black paper evenly over the form and then pressed it to a blank piece of paper. The original's ink was now slightly faded, but I had a perfect copy.

"Have a good day," I said, handing her the copy of the form. As the newly registered necromancer retreated down the hall, the child turned its head to stare at me in an unnerving fashion.

I settled into the quiet, glancing down at the list of appointments. I hadn't intended to overhear, but the sound of Mina's door opening and shutting firmly, and the murmur of voices carrying through the wall caught my attention.

"Captain Voshawk. This is a surprise. What brings you here?" Mina asked.

A masculine voice, rough in texture but elegant in its pronunciation, replied, "Administrator Hereswith, I'm here on official business regarding Necromancer Anya Vedeva. I understand MASHA has records relating to her necromancy, potentially pertinent to our ongoing case."

"It's good to see the City Watch finally acknowledging the resources at MASHA's disposal," said Mina, her tone measured but with a trace of irony.

"We had sufficient evidence to make an arrest," Captain Voshawk replied stiffly. "I'm here merely to dot the i's and cross the t's, as they say. You understand the pressure of managing high-profile cases."

"Certainly, Captain. I would have thought, though, that checking with us before making an arrest might have been more . . . prudent."

"MASHA's involvement is not always necessary. We handle criminal activities, you handle magical malpractices. Sometimes those worlds overlap, but I don't need to remind you that they are not the same."

"Of course not, but perhaps if the Bureau of Magical Inquiries had understood that distinction, it might still exist."

"You know as well as I do that the Bureau's dissolution was political, Hereswith. And let's not pretend MASHA is universally respected. Half the city thinks you're a joke—a bureaucratic layer added to give an illusion of control."

"And the other half sleeps better knowing that we're here. Just take a look at my inbox. We've been inundated with concerns about necromancers."

"If anything, MASHA has only stoked the flames of panic concerning hauntings and possessed artifacts," Voshawk retorted.

"Captain, let's stay focused," said Mina coolly. "You need Anya Vedeva's records? You shall have them. But next time, perhaps a bit of collaboration before actions are taken wouldn't hurt. We might save each other some trouble."

"Point taken," said the watch captain, his tone softened. "Thank you for your cooperation. I look forward to receiving the records."

A door swung open, and Mina's voice called out, "Damon, we may be in different roles now, but just because the old Bureau is gone doesn't mean we have to go our separate ways."

I couldn't catch his reply as the tall man retreated down the hall, apparently unwilling to wait for said records.

A few minutes later, Mina stepped inside my office with an announcement. "Simarron, we need Anya Vedeva's file. Captain Voshawk just left my office, and he's asked for our records on her."

I nodded and stood to join her at the filing cabinet, where I'd just been about to file Helena Thanamara's permit.

I pulled open the drawer labeled with a V and quickly flipped through the files until I found the one for Anya Vedeva. The wooden drawer gave a protesting squeak, but offered up the file without resistance.

I handed the file to Mina, who opened it on my desk, scanning the contents with a practiced eye. The file was thin, containing only basic information: her home country was listed as The Bloodborn Commonwealth, a region known for its rich tradition in the darker arts of magic.

"She's staying at a tavern and inn here in Kami-Nihkia," Mina read aloud, her finger tracing the line of text.

I peered over her shoulder and looked up the address on the map. "No burial grounds nearby," I noted.

"For her school of necromancy, it just lists family ancestry," Mina added. "There's no record of formal complaints or any violations against her. It seems she's been compliant with all local regulations."

Mina frowned slightly, closing the file with a snap. "That's all we have. It's not much, but it does imply that her activities have been above board. I'll relay this to Captain Voshawk, though I doubt he'll be pleased."

I watched as Mina collected the file. "Do you think the City Watch is on the right track arresting her?" I asked, doubt creeping into my voice.

Mina paused at the door, considering this question. "I think he's under a lot of pressure to solve Lysandros Garbor's case quickly. Sometimes that leads to hasty decisions. Let's just hope this isn't one of them."

With that, she left my office with the file tucked under her arm.

I checked my pocket watch, then pulled out my journal and turned to my profiles. It seemed unlikely that Anya Vedeva had used necromancy to kill her business partner. What about Tae Bellwyn? Unfortunately, I still didn't know much about her. I turned the page to Kari Ashmin and Aurelia. What research had Garbor stolen from Ashmin? Could it have involved using alchemy to bind souls to objects, as

Lilimari suggested? Yet if the painting really was a Soul Anchor, it couldn't have been the instrument of his death.

I closed my notes as the time for my next appointment drew near, resolving to return to the storage room as soon as I had the chance.

Chapter Nineteen

My stomach rumbled as the lunch hour approached, and I debated whether I had time to slip into the storage room before the next appointment. Just as I was about to go, a tentative knock sounded at my door. I looked up, expecting Mina—but instead, Lilimari entered, her face pinched with worry.

My fatigue vanished and I was immediately flooded with concern. "Lilimari, what are you doing here? Didn't university classes begin today?"

"Yeah, and Professor Ashmin didn't show up to teach her class," Lilimari said. "We were all worried something might be wrong."

"Did anyone try to reach her via Witchy Whisk?" I asked, frowning.

"She wasn't at her home, or the alchemy hall on Gold Row, and a finding spell turned up nothing." Her voice was quiet, but an undercurrent of fear sent a chill down my spine.

"That is indeed concerning." My frown deepened as worst-case scenarios flooded my mind. I flicked my tail uneasily, hating that I was suddenly as jumpy as a colt, but considering recent events—the haunted painting which may or may not be a Soul Anchor, Garbor's death, and a possible dispute between him and the professor over some research—I couldn't shake the feeling that something sinister was at play. "When I last saw Professor Ashmin, she was running some experiments in her lab . . ."

Lilimari reached into her schoolbag and withdrew an envelope addressed to Professor Ashmin at the university. "I found this in her lab on campus," she said, hesitating for a moment before handing it over.

I opened the envelope and unfolded the paper, revealing a strange drawing. A wobbly circle was bisected by unevenly inked lines. Scribbled symbols and cryptic markings adorned edges of the diagram. "Alchemy symbols."

"Yeah, but the symbol in the middle isn't one that I've seen before," said Lilimari. "Do you have any duplication paper?" She glanced about and grabbed a fountain pen.

I opened the rolltop writing desk and handed her a sheet of enchanted black paper, as well as a white sheet of ordinary paper. She smoothed the duplication paper out evenly over the note and then pressed it to the clean sheet of paper. Setting aside the original, she began adding notes to the copy. Her focus was intense, and for long moments, the heavy silence of the room was only broken by the soft scrape of the pen.

I peered closer at the symbol on the original, a sort of elaborate X, circled many times in a whorl of black ink. It was evocative of the symbol that I'd seen on the model of Château Gorget and in the professor's lab. The frenetic handwriting didn't seem to fit, though. It was so unlike the professor's meticulous nature.

"I've seen it before, although I don't know what it means." I set the note down and rifled through my papers for the file with her workshop permit. "However, I can tell you this isn't her handwriting," I said, comparing the note and the permit request side-by-side.

Lilimari clutched the copy with both hands, pulling it closer to her face as if she could force it to give up its secrets with her dark stare. "So someone else gave the professor this note before she left."

"These symbols must hold a deeper meaning," I said, my mind racing. If only I wasn't such a complete novice when it came to the magic of the two-leggers! I stared at the mysterious chart until my eyes began to blur, my gaze trapped within its lines.

My nostrils flared as the smell hit me then, the sharp and unmistakable odor of decaying wood and blood. "That's it!" I exclaimed. "The haunted painting had this smell." That made this scrap of paper another thing inexplicably linked to the painting—the Soul Anchor. I couldn't see how, but my nose didn't lie.

"Hold on, maybe it isn't some mystical message, but a simple cypher," said Lilimari. "Leaving the strange mark in the center aside, I believe that the alchemy symbols are standing in for numbers."

I suddenly rose to all fours, filled with urgency. "Or coordinates . . . it's a map! And the position and phase of the moon aren't mystical, but simply showing the time to meet at the appointed place."

"Oh!" Lilimari exclaimed. "If these coordinates point to the university, and the city square is here, then this leads to . . ." Our eyes traveled to my map of the city's cemeteries and graveyards still spread open on my desk. "Why, there's nothing here but an old graveyard."

I froze, acutely aware that Director Moosekind had just told me not to go galloping off—specifically, that my job was at stake. My gaze flickered between the orderly map of the city's burial grounds and the other—the mess of unsteady lines of ink, its meaning murky.

One thing was clear, however. If I was fired from my job, it could be difficult to get another one unless I wanted to unload cargo at the docks or pull people in rickshaws, which I didn't. However, if I didn't have any income, I wouldn't be able to stay in the city, and going back home was not an option.

"You have work. I'll go," said Lilimari, sensing my hesitation.

"No." True, I did have work. I saw myself as a safety inspector protecting a city that seemed largely unaware of the risks of magic and alchemy. I wanted to be a gentleman centaur who has a professional job and lives in a nice home, and I didn't wish to jeopardize that, but what could be more important than investigating a professor's safety in a mysterious situation?

My hands twitched toward the paper covered in cryptic scrawl. I picked it up—the original map, in case its scent carried more clues. Carefully folding it into my satchel, I grabbed my cloak and set out down the hall with Lilimari.

"Simarron! Where are you going?" Mina called out as I rushed by her office.

"Emergency safety inspection!" I replied, nearly tripping over my own hooves as I scrambled out of the building and into the street. It was true, after all, in a very loose sense. I felt a pang of guilt at my actions, but not for disregarding the rules. In the choice between duty and compassion, a true professional would have acted without hesitation. I hated that I battled between reckless impulse and selfish desire for my own safety—how very centaur-like of me!

The sky was sunset pink and our faces were flushed with exertion when we reached the graveyard, puffs of breath clouding in the cold air. Our muffled footsteps disappeared in the wet leaf mold that covered the winding walkways and a chilling wind whispered through the overgrown tombstones. The rain from the previous night had left the ground muddy.

As the suns slipped toward the horizon behind a screen of bare trees, the rush of discovery faded and I was left with a deepening sense of concern.

"Goddess, why didn't we go to the City Watch?"

Lilimari exhaled sharply. "I wouldn't trust them to find their own behinds with a map."

"This may be dangerous, Lilimari. You should go back," I said, my voice low with warning.

"What? I'm not afraid," she scoffed. "Besides, anyone would think twice before messing with a centaur, you know."

Our words died quickly in the wind, and I needed to save my breath for hiking the uneven terrain. The cemetery hadn't been maintained for a long time. Where I could still make out the engravings, the moss-covered headstones revealed dates going back to the founding days of Kami-Nihkia. Weathered and worn, they stood as silent sentinels to the passage of time.

The graveyard unfolded in a meandering, organic layout. It looped back in on itself at points and I would have found myself quite turned around if it wasn't for Lilimari's guidance.

"Not many people bother coming out here anymore—just the odd old wizard here and there. People say it's haunted, but I think it's beautiful," said Lilimari softly. "Look at these headstones. They're like ancient relics from when wizard families flaunted their wealth and power. Nowadays, anyone who attends the university can meddle in magic, and alchemists are practically tripping over themselves to make new discoveries."

"Do you visit here often?" I asked.

"I told you, I'm used to exploring the city on my own." She rolled her eyes, then suddenly exclaimed, "Oh!"

"What is it?" I swept my gaze through the encroaching shadows, alert to danger.

"The strange mark in the center of Professor Ashim's map, that X, indicates a missing element," she said excitedly in her nasally tone. "The great work of the alchemists of this century is to find those elements which are theorized to exist but haven't been discovered yet."

"Whoever would be the first to discover element X and make a pact with it would surely become famous then?" I asked.

"You're thinking like a wizard," Lilimari snorted. "The grand goal of alchemy is mastery of all elements without having to make pacts with each individual element. And finding the missing elements will surely help crack the code to the entire Periodic System of the Elements. Any element X would be an important discovery, you know."

"Important enough to kill for," I said as a cold wind sliced between the skeletal trees and rows of uneven headstones.

As twilight cast its shroud, the somber atmosphere settled into an ominous dread filled with the music of shadows: the raw whispers of crickets and the lonely cries of night birds.

"There," said Lilimari, pointing out an ancient mausoleum towering above the graveyard. The imposing structure of dark granite resembled many of the temples to the gods, but its facade had crumbled and one corner was visibly sinking into the ground.

I nodded. Navigating the washed out path, I headed toward it with cautious anticipation, my tail pressed against my body.

"Oh!" Lilimari cried again, this time in pain, as she slipped in the mud and stumbled forward, catching herself on a headstone.

"Lilimari!" I exclaimed, rushing to her side. "Are you all right?"

She winced. "Umb, I'm fine. Just a bit of a twist, I think."

I looked around for a suitable place to rest when I spied a faint light shining from within the mausoleum. The iron gate was slightly ajar, creaking ominously as a gust of wind pushed against it.

With Lilimari leaning on me for support, we closed the distance to the gate and pulled it fully open. The hinges groaned, the sound echoing through the empty graveyard like a mournful wail. Inside, the space was shrouded in darkness, save for the soft pool of light cast on the floor by a meteor crystal pendant.

"Don't look," I said, but Lilimari was already gazing at the scene, her dark eyes wide in horror.

Kari Ashmin lay on the floor, unmoving. There were faint traces of a chalk circle around her, as well as arcane runes.

"A necromancer did this?" I observed as I knelt down and checked the alchemy professor's pulse. Nothing. I gingerly held up the pendant by its chain and shone the light in her face, to no response.

Besides the glowing pendant, she wore another necklace—a locket. Though there were no wounds or spilled blood visible, she was cold and still. Her face was faintly bluish and fixed in a terrified grimace. My lips curled back as Kari Ashmin's slightly sweet, burned scent of carbolic acid and roasted coffee wafted up. There was a sharp smell layered on top of it, like garlic.

After a moment, Lilimari replied tentatively, "I . . . I'm not sure if it's necromancy," she admitted, her gaze still fixed on her teacher.

I slowly and a little unsteadily rose to all fours, tears springing to my eyes. I felt overwhelmed with emotion, not just at my own horror, but as if I had experienced a shadow of the last moment of the scene before me.

"It smells toxic," I said, shaking my head to clear it. Who had lured Kari Ashmin here with the encrypted map and what had she hoped to find in this secluded graveyard?

"I don't smell anything," said Lilimari. "But it's possible that some kind of gas could be dispersed in an enclosed space like this . . . I don't know."

"Let's get you home," I said.

Lilimari shook her head slightly, though it was more of a tremble. "I'll be fine," she said through gritted teeth. "We should probably report this to the City Watch," she added reluctantly.

I sighed and hung my head in defeat. In the end, I was unable to help Kari Ashmin. I felt the weight of the old, crumbling mausoleum bearing down on my chest, constricting my breath. My gaze flickered back to the faint light of Professor Ashmin's pendant. It was evident that the professor had come here at night, using the pendant to light her path. Ultimately, however, it appeared she hadn't been able to see her demise coming. Even armed with my suspicions, I hadn't really expected this outcome.

What did I think I could do, anyway? I was just a MASHA safety inspector. And I hesitated at the prospect of calling the City Watch, having never interacted with law enforcement before. What would they think of me finding Kari Ashmin here? How would I begin to explain the cryptic map?

I slipped my hand into my satchel and pulled out the map, as if it could somehow make this grim scene make more sense. But in the dim light of the meteor crystal pendant, the messy writing refused to yield order.

I startled—nearly spooked out of my skin—at the sound of something cutting through the air above. Glancing out the mausoleum doorway, I saw a silhouette against the moonlight, swooping down from the sky. I tensed, preparing to defend myself and Lilimari, but the approaching figure was not a threat.

It was Mina.

The broomstick landed smoothly. "Really, Simarron? An 'Emergency Inspection' and you thought you could handle this alone?" Mina's tone was a mix of reprimand and concern as she dismounted. Her gaze fell on Kari Asmin's prone body in the remains of the chalk circle. Her red lips parted, aghast.

"Mina," I began, startled. "I didn't think—"

"That much is clear," she interjected, quickly gathering her composure, then softened as she turned her attention to Lilimari. "Let's see what we've got here," she said, examining Lilimari's ankle.

"I brought him here," said Lilimari. "It's my fault."

"By the power of Titanacala…" Tiny beads of light pulsed between Mina's fingers and Lilimari's ankle, tracing a delicate, filamentous path. Greenish-blue metallic lines shimmered on the backs of Mina's hands as she wove the healing spell. The veins, like oxidized bronze at her temples, seemed to glow. "Part of my job is ensuring the proper training of safety inspectors. I'll take you home. Simarron, go to the City Watch immediately."

I nodded, exiting the mausoleum and retracing my steps as quickly as I dared across the uneven ground. A true professional—wiser and calmer, like Mina—would have anticipated this outcome and sought help from the proper authorities right away. But I was never trying to be a hero, I reminded myself. I simply felt like I had to act when I had the chance to do something. Now I would swallow my fear of speaking with the City Watch and report what I'd found. It was what was required of me, and it was the only thing left to do.

Chapter Twenty

My heart raced as I approached the City Watch station on the main thoroughfare. I rapped urgently against the wooden door, and moments later, the door creaked open, revealing the tired face of the watch captain on duty.

"What's the matter, lad?" the man grumbled, squinting at me groggily. As he held up his lantern, I saw that he was a Sireliad with eyes the color of steel and a gray, drooping mustache.

"Professor Ashmin's dead," I blurted out. "In the graveyard."

"Someone's dead in the graveyard?" asked the watch captain, raising a skeptical eyebrow. "Imagine that."

"That is to say, a most recent and untimely death took place in the graveyard." My voice trembled as I recounted following the cryptic map to the discovery of Kari Ashmin's lifeless body in the mausoleum.

The watch captain's demeanor shifted from annoyance to alarm, and he turned, barking orders to those inside the station. "Form up, there's trouble!"

Not a minute later, two more coppers had gathered, clad in their uniforms and gripping swords. The watch captain gestured for me to lead the way, so I hurried from the main street, leading the guards down the twisting paths to the neglected graveyard. I retraced my steps in agony, knowing all too well what I would find this time.

Arriving at the graveyard, the watch captain and coppers spread out, their meteor crystal lanterns casting eerie shadows among the tombstones. I guided them to where Kari Ashmin's body lay in the mausoleum, frozen in death with that terrible expression.

The two coppers exchanged nervous glances as they observed the chalked necromantic runes surrounding the scene. One of them, a young recruit with wide eyes, muttered, "This ain't right, you know. They say this place is haunted."

The other copper nodded, her voice hushed. "Aye, look at the poor woman's face! She looks like she's been scared to death."

The watch captain gave them a steely glare, the lantern light highlighting his weathered features. "Ever since that nonsense with the haunted painting, people's imaginations have been running wild. Isn't it bad enough that we have to deal with real crimes and criminals?"

I grunted, lowering myself carefully to examine something glinting in the light of the powerful lantern. I picked up a wisp of thin, almost invisible filament, surprisingly strong for how insubstantial it felt as I rubbed it gently between my thumb and forefinger. "Indeed. I think she's been killed by more conventional means."

I showed the wire to the watch captain, who shrugged and gathered it in a handkerchief. "I'll notify the coroner. It's her job to determine the cause of death and determine if foul play was involved, whether it be physical or magical," he said firmly. "This is no place to hang around and speculate idly. Could be haunted, after all."

Was he joking? I must have given him a startled look.

The watch captain's lips twitched into a tired smile. "Come on, lad, the coroner will be notified in the morning."

"And what should I do?" I asked.

"For now, you'll need to come with us to the station," he replied. "We'll get your statement."

With that, the two coppers carefully lifted Kari Ashmin's body into a hammock, using it as a stretcher. As we began the somber procession back to the City Watch station, my thoughts swirled with more doubts and uncertainties.

Who had murdered Professor Ashmin? I wouldn't know until I read it in *The Mercury* or heard a bit of gossip from Kai, for it was out of my hands now. It was up to the City Watch and the coroner—qualified professionals—to solve the murders of the two alchemists.

With my hooves dragging in fatigue and my hindquarters heavy with defeat, I was nearly home when I remembered Landlady Lyness's protection spell. The mansion on Slant Row was like an old and venerated member of the Lyness family to her. She had trusted me with a key, but I hesitated as I lifted it to the lock on the front door.

"House, it's me, Simarron," I whispered to the heavy oak door. "I live here, so please let me in without waking anyone up." I gave it a friendly pat before turning the key in the lock.

I made it down the hall to my room without incident and collapsed into my nest of blankets, plagued by nagging doubts and recent memories. I must have drifted off to sleep eventually, for I woke up some time later to find that I couldn't move. There was a heavy pressure on my chest and my limbs weren't taking orders from my mind. Was it the protection spell? *House, I'm not an intruder. I'm simply the centaur who lives in this room.*

My head spun, and suddenly I was a kid lying in bed, blankets pulled up to my chin, fearful of a shadow that lurked just beyond the boundary of my bed. I then knew, with childlike certainty, that the strange noises in my room couldn't be written off as the settling of an old house. The feeling of being watched wasn't my imagination.

Abruptly, a draft rustled the curtain that covered the window overlooking the street. The bright light of the meteor crystal street-lamps faded to the soft glow of oil lamps. The stars spun in the sky and the halo from the lights formed into hoop skirts and daisy chains. I was overwhelmed by a sense of nostalgia.

I shut my eyes, and the light became a green after-image against the background of my eyelids, the circles breaking apart into small dots as they faded to yellow. I felt like a foal, running through a field of buttercups.

What the Hecatonchires? As I slipped back into a half-lucid state, I realized that it was the memory of that other presence. I could feel it flitting about the edges of my mind, with a smell like phosphorus or . . . ectoplasm. Yet what could I do, paralyzed as I was? I surrendered to the ethereal dance of memories that swirled around me.

"It's all right," I whispered, or thought I did. The words may only have formed in my mind. "We can both live here."

I took a deep, calming breath and caught the scent of freshly baked bread. Surely Landlady Lyness wasn't baking at this hour?

"In a way, I'm a lost spirit as well. My parents . . . they told me I'm not welcome in their herd anymore. I'm as good as dead to them." My words stung, but somehow it felt good to uncover the wound.

I continued, "Maybe that's why I feel such affinity for the dead." I had felt something strange when I saw Professor Ashmin's body earlier. A flash of emotion, a shadow of her last moments, almost like what I was experiencing now. Had it been . . . her spirit? Her face, distorted in death, swam up in the current of my thoughts. I squeezed my eyes shut more forcefully, but the image lingered, distorted now by the orange spots pressing against my eyelids.

"I had suspected Professor Ashmin of killing Lysandros Garbor. After all, she had a grudge against him for stealing her work. She could probably concoct all manner of deadly poisons in her lab, and perhaps the ghost story was just a distraction. But now she, too, is dead, and it seems . . . unlikely."

My troubled thoughts continued to gnaw at me as I slipped under the spell of sleep. Did Anya Vedeva kill Lysandros Garbor after all? She was an illusion wizard masquerading as a necromancer and the deaths seemed staged as the work of spirits. The City Watch certainly seemed convinced.

If the City Watch solved the murders, I may still never know what happened to me that day at the castle. Even if they recovered the haunted painting, I might never understand its role in these events. That smell of old blood and decaying wood would haunt me forever. Why was it present on both the painting and the cryptic map? I might never learn what the Soul Anchor truly was, and why some spirits of the dead lingered in Kami-Nihkia instead of continuing on to the Underworld.

This city was friendly to ghosts, far more so than I was used to. Like the Slant Row Boarding House, perhaps it provided sanctuary to those unmoored from their past. In that way, Kami-Nihkia was the perfect place for me, someone who had longed to leave my old life—the Wildlands, the Centaur Post—behind. I just hadn't expected the severance to be so permanent. Perhaps that was the price of finding a place to belong. Yet, like a ghost, I knew my presence here could still be banished, should I stray too far from what my employer would accept.

The spirit sharing my room also reminded me that I wasn't trusting all my senses. I wasn't "just a safety inspector." My instincts, my unique sensitivity to emotions, were part of who I was. They had guided me to this place and this moment, as surely as the map had led me to the graveyard. If I truly wished to solve the riddles that had ensnared my life, including the Soul Anchor, I would need to use all my abilities. There was nothing more in the MASHA storage room or in the pages of *The Mercury* that could replace my own nose.

Chapter Twenty-One

I was greeted the next morning by the aroma of Landlady Lyness's oatmeal porridge. The lowly grain was considered cheap fare, the food of laborers, but she served it in a silver tureen alongside little ceramic pots of spices, jams, and brewer's yeast—which was some kind of miraculous health food, in her estimation.

"Oh, Dani, why didn't you tell me?" Tia sighed as she entered the dining room. "I shouldn't have asked to delay my rent payment. I'll sell a painting. You shouldn't waste good spices on porridge."

"I think it's excellent," I said, settling down on my haunches at my usual place. Serving myself a full helping, I perked up somewhat, despite the ordeals of yesterday evening. I glanced across the table to Lilimari, who dumped an excessive amount of brown sugar on her bowl.

"Thank you, Simarron," said the landlady, who was flitting between the kitchen and the dining room. She placed a bowl of porridge in front of Tia as she sat down, topping it with a generous serving of brewer's yeast. Tia cringed, and Lilimari pulled her own bowl to herself protectively, letting out a soft hiss of disapproval.

"Why do we have to suffer just because your goddess forbids milk and butter?" Tia lamented, poking at her porridge with her spoon. "Vanadar couldn't have salt, and it made meals so annoying. It's ridiculous, these pacts with gods and goddesses, just for a bit of magic."

"Someone's salty this morning," Kai remarked. "I heard you and your beau having an argument about a painting at The Angry Unicorn yesterday. Is everything all right, Tia?" He leaned back in his chair with his cup of tea.

"Forget it. He's not my beau anymore." She sniffed, setting the spoon down and picking up the newspaper from the table. It was wrapped in plain paper, which she carefully removed. I had been avoiding looking at the wretched thing since the Centaur Post delivered it this morning.

Kai's eyebrows rose high above the teacup that hovered at his lips. "Good for you. He can go back to the Kami-Nihkia Club with the other old wizards and leave us be."

"Indeed. Only an old wizard would try to impress a lady by whisking her away in his ancient carriage to a ruined castle haunted by ghosts," said Tia, smoothing out the pages of *The Kami-Nihkia Mercury*, the rustle setting my teeth on edge.

"It's for the best. We all have someone in our past that we'd like to forget," Landlady Lyness said sympathetically, fussing with the teapot. "Now, Tia, don't go reading the newspaper when you're in a foul mood—it'll only make you feel worse."

This earned her a defiant glare. "Here's some news," said Tia, clearing her throat and reading from the front page. "ALCHEMY PROFESSOR FOUND DEAD IN MYSTERIOUS CIRCUMSTANCES."

I froze, spoon halfway to my mouth, exchanging glances with Lilimari while Tia revealed the terrible news that we already knew. Professor Ashmin was dead. My stomach flipped.

"Gods, what would anyone want with Kari?" said Landlady Lyness, blinking away tears from her eyes and dabbing at her face with the corner of her apron. "We weren't close, but my mother and her mother were friends."

Kai set down his teacup with a clatter. Tia continued to read in silence, her fingers white with tension as she gripped the newspaper. Her eyes, those deep green-blue pools that always held a hint of mystery, now darted frantically back and forth across the page as if searching for something.

"It's a tragedy," Lilimari said quietly, carefully setting down her spoon. "Her research was groundbreaking, you know, even if she did have a reputation for causing explosions. Simarron and I . . . we found her last night in the old graveyard."

Tia took in a sharp breath. "You found her . . . body?" she said, leaning away from the table, taking the newspaper with her.

Lilimari sighed and looked down at her sleeves. "I'd been studying with Professor Ashmin for a year before . . . this. She was the only person who truly understood me. The others at the university see me as some curiosity from a far-flung village, a dark prodigy, but no one actually understands my passion. Professor Ashmin did. She encouraged me, even when everyone else, including my family, dismissed my, umb . . . unconventional ideas about alchemy."

"Oh, you poor dear!" said Landlady Lyness, her voice raising in alarm. "Whatever were you doing in a graveyard at night?"

"Do you think it was foul play?" asked Kai, leaning in. "*The Mercury* must have a source at the City Watch, but you were at the scene. Is there anything they're not telling us?"

Daniella Lyness's face drained of color, turning from tear-flushed red to a stark white. "What if the murderer was still there? You could have been killed as well!"

"It seems like a lot of people are mucking about in graveyards lately," Tia muttered.

"It was definitely foul play, but I was safe. I had Simarron with me," Lilimari insisted. "I'd gone to him for help when the professor didn't show up for class. I got worried when the finding spell didn't work, and I found a strange note in her lab."

Frowning, I leaned over Tia's shoulder to peer at the article. It said nothing about me—thank the Goddess—or the note, which I had, of course, handed over to the City Watch. The article contained mostly speculation and few facts, which I gathered was the norm for *The Mercury*. Or more specifically, Manrik Skrift. It read:

"The discovery of the remains of necromantic runes at the scene suggests her death was far from natural. Was the professor meddling in forces beyond mortal comprehension? Or was she lured there by some vengeful rival? Even more troubling are murmurs of internal discord. An anonymous source close to Professor Ashmin claims she had recently confided fears of being overshadowed by a 'rising star' in her own circle. Could jealousy have motivated a protégé to strike down the very mentor who elevated them? This dark possibility hangs heavy over the investigation."

I looked up at Lilimari, horrified. What *anonymous source* was the article talking about? When would Skrift have had time to get a quote between last night and today's printing? And how could he even suggest such a thing?

"What?" asked Tia.

"Nothing," I replied.

"Oh, just take the stupid thing," she said, handing me the paper.

Heart pounding, I read on.

There was also a short article titled, "MISSING HAUNTED PAINTING: IS IT SOUL ANCHOR?" Curse that Manrik Skrift! Had he figured out the truth, or was it simply conjecture for the sake of an intriguing headline? The story went on to suggest that "old magic" wizards sought to use the Soul Anchor in their war against "upstart" alchemists. So maybe Manrik didn't know its true nature.

Did Tae Bellwyn know that the Soul Anchor was created to preserve life, not harm? Although she herself was dedicated to preserving life through her work with the healing sanctuary, I couldn't put it out of my mind that the philanthropist was somehow involved in the events surrounding Lysandros Garbor's death. Perhaps she had hidden the painting somewhere in the Kami-Nihkia Club until things cooled down.

I glanced back at the lead article. The deaths of the two alchemists had to be related: linked by the peculiar odor I'd detected on both the haunted painting and the map to the graveyard.

I was reading MASHA's official statement on safety concerning necromancers and haunted objects submitted by Director Ken Moosekind, when I suddenly caught a whiff of Tia's perfume and flinched involuntarily. It was off—like wilted flowers. Maybe it wasn't her perfume, but something else. She regarded me with a withering look.

"It's nothing," I repeated, a dry, bitter taste in my mouth. I folded the paper and tossed it back onto the table. Feeling colicky, I pushed aside my uneaten bowl of porridge, no longer having an appetite for my favorite morning meal. My thoughts were mushier than my oats, but my resolve from last night held firm. I needed to set aside everything I thought I knew about both murders and trust my instincts from now on.

"I wish I hadn't read that," said Tia, looking ill. "The only way I'm going to be able to unsee that is to feed my memories to an unohdus."

"Whatever that is," I said, rising from the table just as a bell tolled outside. As interesting as this conversation was, I had to get going.

"A hungry ghost that's hanging on to the world of the living," said Tia softly, as if she herself were a spirit barely hanging onto this world.

"Let's not go summoning spirits to devour what little good sense we've got left," said the landlady, shaking her head. "Besides, the City Watch will find this criminal, and soon we'll put all this behind us." She refilled Tia's teacup.

"I've heard unohdus are difficult to summon—and even trickier to banish once they get a taste for head fluff," said Kai. He took a bite of his porridge, sprinkled with cinnamon.

As I left the room to a chorus of goodbyes, I caught his voice in a conspiratorial whisper, "I thought ghosts frightened you, Tia. Yet perhaps I could assist. My abilities help me reveal truths, but never to forget them. And there are a few memories I'd gladly rid myself of."

"They terrify me. But I know where one is—" Tia began, but the landlady cut her off:

"Oh, nonsense!"

Lilimari caught up with me in the vestibule, where the solemn statue of a goddess looked on from her shrine. "Simarron, I want to help you investigate." She showed no indication of her injury from last night.

"No, Lilimari, it's too dangerous. You were a student of Professor Ashmin. By getting involved, you could draw attention to yourself next."

Lilimari narrowed her dark eyes. "My professor was on to something to do with a new element before she died, you know, and I owe it to her to find out what."

"I see. And this element X, it's the one alluded to in the map?" I had been largely ignoring the role of the mysterious element X, yet Lilimari was right—it seemed to play a key part.

"I think so, but I'm not sure. Maybe if I had known, I would have realized something was wrong sooner. I could have stopped it, or warned her . . ."

"None of this is your fault," I said firmly.

"Maybe not," she said with a quaver of sadness in her voice. "But there's something else. She told me once that I might be the only one able to continue her research if something happened to her."

"I understand. If you can do so safely, and without drawing attention to yourself, investigate the mysterious element. If there's a connection between Professor Ashmin's death and her research, we'll uncover it," I replied, shrugging into my cloak. "I have to go to work—and I have a hunch about the haunted painting that I want to follow up on."

I was nervously anticipating talking to Director Moosekind. There had to be a compelling argument that would allow me to investigate the Kami-Nihkia Club, without making it seem like I was shirking my duties or interfering with the City Watch. I could argue that uncovering the truth behind the supposed ghost attacks would not only calm the public's nerves, but also demonstrate MASHA's necessity. More importantly, I could locate the painting and confirm that it was simply a Soul Anchor—nothing to fear.

Chapter Twenty-Two

That morning, I stood before Director Moosekind in his office, my hope of pursuing the haunted painting dwindling with each word he spoke. My arguments, which had seemed so solid on my walk to the MASHA building, fell apart like a wet newspaper.

"I tell you, I've had enough of this ghost business," Moosekind grumbled in frustration. "First it was the haunted painting at the gala, now this bloody graveyard business. The City Watch is being inundated with reports of spirits and specters," he continued, letting out a sigh and rubbing his temples. "No, no. I appreciate your initiative, Simarron, but we have real work to do. It's better to channel that eagerness into your official duties today."

Despite the setback, my resolve didn't waver. I slipped out on my lunch break with the Magical Energies Detector on my back and a wild plan to see if my hunch about the haunted painting was correct—with or without official approval.

Now, gazing upon a dramatic marble-columned archway, I doubted the MED would grant access to this exclusive club. I had been unable to come up with a plausible reason for a magical safety inspection, but I hoped no one would question it . . .

At that moment, a liveried doorman appeared from within, wearing a high-collared coat embellished with diagonal frogging.

"Safety Inspector Simarron, MASHA," I blurted out, and when I realized I was jingling the chain of my pocket watch, I stilled myself.

The doorman cast a brief gaze up at the large case slung over my shoulder, his eyes narrowing with suspicion. "And what's that you're carrying? All deliveries must be logged. Identification, please."

I patted my satchel, searching for something with my MASHA credentials on it, while the colicky feeling in my stomach intensified. Lying, directly disobeying Director Moosekind, and slightly abusing my position as a safety inspector—it was all necessary, I told myself, but it still felt wrong.

"There's been reports of magical disturbances. I need to verify that nothing dangerous has lingered since the haunted painting was displayed during the gala," I said, improvising. "This isn't a delivery, just some equipment I need to set up to do some testing and I'll be on my way. Just a formality, you see."

"Very well, but make it quick. And use the service entrance, for gods' sakes," he admonished, pointing to the side of the building.

With a nod, I adjusted the case on my shoulder and hurried toward the side entrance, before either my deception or the cold wind caught up with me.

Inside the club, a log blazed in a massive fireplace. Oxidized iron busts of wizards, set into wall niches, looked on from their contrasting pedestals of white marble. I passed through a hall carpeted with thick rugs and illuminated softly by meteor crystal lights set in porcelain sconces so delicate they were nearly translucent. When the hall was devoid of people, I discreetly headed for the ballroom.

The blue walls were empty, all the artwork removed from the week before. The chandeliers were unlit, and only the natural afternoon light filtered in through the tall windows. Satisfied that nobody was here, I slipped in and eased the door closed behind me. My hooves echoed on the parquet flooring as I carefully made my way around the room, MED wand in hand.

But the MED registered nothing. I let out a frustrated huff. Taking a steadying breath, I prepared to calibrate it again when my nose was tickled with the by-now familiar scent of decaying wood and old blood. I followed the scent to an empty wall. Suspecting that there might be something hidden there, I felt around the decorative molding until something shifted subtly under my touch.

A door swung out from the wall, revealing a concealed closet. Inside, I spotted a canvas propped up against the wall and loosely covered by a white cloth. I pulled back the fabric. Just one glance at the purple sky told me that it was the enigmatic painting itself, carefully tucked away. There were three scrape marks along one edge. I replaced the cloth, not wanting to see the woman in the painting and trigger the panic I'd felt at the gala.

As I suspected, the painting must have remained here ever since the gala, hidden from prying eyes. I tried to imagine the room as it had been laid out during the art gala. This was more than likely the wall where the painting had been hung.

Footsteps approached, and I quickly looked for a place to hide. I was probably too big to fit into the closet, but I had no other options. I squeezed in beside the painting, trying not to touch it, trying not to breathe its malicious miasma, even as I reminded myself that it was just the Soul Anchor and it posed no danger.

In fact, it was completely inert—the MED hadn't reacted at all! It was my nose that had led me here, not to the scent of the painting itself, but to something else, something interwoven with memories tainted by malice. I let that realization sink in for a moment.

The painting was not magical in nature. It was merely canvas and paint—plainly a fake, not the legendary haunted painting it was purported to be. I realized that it wasn't the Soul Anchor I had assumed it to be, and its eerie aura was more of an emotional impression than a physical smell.

But I wasn't alone in my assumptions about it being a Soul Anchor —hadn't others also referred to it as a "soul painting?" If the killer was attempting to take advantage of the legend of the Soul Anchor to make this painting seem like the murder weapon, they didn't know how this artifact functioned. *Interesting.*

My thoughts began to quiet as I became more aware of my cramped surroundings. It was surprisingly roomy in the back of the compartment. In fact, I couldn't feel the back of it. I shifted uncomfortably on my haunches, moving my hands to find a better balance. In the process, my fingers brushed against something else tucked into the secret room. My hand closed around a glass vial and I heard several more clink together softly in the darkness.

I pressed back as far as I could, breath held, as the footsteps drew closer. My heart hammered in my chest and I hoped they didn't notice the door panel was slightly ajar. As the footsteps moved past me, the dial on the MED jumped in the dim light of its small meteor crystal. At the same time, I noticed a shadow pass over a small, nearly imperceptible hole in the panel, blocking a pinprick of light.

I inhaled as deeply as I dared, but smelled nothing unusual from the passerby, and I could not see who was causing the reaction on the MED without giving myself away. The footsteps paused and a door somewhere creaked open and then closed. Quickly, I stuck my head out of the closet, but whoever it was had already moved into the adjoining room.

I glanced down at the vial in my hand, marked with the alchemical symbol for *arsenic*. I doubted it was for clearing up complexions, or even as part of a cleaning solution. The dim illumination of the MED's meteor crystal indicator glinted on the vial, empty remnants from the murderous plot that had been executed through the pinhole. But how?

As far as I knew, arsenic was an odorless white powder. There was no visible residue in the vials. The element must have been concocted into a gas, as Lilimari had suggested in the enclosed space of the mausoleum. Somewhere in this deadly process, it took on a garlicky smell. One thing was certain—the killer was adept at poisons.

Who would, or could, do such a thing? They were not merely a poisoner, but also a machinator, favoring clever mechanisms to ensnare their prey. It had to be someone with access to this room, too—perhaps a member of this very club.

Further examination of the compartment revealed that it extended for some way, narrowing as it went. It was, in fact, a passage. Unfortunately, my frame was too large to travel through it and find out where it led. The murderer was clearly someone smaller than me, and probably better-educated and wealthier, too, as a club member. But they weren't smarter. I might only be a safety inspector, but I would sniff out the killer and bring them to justice.

I cursed myself for hiding when I should have leaned into my role as a safety inspector. After all, the worst that could happen is that I'd be asked to leave this exclusive club. I climbed out of the hidden room, stretching my cramped limbs as I extracted myself. Clapping my hands on my front kilt to dust myself off, I headed in the direction I'd heard the footsteps travel.

Chapter Twenty-Three

I found myself near a set of richly appointed rooms where games of cards were taking place. The soft hum of conversation and the clinking of crystal glasses filled the air as club members enjoyed the early afternoon in leisure. The dials on the MED quivered inconclusively, as inscrutable as the faces of the players clustered around the gaming tables. I breathed in the scent of polished leather and old money, surmising that the affluent had the means to enhance their appearances with various glamour spells and charms.

"Simarron, MASHA safety inspector," I announced, mustering every bit of self-confidence I had. I could not hide; I had to take up space like I belonged here.

I heard some disdainful murmurs. How dare a tradesperson invade their private gaming room?

Benefactor Tae Bellwyn looked up from her cards at one of the tables, her eyes mirroring my surprise. Her pointed Helvenkin ears peeked through auburn waves of hair, adorned with delicate gold cuffs. "Simarron, is it? Please, have a seat. We could use another player," she said, clearly not recognizing me from the art gala. "Three-Handed Fool's Gambit is entertaining, but it lacks the finesse of a proper four-handed game, wouldn't you say?"

I hesitated for only a moment. Speaking with a person of interest could potentially reveal much more than my device. "I suppose one round couldn't hurt."

Replacing the MED in its case, I sat down at the table and exchanged pleasantries with the others seated in brocade chairs around it. I was partnered with Tae Bellwyn. Aurik adThornevar was a Bloodborn with a face that was all angles and straight lines, much like the tailored cut of his velvet waistcoat. And his partner was . . .

When he looked up at me with those unnatural green eyes, I recognized Vanadar immediately. "We meet again, Safety Inspector."

As the cards were dealt, Vanadar watched me furtively, his smirk betraying amusement at the unconventional situation. Aurik maintained an air of polite disinterest, while others around the room glowered in disapproval or smiled bemusedly.

Tae Bellwyn smiled as she primly arranged her cards. "I find tradespeople so interesting. What is it that you do as a, what was it, MASHA safety inspector?"

"Benefactor Tae," I addressed the wealthy philanthropist with polite firmness, hoping I sounded convincing. "The haunted painting has stirred quite a bit of concern. There are whispers suggesting it might be hidden nearby, or even that its spirit might have found a new host. Have you observed any disturbances or anything unusual since the painting was displayed at the gala?"

Tae Bellwyn leaned toward me, her full figure pressing against the table as she considered my partially truthful bait. "A new host?" she echoed.

Vanadar's smirk faded into a tight-lipped smile. "Of course, the unfortunate incident with Alchemist Garbor at the gala was a true tragedy. Such occurrences do tend to add to the legend of such artifacts, don't they? The idea that a mere painting could wield such power . . . But surely, if the painting were here—which, I assure you, it is not—it would have been secured by now."

"You know every hiding place in this building?" I asked.

Tae Bellwyn glanced at Vanadar and let out a small laugh. "The idea is quite preposterous, isn't it? I must admit, the night of the gala had its share of peculiarities, but nothing since then. This building is quite safe, Safety Inspector, although your concern is charming."

She paused and, after sharing a concerned look with Aurik, added, "Still . . . disturbances, you say?"

"Yes indeed," I continued, keeping my voice measured as I selected a card from my hand. "The collector who owns it didn't warn you of the risk with such an artifact?"

"No, I'm afraid it was all rather mysterious, but the art world is filled with enigmatic patrons, isn't it? The opportunity to showcase such a rare piece was too tempting to refuse," she said, her tone casual but guarded. She then played the Fool card, carefully setting it aside as she avoided following the suit in play, signaling her intention to retain it. Its painted face appeared to mock me.

"And the patron's penchant for secrecy was so profound that they did not attend the gala in person, am I correct?" I doubted there really was a collector. I played a lower trump card, keeping my stronger ones for later.

Vanadar and Aurik, following the basic strategy, also played throw-away cards.

"That's right." Tae Bellwyn played a Queen. "I believe she said she was leaving on an extended trip abroad. She was quite eager to lend her support to the healing sanctuary, the beneficiary of our gala."

"And yet," I interjected sharply, "the painting disappeared after the gala, despite much interest from prospective buyers."

She seemed momentarily flustered by the directness of my inquiry. "Yes, most unfortunate about the disappearance, although it was never intended for sale. It performed admirably as a draw to the event. I'm assured the City Watch is doing everything it can to recover such a priceless artifact. Now, I believe it's your move."

Vanadar and Aurik exchanged uneasy glances, and I heard a few nervous chuckles around the room.

"Of course." I hastily led with a Nine, my mind divided between the game and my line of inquiry. "It's just that MASHA takes the magical and alchemical safety of the city, especially of its most prestigious citizens, very seriously. Your response with healing magic that night was quite timely." I gave her my best, most charming smile.

"I am a trained physick and I did what I could to assist," she said, her expression tightening as she followed with the Knight of the same suit.

The game continued, but a subtle tension lingered in the air. I was a terrible Fool's Gambit player. Long-enamored of the game, I had often tried to play it by myself, but it turned out I was no match against practiced players. My attempts to outmaneuver them fell flat, and in the end, Vanadar, with his strategic use of trumps and a well-timed Fool card, took the most tricks and secured the victory.

"This game has gone cold," Aurik remarked stiffly. With that, he nodded politely and excused himself from the gaming room.

"I need to get back to my duties," I said, rising from my haunches to stand on all four legs. Only a member of this club could have set up the trap and concealed the painting in the hidden compartment. If Tae Bellwyn honestly didn't recognize this person, it could be due to a strong glamour spell—which I hoped the MED might pick up among the people here tonight.

"Oh, you mustn't go on waving that thing around in here," said Tae Bellwyn, dropping her voice. "We can't have the members thinking a spirit is lingering in these esteemed halls."

I looked at her, surprised that she had believed my white lie; now to shade it even more. "This is a magical safety matter threatening your esteemed halls," I said.

She opened her reticule and pulled out a tiny card, no bigger than a thumbnail. "Although a foreigner, Elia Ariagwen seemed perfectly fine in my assessment. Besides, wouldn't the spirit haunt, you know, the castle from whence it came? The very castle that poor Lysandros Garbor had recently come into possession of?" she continued, uneasiness creeping into her tone. "The painting vanished after the gala and I wouldn't be surprised if it reappeared in its ancestral halls."

I took it from her outstretched hand. My nose twitched as I breathed in the complicated scent of paper that had exchanged hands. While it had taken on the distinctive fragrance of Tae Bellwyn's peony-scented perfume, there was something else lurking behind it, something damp and ethereal. I tried to link it with the scent of the painting or the map, but the pieces wouldn't jiggle into place in my memory. The text was too tiny to make out, but I knew one person who could craft something that incredibly small and detailed.

"I'm afraid you have been duped, Benefactor Tae," I informed her, pinching the tiny card between my fingernails and extending it toward her. "Elia Ariagwen, if that is truly her name, lives no further than Misty Vale. And she won't be coming back for the haunted painting. I intend to find it, and put the reports about its ill curse on your club to rest."

Tae Bellwyn's face pinched with concern. "This is most unsettling news. If what you are saying is true, we must get rid of it immediately, if only to dispel these rumors once and for all."

"Indeed," I said. "Shall we search the club together?"

"Bellwyn, this is preposterous!" Vanadar interjected as he stood from the table, his mask of cool contempt slipping into open hostility. "Inviting scrutiny over such stories could cause unnecessary panic or . . . worse! In his day, Thaddeus, our club's founder, would have never taken such nonsense from a tradesperson—and a centaur, no less. I must object!"

But Bellwyn, now intrigued and perhaps a little alarmed by the thought of hosting a malevolent artifact, stood up from her chair decisively. "No, Vanadar, we owe it to our club's patrons to prove that there is nothing malevolent here. We will search the club thoroughly with the MASHA safety inspector."

Vanadar's gaze darted about the room. "Fine. We'll split up and get it over with more quickly," he said, stalking away from the table.

I watched him retreat with narrowed eyes. Did he know the painting was still here, and was he planning to reach it first? However, he disappeared in a different direction than the ballroom.

I caught a whiff of it then, that malignant spirit that carried the essence of decaying wood and old blood. Was it Vanadar? Tae Bellwyn? Someone else in this club? It struck me that the source was not strictly a person, but rather a malevolent . . . intention. The story I had told about a spirit lingering in this club may have been a fabrication, but apparently I wasn't totally wrong. Someone here was possessed by an intent to kill, and it sent a chill up my withers.

It faded before I could fully grasp it. Tae Bellwyn led me away from the gaming room, her steps quickening as we ventured deeper into the corridors of the club, the plush red carpets muffling our footsteps. I followed with the MED, wishing it could detect if the esteemed benefactor was leading me on. She did a methodical search of each room, each more opulently furnished than the last, showing no special concern for any area.

I have no explanation for what happened next. A sudden thumping sound echoed throughout the hall. Tae Bellwyn stopped abruptly, spinning to face me. "Did you hear that, Safety Inspector?"

"I did," I replied. "It seems we are not alone in our quest. Continue, please."

We pressed on, the strange sounds intermittently accompanying our journey through the club. With each mysterious noise, Bellwyn's resolve seemed to strengthen, her initial trepidation giving way to a determined curiosity. "We must find this painting. The safety of the club's patrons could be at stake."

As we entered the ballroom, my anticipation grew. "I believe the painting is nearby. Please continue," I encouraged her.

At her side, I subtly led the way to the concealed compartment. She betrayed no familiarity as I reached for the hidden mechanism in the molding. With a soft click, the section of the wall panel swung open.

Bellwyn gasped, stepping closer to examine the compartment's interior. "I had no idea," she whispered. Her hands hovered hesitantly at the edge of the cloth cover, peeling it back slightly before dropping it like a dirty rag. "I didn't know about any of this."

"Benefactor Tae, your reaction suggests that you were truly unaware of this compartment's existence," I observed, watching her closely.

"Yes, Safety Inspector. I assure you, I was," she replied earnestly, meeting my gaze.

"Send for the City Watch. They'll handle it from here."

She thanked me and rushed off to her task.

"Thank you, Benefactor Tae. This has been incredibly helpful."

The arrival of the City Watch was swift, their copper badges and dark uniforms standing out in stark contrast to the opulence of the Kami-Nihkia Club. Shocked murmurs mixed with curious whispers and mild outrage filled the halls.

Captain Damon Voshawk addressed Tae Bellwyn in his low, gravelly voice. "So, you're saying that the painting you reported missing . . . was here the entire time? Well, that was easy." He was a tall man, exuding authority independent of the copper badge pinned to his sharp brown suit.

A ripple of laughter ran through the coppers, but Bellwyn's expression remained poised. "You misunderstand, Captain. The painting was hidden, not stolen," she said. "I had no idea it was in this building until Safety Inspector Simarron uncovered it."

Voshawk's red eyes shifted to me, one brow lifting. "Did you now?"

I flicked my tail in irritation. "More importantly, Captain, this painting is a piece of evidence in the death of Lysandros Garbor. It should be examined thoroughly." I nodded toward the secret compartment, its door still ajar in the ballroom wall. "There were vials stored with it as well."

Voshawk turned to his officers. "Bag everything."

A pair of coppers stepped forward, holding sacks covered with magical containment runes.

"We've been seeing you around a lot lately, Safety Inspector," said the watch captain, his tone edged with dry amusement. "Just remember, the City Watch investigates crimes."

"Understood. I'll head back to work."

"Don't go too far. The coroner may have some words for you during her inquest."

I nodded and took my leave. Glancing at my pocket watch, I was horrified to see how much time had passed. I was dreadfully behind schedule, but I comforted myself with the idea that today's discoveries would be worth it.

Chapter Twenty-Four

The next day at MASHA, the initial thrill of uncovering the painting quickly evaporated. Lingering questions gnawed at me—who had accessed the hidden compartment and deployed the poisonous gas that killed Lysandros Garbor?

I was now certain the gas was also the source of the garlic odor I had detected on Kari Ashmin's body in the mausoleum. She had been lured there by the map, just as Garbor had been drawn to the haunted painting. If Ashmin was on the trail of the missing element, had Garbor pursued the same goal? And who stood to gain by removing them both?

I glanced at the map on my desk, the copy that Lilimari had made the previous evening, but it refused to yield any more answers. It nagged at me while I tried to focus on my work, meticulously documenting my site visit to North Star Remedies and cross-checking my notes with their permits and compliance records. My productivity lagged as my attention kept being dragged back to the map and its messy X in the center.

After my discovery of the haunted painting hidden in a secret passage at the Kami-Nihkia Club, I was certain that someone at the club was responsible. I opened my journal to the page with Tae Bellwyn.

She was wealthy and influential—could she have wanted something from Garbor, perhaps connected to Château Gorget? My senses had picked up something in the gaming room—malicious intent, I believed —but it had faded before I could pinpoint the source. And the MED readings were inconclusive, clouded by glamour spells on multiple people, including Tae Bellwyn and others at the table.

Yet she had seemed genuinely shocked when the secret compartment was discovered. More importantly, she had called the City Watch when I directed her to.

If not her, then who?

I tapped my pen against my desk. Should I consider Vanadar and Aurik adThornevar suspects? Something was rotten in that club—I trusted my instincts on that.

Mina's voice cut through my thoughts.

"Simarron, I'm sorry about what you went through with Kari Ashmin."

I jolted, a twinge of guilt catching in my chest. I hurriedly tucked the copy of the map into my journal and snapped it shut.

"It can't have been easy finding her like that, especially after everything you did to try to help," Mina continued gently. "However, I'm concerned that this pursuit of yours is taking away from your duties as a safety inspector."

"I understand, but it's important that the City Watch doesn't waste time when a killer is out there, murdering alchemists," I said.

"You gave the City Watch your statement, didn't you? Including all the leads you have? Determining what happened could take some time."

"I did," I said, shifting uncomfortably. In the excitement at the Kami-Nihkia Club, I realized I had not told the coppers about a certain naiad, a miniatures enthusiast who was surely involved in the hoax surrounding the haunted painting—the fake Soul Anchor.

"Maybe you need some time off," my supervisor suggested, not unkindly.

"No, I want to work. I need to keep occupied." I needed the access that being a safety inspector provided.

"Simarron, are you worried that you might be targeted? Is that what this is about?"

It hadn't occurred to me before, and I was startled at the implications.

"If we are dealing with a magical miscreant, it's likely your interference has been noticed by now," she said. "Would you like to learn a defensive spell?"

"You can teach me magic?"

The morning sun smiled down on the quiet courtyard behind the MASHA building. The neighboring buildings enclosed the area, their backs turned toward us, arched windows on their ground floor and tall, narrow windows on the upper levels. Lacking their street-facing facades, they were nearly indistinguishable from one another.

The bricks beneath my hooves were warm terracotta, and potted plants scattered about were beginning to show evidence of spring. A pillar of basalt served as a focal point. It was beautiful, and I wondered why I hadn't been out here before.

Mina was carrying a blue earthenware bowl, which she set down in the shadow of the rock. Then, picking up a stick, she scratched out an equilateral triangle in a patch of bare earth.

"The universe, as classically understood, is made up of three indivisible elements: fire, air, water," she began, tapping the points of the intersecting triangles. "And combined, they made earth," she added, circling the center of the diagram. "We now know that the earth is also full of metal, a large family of unique elements, each unable to be broken down into other substances."

She really looked like a wizard now, I thought, about to perform a spell with a makeshift wand. Or an instructor at the university, using a pointer to draw attention to specific points on the chalkboard to a class of magic students.

"Now, I'm not going to be able to teach you how to summon fire," she continued. "But at its core, wizardry is probably not too different from the magic of centaurs, traditional witches, or anyone else. Like all practitioners of magic, the spellcaster must first understand that elements are non-human entities possessing will and agency. Magic is cooperative, requiring a pact with the element."

I nodded. "It is the same with centaur magic, only less formal."

"Titanacala is a protective metal that provides strength and defense. She readily forms pacts with those magically inclined. Once you've formed a bond with her, you can call upon her to influence the world around you both."

"I'm not familiar with that goddess," I said, mentally sounding out the five syllables in the name of the foreign deity. I briefly recalled Mina speaking it, however, when she had healed Lilimari.

"Titanacala is in the earth all around us, but she especially favors granite, basalt, and sand," Mina continued, her voice shining with a passion that I hadn't seen in her before. "Magic, at its core, is deeply personal. Each pact, each spell we cast—it's a reflection of who we are and our relationship with the deity."

I felt a warmth spread through me, not from the morning sun, but from Mina's belief in me. "My mother had a special gift with nature spirits, which she tried to teach me, but I've never really understood the magic of wizards before," I said.

Mina smiled. "We'll go slow, and I'll be here to guide you. Titanacala is patient and forgiving to those who respect her. You must first cleanse your hands with water and clear your mind of wayward thoughts, holding only the mental image of a bright flame."

She handed me the bowl of water. On the inside, the deep blue glaze had been allowed to drip down the bowl. The firing process had preserved the trails and droplets, darker still where they had pooled at the bottom. I set it down and dipped my hands in the water, flicking off the moisture.

"Next, anchor yourself to the earth and repeat in your head, after me." She nodded toward the rock. The rust-colored column of basalt had five uneven sides and came up to my knees.

"Titanacala, I wish to form a bond with you. I seek your protection, and in return I promise to aid you as well," Mina intoned.

I tried to focus on the rock while letting the image of a white flame burn away any other thoughts. I didn't know how I could aid Titanacala, but as I mentally repeated the words, I felt I was forming a bond—not just with the element, but with Mina, too—bridging the gap between pupil and mentor.

A chemical scent, reminiscent of disinfectant mingled with ground nuts, tickled my nose. The aroma transported me back to Professor Ashmin's lab. Had there been a large brown menacing spider lurking in the corner? The image flitted through my mind, vague and unsettling. I shook my head, attempting to refocus on the rock before me.

"That's it, you're doing well . . . What's wrong?" Mina's voice broke through my confusion.

"I don't know if it worked. I got distracted," I admitted. "Sorry, I started thinking about spiders for some reason."

"Oh?" Mina raised an eyebrow. "Titanacala is probably telling you something about spiders, most likely not to harm them. Now you must remember to honor your pact, or she will remove her protection from you."

I hadn't realized that I'd be making a pact with a minor deity today. Now it was done, apparently, and I didn't know how I felt.

"I sense . . . something," I said after a moment, a shiver running down my spine from neck to tail.

Whatever Mina said in response, it sounded muffled, like she was far away. Suddenly, I sensed a presence behind me. I spun around, but there was nobody. Turning back to Mina, a sudden gust of wind swept through the courtyard, upturning the bowl with a clatter.

"What's the matter?" Mina asked as I jumped.

"Titanacala felt cold and . . . angry," I stammered, staring at the overturned bowl, my instincts on edge.

"Simarron, that wasn't Titanacala," Mina said, her tone grave.

"Then what was it?"

"I'm afraid I must apologize. We should have gone outside the city to perform the bond rite. I didn't consider the fact that lowly spirits can lurk even here. You do not want anything to do with these spirits of the dead, Simarron."

"Spirits of the dead? You mean that was a ghost?" I coughed, my throat dry.

As the words left my lips, we both looked down at the upturned bowl. On top of it sat a wispy blob of gauze-like substance. It had an acrid, phosphorous scent.

"Ectoplasm," said Mina. "I take it back. That was no lowly spirit, that was a powerful ghost."

"Why do your people let the spirits of the dead hang around in the world of the living? Isn't that dangerous?" I asked.

In the Wildlands, we did not encourage the spirits of the departed to linger. The clan of the deceased held a party, a great sendoff complete with feasting and games of sport. If the spirit did not know it was dead, it was believed that this realization would come when it could not consume the offerings of food. No longer confused, it would then hasten on its journey to the Underworld.

"In Sireliad culture, we honor our ancestors without letting them interfere in the living world. They're revered, not feared," Mina insisted.

As I knelt to pick up the bowl, my head spun with the revelations of this encounter. The ectoplasm found at the castle site wasn't only a component in an alchemical concoction—it was the residue left from summoning a ghost, similar to the one I'd just encountered. This ghost had made me think of spiders, much like the ghost in my room could impress me with memories. I realized that a potent spirit at the castle could also have meddled with my mind, perhaps wiping my memories of the castle itself. And hadn't Tia mentioned something about feeding memories to a hungry ghost?

My thoughts were interrupted by the swift descent of a witch on a broomstick, her dark hair flowing behind her. She was dressed exactly the same as the Witchy Whisk messenger who had come last week.

"Safety Inspector Simarron," she called out as she landed, her broom kicking up a swirl of dust. "Your presence is requested at the coroner's office at Shetland Yard. Please come at your earliest convenience."

The sudden arrival of the Witchy Whisk messenger—quite literally appearing from thin air—and her urgent tone sent my heart pounding. What would the coroner require from me in her inquest?

Chapter Twenty-Five

Shetland Yard, the headquarters for the City Watch, was an imposing stone building facing a courtyard that bustled with activity. The building's high arched windows and crenelated roof lent it the air of a fortress. Coppers wearing polished breastplates stood at attention before the heavy wooden doors, their postures as unyielding as the walls behind them. A raven soared above before wheeling out of view behind the building. The sun had been shining when I left MASHA, but now hid itself behind a gathering veil of clouds.

A horse whinnied, drawing my attention to the large stables nearby. It housed the powerful horses that pulled the City Watch's wagons. Above the stables rose a bell tower, its sharp silhouette piercing the sky. The bell sounded only during dire emergencies; it had remained silent for nearly half a century. Although Landlady Lyness had not even been born during the Storms of Wrath, she had recounted to me the tale of devastation wreaked on the city.

A statue of the goddess Cualaith watched over the City Watch building dedicated in her honor. She bore the sword of justice and the shield of protection, both forged from copper—the sacred metal representing the officers who carried out her will. The shield was emblazoned with the founding year, and I realized that the City Watch itself had been established after the storms, making it barely older than MASHA.

As I watched, a siren led a group of coppers in a horse-drawn wagon, her wail clearing a path through the crowd of pedestrians who hurried to make way. The wagon rattled over the cobblestoned courtyard as the driver shouted and the pair of horses picked up speed.

"Ah, Simarron, MASHA's new centaur safety inspector. What a coincidence," a smooth voice cut through the noise as its owner strolled around the corner of the building.

I skidded to a halt and turned to see a dark-haired man, his sleek black tailcoat catching the light to reveal a faintly iridescent sheen. He looked familiar, but I couldn't place a name to him. There was nothing remarkable about his features. At first glance, he looked like he could be of any two-legger lineage, yet I felt that somehow he was not one at all. His movements had a quick, darting energy, and his beady black eyes studied me with unsettling focus. A dry metallic scent surrounded him, something I could only compare to dust.

"Manrik Skrift," the man offered, his smile sharp as the nib of a fountain pen. He wore a silver pin shaped like a quill that shone in the light. In the grip of his long, spindly fingers was a leather satchel similar to my own.

"You're a writer for *The Kami-Nihkia Mercury*," I said, piecing it together. I recognized his name from the byline of the articles breaking the news about Lysandros Garbor's death and the haunted painting. Those articles had been sensationalist at best and misleading at worst.

"Indeed," Manrik replied with a theatrical bow, much deeper than was customary. "What brings the illustrious MASHA to Shetland Yard today? Surely not a magical safety check?"

I dipped my head politely, but I felt my tail swish in agitation. "I'm wanted by the City Watch. I mean to say—" I stammered, "my presence was requested by the coroner. And you?"

"Oh, just following a thread of inquiry," said Manrik, his voice as slick as oil. "The Soul Anchor. An artifact whispered to grant immortality, although one must wonder at what cost. I have a lead that ties it to the Lyness family mansion, which, I hear, is now a boarding house for misfits and . . . centaurs. Coincidence? Perhaps."

I stiffened. "I don't know what you're insinuating, but I have no comment." The warmth I'd felt on my walk here had faded; now, standing in the cold, I felt a chill creeping in.

"Comment? I haven't even asked a question," Manrik said, smiling. "But if you'd like to save me the trouble . . . perhaps you've seen it yourself?"

"Sorry, I don't have time for this." I realized I was shifting from hoof to hoof and forced myself to still. I hated how anxious I seemed. I had never interacted with a news writer before. Were they all like this, pecking and probing?

Manrik Skrift tilted his head. "You know, when someone refuses to answer, it often says more than words ever could. You know something, don't you? Or is MASHA itself hiding something? Whatever happened to those old Bureau of Magical Inquiries case files, anyway?"

I inhaled sharply. Of course, I knew exactly where that cold case was filed. I'd believed that the haunted painting was a Soul Anchor, but it was only a pale imitation. I was aware of the connection to the Lyness family, but I had promised myself that I would be respectful of my landlady's family history. Skrift would have no such compunction. Her family had already been scarred by this artifact; the last thing she needed was her name splashed across *The Mercury* as part of a fresh scandal.

Drawing myself to my full height, I said, "If you have questions about public safety records, take them to MASHA." I could only imagine Mina's cold displeasure at dealing with such a person, and Moosekind's exasperated sighs.

Manrik's grin widened. "Oh, don't worry, I will. But remember, Safety Inspector, the truth has a way of finding the light."

Before I could retort that his stories had a flexible view of the truth, Manrik sidestepped around me and went inside the building.

I hesitated as I followed him inside, the wooden doors closing behind me with a heavy thud. What did Manrik really know about the Soul Anchor—and how much more trouble would his pursuit of a story cause? I drew a steadying breath and attempted to shake off the sense of foreboding that had crept into my chest.

The inside of Shetland Yard was spacious, with high ceilings and great arched windows that let in light. A guard escorted me past a pointy-eared woman arguing with a sharp-fanged copper behind the reception area, to a large open room where coppers worked at wooden desks arranged in neat rows. At the moment, many of them seemed distracted from their work by the glamorous woman who was in custody.

Anya Vedeva was handcuffed to a chair, being questioned in front of a group of officers. At our arrival, she nonchalantly slipped out of her bonds and handed them to the watch captain. Together, they made quite the pair.

Captain Voshawk's frame was as long as a languid summer day, his face a black diamond—sharp-angled, rough and impenetrable. He radiated command, and when one officer began to applaud the stunt, he was immediately silenced with a mere glance from the captain.

Anya, petite and elegant as ever, bowed deeply. Her sharp white teeth flashed against her tan skin as she smiled. "Thank you, thank you. I'll be here all week."

The captain, looking less than impressed, handed the handcuffs to a junior copper.

"Quite a spectacle, wouldn't you say?" a familiar, smooth voice murmured near my ear. Startled, I turned to see Manrik Skrift standing at my shoulder. He held a small leather-bound notebook in one hand, a pen poised in the other. His beady black eyes glimmered with delight at the unfolding drama.

"Just what are you doing here anyway, Skrift?" I hissed.

"I told you outside—following a lead," he replied, his tone infuriatingly nonchalant. "Captain Voshawk and I have a kind of agreement. He grants me exclusive access in exchange for any information I happen to uncover in my line of work."

"And does he know how you twist the truth?" I briefly considered how the news writer might spin the tale of my recovery of the painting, but squashed the thought.

"You wound me, Safety Inspector!" Manrik pressed a hand to his chest theatrically, still clutching his pen. "I am required to keep certain details off the record, of course. But surely the good captain can't object to me adding a few of my own."

I clenched my jaw, aware of the guard beside me glowering at us, clearly displeased that we were whispering during the interrogation. Before I could fire back another retort, our hushed exchange was interrupted by the raised voice of Captain Voshawk.

"I'll ask one more time," the captain thundered, his tone sharp enough to slice through the murmurs in the room. "Explain to the officers of the watch how you commanded the spirits to vanish the monument in the city square!"

Manrik, scribbling away furiously in his notebook, leaned toward me conspiratorially. "Do you think The Incredible Spectra could have used the Soul Anchor to amplify her power?"

I glared at him in silence.

"Necromancer Anya Vedeva," Captain Voshawk addressed her formally, "we've got quite a situation here. You were seen near Alchemist Lysandros Garbor before he collapsed at the gala. Witnesses claim to have heard strange whispers, with Garbor exclaiming: 'If this is what awaits us in the afterlife, I want no part of it.' Your show involves communing with spirits. Care to explain?"

"Captain, my act is open to interpretation. People see what they want to see. As for Garbor, I'm as shocked as anyone about what happened to him."

"Now, Garbor was developing business plans with you. His death complicates things. What do you have to say about that?"

"I've lost a business partner, and my plans are now in ruins. I have nothing to gain from his death," she replied, frustration creeping into her voice.

"He was a wealthy man, yet his fortune seems to have disappeared."

"He gambled his money as quickly as he earned it," she said through gritted teeth.

"Is this a result of some personal vendetta?" pressed the captain, leaning in.

Anya refused to back away. "Captain, I don't have any personal enemies. And my act is purely for entertainment."

"Prove it! What spells did you use, and what are their magical components? You know we found suspicious materials when we searched your room at the inn."

"I won't reveal my methods," Anya said firmly, golden bracelets jingling as the junior copper stepped forward to put the handcuffs back on—tightly, by the way she winced. Or maybe that was part of her act.

"We're not done here, necromancer. If we find anything that connects you to Garbor's death more than you're letting on, things won't go well for you," Captain Voshawk said forcefully.

He turned to his officers. "Take her back to her cell."

As the coppers moved to follow his orders, Captain Voshawk's piercing red eyes swept the room, landing squarely on Manrik Skrift. His acknowledgment was subtle—a brief, curt nod.

"Manrik," he said, his gravelly voice carrying an edge. "I'll see you in my office."

"Of course, Captain," Manrik replied smoothly, but Voshawk was already turning away, his long strides purposeful and unhurried. The watch captain seemed never to wait for anyone, always moving to his own cadence.

Manrik watched him for a beat before turning to me, a glint in his beady, black eyes. "Go on, Safety Inspector. I'd hate to delay a centaur of your . . . importance." He stepped aside with an exaggerated bow, letting me move past him.

My escort led me once more as the coppers hurried back to their tasks. We passed Anya being led back to her cell. Eyes straight ahead, her mouth set in stubborn denial, she walked as if trudging through turbulent water. I ached with empathy, feeling equally powerless to influence the tide of events in this strange city that threatened to subsume us.

Chapter Twenty-Six

Inside the coroner's office, I was greeted by the heavy scent of herbs and chemicals and the unconventionally attractive coroner of the City Watch. She was tall, with a very pale complexion, widely spaced dark eyes, and a long nose that nevertheless suited her face. Her brown hair was pinned back to reveal the pointed ears of a Helvenkin. A long white apron, the kind worn by sanctified physicks, was tied over her black robes.

"Safety Inspector Simarron, thank you for coming swiftly. I am Coroner Rin Heartbloom," she said with a slight bow. "We are facing a mystery, and your insight may shed light upon it." Her office was filled with homely wood furniture stuffed with books, bottles, and medical equipment. More brown bottles lined the window sills, glowing in the afternoon light. It seemed far too cozy for her cold profession.

I dipped my head, returning the bow. "I'm happy to help, but . . . could I ask why Anya Vedeva is still here? The painting should prove that she wasn't involved in Lysandros Garbor's death. It doesn't possess dangerous magic, and she couldn't have administered the arsenic gas while attending to him during his collapse."

"Please, sit down. It sounds like you have been conducting your own investigation," said Rin, offering me a rug to sit on, instead of the bare floor, which I appreciated. She didn't seem critical—more intrigued—but heat rose to my cheeks. Had I overstepped my role?

"Let's start at the beginning. How well did you know Professor Ashmin?" she asked me once I had settled on the rug. She poured a cup of tea and passed it to me—a steaming brew that smelled deeply earthy, like damp leaves and old roots.

"Well, I met her twice, in her lab at the university. She mentioned that she had a right to know what Lysandros Garbor was doing at Château Gorget. She followed him in death shortly after starting her investigation—that can't be mere coincidence."

"So the two victims are linked," she said, tapping her spoon against the edge of her cup. She leaned forward over the desk, the steam from her tea curling in the space between us, her eyes narrowing in thought. "Still, Anya Vedeva remains a person of interest. The painting turned out to be mundane, but she could have killed Garbor using dangerous magic or even toxic components from her performances. And unfortunately, she has been uncooperative with Captain Voshawk."

I snorted in disbelief. "There's nothing in Anya's MASHA file to suggest she's ever engaged in dangerous magic. However, someone hung the painting against a concealed compartment from where a lethal poison was dispersed." I detailed how I discovered empty vials labeled "arsenic," which carried a distinct garlic odor.

The coroner let my words tumble out in a nervous rush. She sipped her tea, listening with unwavering focus. Though she didn't take any notes, I could sense her filing away every word. Warmth bloomed in my chest. She trusted me with information she didn't have to share. From the very first moment, she'd acknowledged my intelligence—not my height, as Director Moosekind had, nor my clothes, as Kai had, nor the fact that I was a centaur, as most two-leggers did. She wanted my help, and I desired nothing more than to give it.

"The same odor was on Kari Ashmin's body," I continued. "It could be a gaseous compound of arsenic. The two deaths have to be connected," I finished, feeling calmer as I spoke. The unsettling tension from my interaction with Manrik and seeing Anya in custody began to ease. Here, in this space, I finally felt grounded again.

"Interesting theory," said Rin thoughtfully. "I am having the university lab test for poison as part of the inquests in both cases. But as you must know as a MASHA safety inspector, alchemists often expose themselves to toxins."

I nodded solemnly. Lysandros Garbor hadn't seemed to possess the healthiest physique, and I'd witnessed Professor Ashmin first-hand conducting very unsafe behavior in her lab. How could the coroner determine if the killer had used poison, if alchemists insisted on subjecting themselves to these conditions on the regular?

"Surely she can't have murdered Kari Ashmin while in custody." Why was it so clear to me but not to the City Watch? Or did they think that she could somehow have reached beyond her cell walls to commit another crime?

I thought back to Anya's arrest at the Spring Equinox Fair, the way she was dragged off the stage while whispers and gasps rippled through the crowd. It had all been so dramatic, so perfectly orchestrated to make a point. The watch captain hadn't even requested her MASHA necromancy file until after the fact, as though scrambling to justify the spectacle retroactively. Did he truly believe she was capable of such wicked crimes, or was this about appearances? I supposed Captain Voshawk didn't want to admit he'd made a mistake, especially if it would end up splashed across the headlines of *The Mercury*.

"You're truly convinced that the killer of Kari Ashmin and the killer of Lysandros Garbor are one and the same."

I hesitated. How could I explain it? "Yes. When viewing the painting, and when I revisited the Kami-Nihkia Club, I caught a . . . sense, an emotional scent of what I believe belongs to the killer. The same one I smelled on the cryptic note. Garbor and Ashmin must have been targeted by the same person." The words felt absurd even as they left my mouth. And yet, they rang with an inexplicable truth. "My instincts don't lie."

"And what was that 'emotional scent?'" prompted the coroner, genuine interest reflected in her dark eyes. She really was quite pretty, I couldn't help noticing.

"It's hard to describe, kind of like decaying wood mixed with the metallic tang of blood. But it doesn't just hit my nose. It feels like a punch in the gut, like a seething ball of . . . pure avarice. If I smelled it again, I'd recognize it," I managed to say. Embarrassed, I felt that I needed to shift the focus of the conversation away from myself and my strange ability. "Did you discover who delivered the note to the professor?"

"It was delivered by Witchy Whisk. Unfortunately, however, the sender used some kind of enchantment on the messenger. The poor girl could not remember anything between arriving at Château Gorget and leaving with the note."

"She had her memories of Château Gorget tampered with?" A cold familiarity settled over me.

"It is troubling, as Witchy Whisk is normally very secure," said Rin Heartbloom. "Their messengers are carefully screened, and protected by defensive magic. They're trained to detect curses. Of course, if anyone uses the service to commit mundane crimes like blackmail or fraud, such persons usually find themselves thwarted. That's why it's so disconcerting that someone managed to bypass these measures."

"Are there any leads at all?"

"I contacted Lysandros Garbor, but unfortunately he had already passed far into the Underworld and his voice was very weak. Should we ask Kari Ashmin if she saw her killer?" Rin suggested cheerfully.

I blinked, my mind stumbling over the weight of her statement. "You can do that?" The words came out before I could stop them, incredulous and tinged with disbelief. "And . . . you want me to accompany you while you summon Professor Ashmin from the Underworld?"

"You're very observant, Simarron. I think you can help me while I attempt to speak to her spirit via séance."

"But how can I help you talk to a spirit?"

Rin smiled. "You just said yourself that you have a sense of smell that's beyond the natural."

"Just the other day, I issued a necromancy permit," I said, chuckling nervously, "but I'm not a licensed necromancer myself. I'm not sure how I could possibly contribute."

"You underestimate yourself, Simarron." Rin's voice carried a sincerity that was unsettling but oddly invigorating. "Do you trust me?"

I hesitated, gazing at the steam curling up from my untouched tea. Did I trust her as much as she seemed to trust me?

"I'm still not sure I'll be much help, but I'll do what I can."

"That's all I ask," Rin said, rising from her chair and gesturing for me to follow. "Come. Let's see where this leads."

The corridor beyond the coroner's office dimmed as we entered an older part of the building. I followed Rin to the morgue, wondering what revelations awaited me in the séance. Would I really be able to use my sense of smell to help find Professor Ashmin's killer and prove Anya's innocence? I wasn't so sure, but Rin's unwavering belief in me made me want to try.

Chapter Twenty-Seven

The morgue was a clean, open space with two gleaming tables in the center—like those used by physicks in the healing temples, only clearly meant for patients no longer living. A long sink took up one wall, shelves full of equipment lined another, and a deep cabinet of large drawers dominated the far wall.

Rin approached the wall of drawers and slid one open. The last time I'd seen Kari Ashmin alive, I'd told her to be more careful. Now here she was. I swallowed hard, wondering if she'd be more or less forthcoming with information this time.

Rin pulled the heavy curtains shut and shadows enveloped the room, cast by the light from a single meteor crystal lamp. Continuing in silence, she pulled a stool over to one of the tables gleaming in the lamplight, and I settled down on my haunches to observe as she arranged some items before her: an hourglass, an incense burner, a bell, and a pen and paper.

"Do you have permission from Professor Ashmin's family to contact her spirit?" I asked, flashing a quick smile to mask my discomfort. *This is fine and not weird at all.* Necromancy. I had so far thought about it in the abstract, something neatly confined to MASHA's *Rules and Regulations*. But this was real. Summoning a spirit from the Underworld was no longer a line item on an authorization form, it was a ritual I was being invited to witness, even assist with.

Rin smiled. "I knew I wanted a MASHA safety inspector here for this," she said, producing a sheet of paper. It was a consent to necromancy form, signed by Kari Ashmin's sister.

I nodded, but still felt uneasy. I didn't like thinking about the alchemy professor having a family who she'd left behind.

"Please, use your special sense to help me sniff out the truth," Rin said, lighting the incense.

The distinctive aroma of frankincense masked the smell of carbolic acid used as disinfectant. Rin was very close, I realized suddenly, catching a waft of calendula from her robes. She carefully turned over the hourglass and began the summoning spell. I did not recognize the name of the god or goddess she invoked. Upon hearing it, the sound slipped through my mind like quicksilver and was lost to me. I was struck by another realization: Rin was a necromancer, after all.

"Kari Ashmin, follow the sound of my voice and let the ringing of the bell guide your spirit back to the world of the living." She gripped the bell by the handle and gently tilted it back and forth, releasing a series of clear tones that resonated through the room. Sand trickled into the bottom lobe of the hourglass.

The silence stretched as I waited, my gaze shifting between the pendulum swing of the bell and the open drawer. I listened to the chime die away and smelled the incense offering, scarcely daring to breathe. I had to wonder if it was truly possible to bridge the gap between the living and the dead in this way. The ancestral spirits of the centaurs guided and protected us from the final hunting grounds. Here, the boundaries between life and death blurred. Ghosts lingered in the material world for reasons I couldn't yet fathom. Yet despite my skepticism of the death magic of the two-leggers, I was hopeful—desperate, even, for answers that possibly only Kari Ashmin could provide.

Long moments passed and I anxiously looked at Ashmin's corpse, half expecting her to sit upright, but she lay still. The only movement came from an ethereal orb that began to flicker into being, hovering near us. It was small and faint, giving me the impression of starlight reaching us from a distant world.

"Greetings," Rin greeted the spirit, her voice soothing and gentle. "I'm Rin Heartbloom, Coroner for the City Watch, here with Safety Inspector Simarron. We're here to help you find peace, to understand what happened to you. Can you tell me your name?"

Rin nodded to a voice only she could hear. "Thank you for coming to my morgue, Kari Ashmin. Do not be afraid. We simply want to ask you a few questions before you return to your journey through the Underworld. Can you tell us what was the last thing you saw before you died?"

Kari's spirit form wavered as if struggling to maintain coherence. Rin leaned forward, her pen poised over the paper. It struck me that this, too, was a novel way of listening—one that gave the dead a voice.

"It's all right, take your time," she said gently. "A stone in an uneven row of many, leading to a small house." Her gaze flicked to mine.

"The mausoleum in the graveyard," I whispered.

"What else did you sense?" Rin began writing swiftly, her script neat and dotted with abbreviated words. "A whispered fracture beneath your steps . . . What could that be?"

I hesitated, uncertain.

Rin frowned. "Who whispered? Did you sense anyone?"

"Ask about the smell," I prompted. I couldn't hear Professor Ashmin, but beneath the smoldering incense, I caught the familiar aroma of coffee mingled with chemicals—it had to be her. I pictured the mausoleum as it must have looked from her eyes, lying on the cold ground, and felt a stab of emotion—sharp and raw, like I'd experienced before with the spirit in my room and the one in the courtyard. What Rin said next affirmed my belief that the contact was legitimate.

"A choking cloud of garlic and feet," she said after a few moments, meeting my gaze.

I nodded. The arsenic gas—but who was the mastermind behind the trap?

"Did you suspect who sent the note?" Rin quickly began writing names, but paused as the list of possible offenders overflowed the page.

"I see . . . you have many academic rivals. What were you investigating in the time just before the note appeared?" Rin flipped to the other side of the sheet of paper as she prepared to record the circumstances surrounding the professor's death.

There was a pause, a breathless stillness in the morgue. As my eyes adjusted to the darkness, the outlines of the drawer containing Professor Ashmin's earthly form became more clear. Rin's pale face dominated the solemn scene, illuminated by the lamplight as she bent over her writing.

"Please understand that I ask purely for context, and that your research is safe with me," said the coroner, as the silence stretched on. "I understand, you were working on analyzing samples."

"And what did she find?" I asked, my voice barely above a whisper.

Rin, apparently listening to the professor, nodded and wrote down "element X" and circled it.

This confirmed my hunch. "Someone else suspected what she was researching and wanted to stop her," I said softly. "In fact, they counted on it when they created the map and encrypted it with an easily-solved code, promising more. But what were the samples from?"

Rin kept on writing. Her lips were pressed together in a stern line, but her eyes danced with excitement in the lamplight as she wrote:

Locks from an ancient, dark-haired woman, where pigments hold secrets more than skin-deep.

What did that mean? I was still puzzling over this revelation when Rin continued, "I'm so sorry, Kari, that must have been terrible. Yet you weren't afraid of any harm coming to you in the graveyard. Why was that?"

My agitation grew as the cold silence stretched on, broken only by the scratching of Rin's pen and the nearly imperceptible flow of sand into the bottom lobe of the hourglass. Our time was nearly up.

"Do you have anything else you'd like to say?" she urged.

"Yes, I'll give your message to your sister. Thank you, Kari Ashmin, for sharing your experiences and knowledge with us," said Rin, setting her pen down. "I assure you, we will do our best to bring your murderer to justice."

She then picked up the incense burner and waved it in a wide arc, the smoke trailing in gentle swirls before extinguishing it. "I cleanse this space, and with gratitude, I release you from this calling." The woody, spicy fragrance tickled my nose.

Rin turned the hourglass over again, letting the fresh sand start its descent, a symbolic gesture marking the end of the communication. "Go now, back through the veil to the Underworld, and be at peace."

She rang the bell softly three times, each chime echoing in the morgue. The sound seemed to usher the remaining presence of Kari Ashmin away, the spirit light fading into nothingness.

Rin was smiling. "That was by far the clearest connection I'd ever had with a spirit of the dead. She said something about being protected by the Soul Anchor. Do you know what that is?"

"The Soul Anchor?" It couldn't be. I peered at the coroner's notes, and there it was, written in her precise hand.

Where whispers of the past echoed in the tombs of forgotten wizards, I felt invulnerable, wrapped in the cloak of eternal life bestowed by the Soul Anchor secured around my neck.

"She apparently tried to tell you before, in the place of red bricks," said Rin, indicating the next line.

It wasn't a cloak of safety but a wrapping, ensnaring me to the world of the living. Like a spider's web, intricate and strong, yet easily torn apart. To free my spirit, you must sever the threads that tether me to this world.

The powerful ghost in the courtyard, the vision of the spider—that had been Kari Ashmin trying to tell me that her spirit was trapped.

The room seemed to contract, focusing all energy on the glowing center where Rin sat, her pale face and long, pointed ears illuminated by the lamplight.

"It's a lot to take in," said Rin gently, her gaze shifting to my trembling hands. "When you're ready, I'm listening."

"Yes, I'm familiar with the Soul Anchor," I said, clenching my fists to still them. "It's supposed to grant eternal life, but it seems that it quite literally anchors souls to the mortal world, preventing them from passing on." This was bad, very bad. No wonder the Bureau of Magical Inquiries had opened an investigation into the Soul Anchor in the past.

Rising from where I sat near the table, I approached the open drawer containing Kari Ashmin's lifeless body. Around her neck was a pendant hanging from a silver chain. Was this the Soul Anchor? I'd seen it when I'd discovered her body, but I hadn't given it much consideration. Her killer had apparently not been concerned with it either, seemingly also unaware of what it was. Yet I was certain that somehow the Soul Anchor fit into all of this. And because of Manrik Skrift's article claiming that wizards were trying to use it against alchemists, well, that was just giving people ideas.

"It seems like you might know more than you're letting on. If there's anything else you can share, please do," said Rin, sensing my hesitation.

"Others will be looking for the Soul Anchor, and it might not take long for them to find out that Ashmin had the real one," I said, taking the locket and closing the drawer with a thud. I didn't know how close Skrift was to exposing the Lyness family connection to the Soul Anchor, but Daniella Lyness had mentioned that her mother was involved with its creation somehow. And hadn't her mother known Kari Ashmin's mother?

"Simarron?" Rin's voice rose slightly. She stepped closer, her hand outstretched as if to retrieve the locket.

My instinct was to step back, but the confines of the morgue left little space, causing me to loom unintentionally over her. I saw her flinch slightly, a subtle but unmistakable reaction to my imposing stature.

"There's no doubt what it is—the reason her spirit is so strong is because of the Soul Anchor. As a dangerous magical artifact, it falls under MASHA jurisdiction to contain it—Regulation 7.4.2, subsection C," I said.

Rin's hand dropped to her side, but her voice remained firm. "It's also potentially evidence. Captain Voshawk won't be pleased. I can't let you remove it without informing him first."

"You're right, Captain Voshawk will never let MASHA interfere, despite the danger," I said, my grip tightening on the locket. "But you saw what it did to Professor Asmin's spirit. The Soul Anchor is a threat to public safety, and it's my duty to neutralize its power."

She shook her head. "And what if it's also a key to solving Ashmin's murder?"

"Kari Ashmin begged us to destroy it and free her trapped spirit. If we wait for Captain Voshawk's approval, that might never happen."

Rin studied me with her warm brown eyes, and I saw a familiar conflict between duty and compassion flickering within them. Finally, she sighed.

"You're asking me to delay telling Captain Voshawk what we've discovered," she said. "Fine. You have two days to follow MASHA protocols."

"I must destroy it." My words hung in the air like smoke from the incense, a promise to whatever spirits or gods were listening in that dim chamber.

Chapter Twenty-Eight

I drifted home that evening like a formless specter, my mind so awhirl that it felt disconnected from my body. My legs moved automatically, taking me to the mansion on Slant Row with the withered tree out front. I passed through the door flanked by columns, barely noticing the shrine to the goddess Prismuth in the vestibule.

A clock chimed, grounding me back in the present. My fingers curled around the cold form of the locket—the Soul Anchor—in my vest pocket. I stepped into the warmth of the parlor, where the flicker of the fireplace cast a cozy glow.

Gathered around the fire, I held the attention of my housemates as I recounted my recent séance in the morgue. Lilimari peppered me with questions, wanting to know every detail of how the coroner used necromancy to investigate deaths.

"Lilimari, do you know who this might be? Professor Ashmin was testing 'locks from an ancient, dark-haired woman, where pigments hold secrets more than skin-deep.' Did you find out what she was researching before she died?"

"Yeah, I was waiting for you to get home so I could tell you," Lilimari said, her words picking up speed with excitement. "She was working on uncovering an unknown element—after a hiatus when a rival stole some of her research. But her life's work was the intersection of alchemy, the material world, and necromancy, the spiritual realm. So of course she took paint samples from the haunted painting to test them."

She paused for a breath, then added, "Umb, didn't you say the painting was of some old lady with dark hair and creepy eyes?"

"The haunted painting . . . of course! The woman in the portrait. The pigments used in the paints." I paused. "Before, when I asked Ashmin if Garbor's death could be connected to the haunted painting, she was dismissive of the idea," I said, thinking back to that day in her lab. "Either she was being very guarded, or she had already debunked the painting's magical qualities. And what's more, she suspected its pigments contained traces of a new element."

"That's why she was lured to the graveyard with the map marked element X," concluded Lilimari.

"She was wearing this locket, thinking it would protect her." At last, I had arrived at the true purpose of this conversation. I took a steadying breath. "Daniella, I need to ask you something. Where did this come from?" I asked, producing the Soul Anchor from my pocket. It felt far heavier than it should as I held it out to her.

The landlady blinked, taken aback. "Where did you find that? It's been missing for years!" she exclaimed. "I thought the Bureau of Magical Inquiries had locked it away for good."

"I found it with Kari Ashmin. Do you know what it is?" Its metallic surface gleamed in the firelight.

"Ashmin?" Lyness's voice trembled. "Her mother worked at the BMI. Did Neda Ashmin confiscate the Soul Anchor, only to have it end up in the hands of her daughter? Neda was a friend of my mother's . . ."

Lilimari sprang up from her chair, her dark eyes alight with curiosity. "Can I see the Soul Anchor?" Her enthusiasm cut through the heavy atmosphere. "There's so much I could learn from it about binding spells and spectral retention!"

Tia, who had been silently sketching in her notepad, looked up sharply. Her hand paused mid-stroke, pencil hovering in mid-air. "The soul painting is real, then?" she murmured, more to herself than to anyone in the room. Her gaze flicked to the locket and back to her drawing.

"Why do you call it that?" I said. "The Soul Anchor is very real, but the haunted painting was a fake. I discovered it yesterday, where it was hidden at the Kami-Nihkia Club."

"It's not a fake," said Tia, her tone a mix of disbelief and defensiveness. "I thought the soul painting was just a legend, that's all I'm saying." She rose from her chair and began gathering her drawing supplies.

"But it was meant to evoke the legend of something powerful and real," I said. I glanced at her retreating figure from the side of my vision, suspicious.

Kai's eyes darted between the locket and the landlady, a flicker of concern crossing his face. "Is it dangerous?"

"Yes," I replied. "Kari's ghost is eternally trapped in the world of the living, and she wants me to destroy the locket so she can rest in peace."

The tension in the room grew as Daniella Lyness, with trembling fingers, finally opened the locket. Inside, the small portrait revealed itself to be ingeniously crafted, its image shifting with the light and angle. From one perspective, it clearly depicted Kari Ashmin, her features softened by youth. As the locket tilted, the image morphed, revealing another face—one that was strikingly different.

"It's been altered," Daniella murmured. "From this angle, it's Neda Ashmin's daughter, and this way . . . it's someone else."

Lilimari leaned in closer. "Your mother made this? That's some sophisticated magic, not to mention artistic talent," she noted in awe.

"I need to keep this for a little while," said Daniella, her gaze locked onto the shifting portrait. "There are things I need to understand about it first. But I promise, it won't be long. We'll destroy it soon, to free Ashmin's spirit and . . . that of the other person bound to it."

"I'd love to learn more about it, too," said Lilimari.

"I can't let you do that," I said, shifting from hoof to hoof.

"I'd rather it was destroyed as soon as possible," said Kai, his fingers brushing the amulet at his neck.

"She was important to me, and this is my last memento of her. I just want a little more time," Daniella pleaded. Closing the locket, she gently polished the outside with a corner of her apron.

"You have until tomorrow evening," I said firmly. "Then I must destroy it, in accordance with MASHA protocol in regard to dangerous magical artifacts." Coroner Rin Heartbloom had given me two days, so I reasoned it would be fine. Probably.

The locket disturbed me, and not just because my sense of duty clashed against my feelings of compassion for Landlady Lyness. It was the way it shifted between two portraits, the way it was created to preserve life but became a curse. To her, it was a sentimental family heirloom that represented closure; to me, it was a dangerous artifact. I trusted Daniella with it, but the weight of that trust pressed heavily on me.

Despite feeling that I needed to retire early that evening, sleep wouldn't come. I shifted uncomfortably, my chest upright and my legs folded underneath me. The mattress on the floor, adorned with pillows in decorative covers Kai had knitted, shifted under my weight.

I released a heavy sigh and breathed in the scent of old wood, linseed oil, and the faintly dusty smell of the rich blue curtains. The patterns in the well-loved yellow wallpaper faded into shadow as the light receded. Outside my window, the branches of the tree out front danced in the wind, their movements accompanied by the evening songs of birds.

I picked up my book of MASHA *Rules and Regulations* and idly flipped through the pages. There was a large section of appendices at the back, including a classical chart of the elements, as well as the modern Periodic System of the Elemental Metals.

I paged through the book aimlessly, unsure of what I sought. In any case, reading dry material in bed proved to be the perfect remedy, and I soon nodded off in my nest of blankets.

I woke up some time later, confused. The faint blue light of pre-dawn cast a ghostly glow across my room. Had I slept until morning? I took a deep calming breath and reached out with all my senses for any sign of ghosts, for I had the dreadful sense that I wasn't alone. The shadows seemed to shift, and if I trained my focus on any spot long enough, all manner of shapes seemed to form out of the darkness. In the dim light before sunrise, the once-familiar stains in the wallpaper resembled ominous eyes.

"Is that you, ghost, flitting about the room?" I whispered.

I felt a bright, clear sensation, like the reverberations of the bell the coroner had rung in the morgue. My reaching out had definitely resonated with someone. I shivered.

"Who are you?"

I felt a sudden terrible emptiness that consumed my very being.

"Why are you here?"

Again, a soul-consuming hollowness with only a single pinprick of light, as I conceptualized it. But then, a second little metaphorical ball of light joined it. *Ah, that's right.* I remembered promising in my previous half-asleep encounter with the entity that we could share the space.

"I meant before that. Listen, if we're going to be roommates, I need to call you something. How about . . . Flit?"

I felt the bright sensation again, small but vibrant, like little sparkles against my mind.

"Are you stuck here because of the Soul Anchor, too?"

A wave of joyful bubbles carried on a tide of sadness.

"That was you who revealed that note about the Soul Anchor during the storm, wasn't it?"

I suddenly felt awash in emotions that weren't mine, I was drowning. I reached out to the wall to steady myself.

"Is Kari Ashmin haunting me too?" That was her spirit in the court-yard. Had she latched onto me when I'd discovered her body at the graveyard? Was she here now? A chill ran down my withers as I peered into the dim confines of my room.

I felt a shift from Flit, like a shrug.

To think if Professor Ashmin, unable to find eternal rest, was going to follow me around until I destroyed the Soul Anchor . . . An icy dread settled in my chest as I reflected on the artifact that had ensnared Ashmin's soul, the séance in the morgue, the ghost that had devoured my memories of the castle, and all the other necromantic events of late.

But in the end, none of it truly mattered in the murders themselves, did it? The haunted painting was a fake, meant to make Garbor's death appear like the work of necromancers—just as the necromantic runes around Ashmin's body had been designed to do the same. Was the killer a wizard pretending to be a necromancer, staging fake hauntings? Or a necromancer disguising their craft by being terrible at it? Yet neither explanation accounted for what I now knew.

"No, the real link isn't necromancy—it's element X," I whispered.

Kari Ashmin had been studying the intersection of necromancy and alchemy, and she had taken samples from the haunted painting. But there was nothing magical about the painting itself. What she *did* find was element X. That was why she was killed.

Lysandros Garbor had previously stolen her research. Presumably his death, too, led back to element X. The killer wasn't some charlatan playing at magic—they were someone dangerous with a strong inter-est in keeping the discovery of element X from both alchemists.

My conclusions left me feeling chilled. Unable to return to sleep, I pulled myself off my bed. *Rules and Regulations* was lying on the floor, open to the chart of the Periodic System of the Elemental Metals. A drop of wax had fallen onto the page, on a gap in the column contain-ing Chromia, noted as X51. An element X.

Chapter Twenty-Nine

Seated in my windowless office at MASHA, surrounded by the heavy wooden filing cabinet of organized files, and my desk laden with papers less so, everything from the previous day felt like a surreal dream—Mina attempting to teach me magic in the courtyard, the brush with Kari Ashmin's spirit instead, witnessing Anya Vedeva's interrogation at Shetland Yard, the séance in the morgue, the encounter with Flit. But I knew it was all real, as solid as the fountain pen in my hand, hovering above the paper as I attempted to write.

It was difficult to focus with my thoughts galloping in all directions. I took a deep, steadying breath. If there was one thing I had learned lately, it was that my mind needed to be corralled before I could fully rely on my senses.

What about the emotional scent of the killer—the one I had detected near the haunted painting, on the cryptic note, and in the Kami-Nihkia gaming room? I latched onto the memory of its unique yet elusive aroma.

My conversation with Rin Heartbloom had uncovered another possible source of that scent. The note Professor Ashmin received—it was delivered by someone who, like me, had a mysterious experience at Château Gorget.

Slowly, an idea began to take shape, like ink spreading on paper and gradually forming into a legible letter.

I turned, then nearly jumped out of my skin when I noticed Secretary Ami sanMaelthara had materialized in the hallway outside my open door. She remained there quietly, seemingly oblivious to my presence. The silence between us stretched uncomfortably until I noticed her gaze fixed intently over my shoulder, her lips moving slightly as if deep in silent conversation. Despite her recovery from the other morning, something still seemed off.

"Is there something wrong, Ami?" I asked, turning to follow her stare, expecting perhaps a spider on the wall. Instead, I found only an old portrait.

When I looked back at her, she gazed at me with a quizzical expression, like I was the one doing something strange. "Oh, it's nothing, Simarron," she said, her voice quiet and rustling like aged parchment. "Can I help you with something?" She offered a faint smile.

Regaining my composure, I nodded. "Yes, could you please fetch me a Witchy Whisk token?"

Without a word, Ami turned and disappeared down the corridor. Moments later, she was back, almost too quickly for someone who had just walked the length of the building and back. She extended her hand to me, holding the token.

As our hands touched, I flinched at the icy coldness of her skin, but I thanked her, masking my discomfort with a polite smile.

"Do you require anything else?" Ami asked, her expression unreadable.

"No, thank you," I replied hurriedly. She nodded and vanished as quietly as she had arrived, and I had no time to ponder our enigmatic secretary, for I was already invoking the magic I needed for another matter.

"I summon thee now, Witchy Whisk!" As the last words of the spell died on my lips, I began pacing my office in restless anticipation. I should have noticed before that the cryptic note had been in an envelope containing a full address—this was not the norm for Witchy Whisk. With the messages delivered individually, the witch could be counted upon to remember the intended destination. By writing the address out fully, it was as if the sender anticipated the messenger would not recall this information.

The witch appeared. She was not the one who had delivered the note from Château Gorget, but promised to ask the messenger who had. She also informed me that if any customer tried to attack her, it would go very badly for them. I did not doubt her abilities as I scrambled a step back from her dramatically gesturing finger.

Yet the killer hadn't attacked me or the messenger at the castle—at least not directly. A ghost had drained our memories of Château Gorget, or so I suspected. Otherwise, our magical safety gear or Mina's pact with Titanacala surely would have protected us. Coroner Rin Heartbloom had said that the Witchy Whisk messengers were normally protected from harm, too.

No, the murderer preferred indirect methods.

A little while later, the other witch arrived. It occurred to me how terrifying it must be to return to work after the experience she must have had, but she did not appear frightened.

"Witchy Whisk, at your service," she said brightly.

"Thank you for coming so quickly. Please, have a seat. I want to ask you a few questions about a delivery you made, that's all."

Her smile faded. "What delivery?"

She propped up her broomstick against the wall of my office, but remained standing stiffly.

"I need to ask you about a message you delivered three days ago to Professor Ashmin at the university."

The witch's eyes widened. "I already told the City Watch, I can't clearly recall anything that happened between arriving at Château Gorget, and leaving with the note," she said with a tone of finality.

"Do you remember the castle? I'm asking because . . . the same thing happened to me."

Her posture eased and her tone was softer as she replied, "Not particularly, but everyone knows the old castle up there, Safety Inspector."

"Do you still have the token that was used to summon you for that delivery?"

The witch reached into the pocket of her tailored coat and retrieved a silver disk. "Yes, I do," she replied, handing it to me. "It felt . . . strange, somehow. I couldn't bring myself to exchange it for a regular coin. It's as if it carries a certain . . . energy. I kept it to remind myself to trust my instincts if a place seems off."

I examined the token in my hand and brought it close to my face. Although it had been riding for over three days in the pocket of a flying messenger, and had not been present for the crime it had been used to facilitate, it did retain a certain emotional quality. I smelled the lingering malicious intent, like a faded bloodstain on decaying wood.

"Thank you, Witchy Whisk. You've been most helpful," I said, moving to hand it back.

"You keep it," the witch said, stepping away and offering me a half-smile. "I hope you find what you're looking for, Safety Inspector."

She retrieved her broomstick and headed out the door of my office.

I began to pace again. My hooves carried me down the hall, where I paused at Mina's door. The hairs on my withers stood up and, hand raised to knock, I glanced back down the corridor. There was a flutter of movement that seemed out of place. Was it the secretary and her unsettling way of appearing and vanishing?

I moved swiftly toward the figure emerging from the storage room, my hoofsteps loud on the polished floor. For a brief moment, I didn't recognize him, as he had the sort of face that was instantly forgettable. But as I drew close, I caught the distinctive scent of metallic ink and dry dust.

"Manrik Skrift!" I called. "What are you doing here?"

Yet something was off about him, as if I were remembering his scent wrong.

"Ah, Safety Inspector," the reporter said smoothly, his thin lips curling into a self-satisfied smirk. "I must thank you for your advice to take my questions about public safety records to MASHA. What a fascinating story this Soul Anchor business has turned out to be. I've uncovered some very interesting history about the Lyness family, which I'm sure the public will find quite illuminating."

My tail lashed behind me. "Leave Daniella Lyness alone."

"Don't worry, I'll let the City Watch handle the details. I'm just doing my civic duty to keep the public informed," Manrik said, his grin widening. "I'll see myself out."

I followed to make sure he really did leave, then retraced my steps to Mina's office. I was surprised she or Director Moosekind had let the news writer into the old storage room with the cold case files, but I had other matters on my mind.

"Come in," Mina called in response to my knock.

I stepped inside to find the administrator seated at her desk. The glowing eye on the pen stand swiveled toward me.

"Simarron, how was your visit to the coroner's office?" she asked.

"Coroner Rin Heartbloom wanted my help in her inquest. And . . . well, it's unlike anything I've ever witnessed before. She had me observe a necromancy session where she contacted Professor Ashmin's spirit. Is that . . . normal?" It still didn't seem real.

Mina's brow furrowed. "A séance is the usual procedure in a murder with no witnesses."

"She called Professor Ashmin back from the Underworld, and for a moment, she was there—flickering at the edge of existence."

Mina nodded solemnly. "And did she tell you anything useful?"

"She remembered the mausoleum. The uneven stones leading to the entrance, the scent of the arsenic gas." I exhaled, recalling how the spirit's presence had wavered like she was struggling against some invisible current.

Mina shuddered. "No need to tell me any more. I'm glad the City Watch has a use for them, but a lot of us find necromancers, well, creepy."

I didn't entirely disagree, but necromancy seemed like a useful tool in the right hands, much like the Magical Energies Detector.

"I just thought of something that may help. May I borrow the MED?"

The eye on the pen stand squinted at me as if taking measure of my intentions.

"Help with what? Let me guess, you want to revisit Château Gorget," Mina said flatly.

"Mina, is there a reason you're particularly against going back? It seems unlike you to limit yourself to the boundaries of our duties and shy away from discovering the truth."

She took a moment before responding, like she was choosing her words carefully. "Simarron, there are things in our line of work that can leave lasting marks, not just physically but mentally. Years ago, I was involved in a complex Bureau of Magical Inquiries case, investigating a daring robbery of rare artifacts. The only witnesses had their memories erased—magically. We never solved it because those involved couldn't remember anything useful. It was the first case I worked on, and it serves as a constant reminder of what's at stake."

"I'm sorry you had to go through that," I said. "But Mina, it's precisely your experience that makes you such an effective administrator. You're determined to do better than the Bureau of Magical Inquiries."

"It's not just about doing better than the Bureau," Mina said, her voice firm. "It's about preventing harm before it occurs. And right now, I do not believe revisiting the site is prudent."

"I'm ready," I pressed, hoping to convince her. "You've guided me with knowledge and wisdom, and allowed me to learn from my mistakes—like when I impulsively ran after Kari Ashmin and later faced the responsibility of reporting directly to the City Watch. You've prepared me well, Mina."

She shook her head. "We have an entire city to protect, and we cannot afford reckless actions. Continue your safety investigations here, within the parameters Director Moosekind and I give you." She gestured at the papers on her desk. "Once I finish this paperwork, the castle will be condemned—no one will be allowed up there. Moosekind and I will place magical wards to seal it off."

"Understood, Mina," I said, disappointed.

"Administrator Hereswith," she corrected me, her tone as cool and professional as the day we'd met. It sliced through me like a knife, and I realized that I was jeopardizing everything if I continued to investigate.

Head hung low, I returned to my office and closed the door. The old portraits on the walls looked down at me, stern and disapproving. I forcefully pressed on the brass lever of the hole punch, biting holes in papers that needed to be bound. Ink bled from my fountain pen as I dragged it across paper in an unsteady hand. Drawers squeaked in protest as I fetched and returned files.

Château Gorget was to be condemned, forbidden to all. If I went there, I'd probably lose my job at MASHA and would have to go back to the Wildlands, where I'd now be even more of an outsider. I never fit in with the wild ways of my kind. I didn't enjoy hunting for sport or engaging in contests of strength and speed. I wouldn't be able to talk to anyone about my experiences here because they wouldn't under-stand why anyone would want to live in a city.

I fiddled with the brass key to my room at Slant Row Boarding House, spinning it between my fingers. It wasn't just a key, but a symbol of the belonging I had found. Meanwhile, the copy of the map represented knowledge—and ruin. I kept stealing glances at it while I worked, that cursed map that had led Kari Ashmin to her death in the graveyard. In the center, the dark ink marking element X appeared to shine in the lamplight.

Finding the truth was important. After all, condemning the castle and sealing it off wouldn't stop the murderer. I believed Professor Ashmin had been killed because she got too close to the truth, and there was no reason to think the deaths would stop now. Yet if I pushed forward with the investigation, challenging Mina's direct orders, I risked everything.

I was faced with a decision: I could adhere to Mina's directives, or I could follow my instincts, which screamed that the answers lay at the castle. My tail swished in agitation.

Caught in thought, my fingers slipped, and the key clattered to the floor, falling under my desk. The metallic sound echoed in the quiet of my office, a stark reminder of what I stood to lose: my job, my reputation, my home.

The room felt smaller, the air oppressive, as if the painted eyes of the portraits could really see and judge my actions. They were old Bureau of Magical Inquiries bigwigs, I supposed, based on their voluminous wigs. What would they think of this replacement organization and its newest safety inspector, considering trading in the pursuit of truth for personal comfort? Accepting that a castle was sealed off for public safety while allowing a villain to continue menacing the public?

Then, with a heavy sigh, I knelt down awkwardly, my hands searching blindly behind the desk. My fingertips brushed against the cool metal of the key and I pulled it back into the light of the meteor crystal lamp.

Bracing one hand on my knee and one on the edge of the desk, I pulled myself up. I deliberately placed the key on the desk next to the map. Whatever I decided, I needed to do it quickly. Once the magical ward was in place, it would likely be too late to pursue that path.

As the hands on my pocket watch marked the end of the workday, I reached a shaky decision. I grabbed my coat, knowing that as I stepped out the door, I might not be able to return to this office. But the truth was worth the risk, or so I hoped.

Chapter Thirty

Supper was a tense, quiet affair that evening. Kai and Tia were absent, along with their comforting chatter. Lilimari spooned mushroom catsup all over her bowl of stew, a spicy sauce made by the landlady that the university student claimed was more magical than any potion she'd brewed in class. I stirred my pottage in rapid motions, impatient for it to be cool enough to eat. I needed to eat quickly, gather some supplies, and be off to Château Gorget as soon as possible.

The landlady herself was just about to sit down when there came a knock, firm and insistent, at the door. It didn't sound like the knock of a casual visitor, or either of our two missing housemates, as it reverberated through the hall. Daniella paused, frowning. She crossed through the parlor to the front window and, glancing outside, bustled to the door.

When she opened it, the watch captain's gravelly voice rolled out of the threshold. "Captain Voshawk, City Watch. Wiz. Daniella Lyness? I hope this isn't an inconvenient hour."

"To what do I owe this visit?" she replied.

"I'm here on official business. May I come in?"

"We were just about to have supper," she said, her tone polite but wary as she ushered him into the dining room.

The warmth seemed to dissipate from the room, the glow from the chandelier dim. Captain Voshawk ignored her gesture to take a seat, but he removed his hat. I'd always thought of her as "Landlady

Lyness," but I noticed that Voshawk referred to Daniella by the honorific for witches and wizards. Although I'd never noticed her cast a spell, she kept a shrine to Prismuth and came from one of the old wizard families, after all.

She had always seemed unflappable, a steady presence in our eccentric household. For the first time, I saw her through Voshawk's eyes—not as a landlady, but as a wizard with a powerful legacy of secrets.

I stood, uncertain if I should stay or give them privacy. But one look from Damon Voshawk's stormy red eyes rooted me in place. I slowly sank back down to my haunches, feeling exposed.

"I need to ask you a few questions regarding the artifact known as the Soul Anchor. It's come to my attention that this object has a connection to your family—that, in fact, it may be in your possession. Hand it over now, and the law will look favorably upon you. But if I have to come back and search the entire mansion, my people will not hesitate to tear this place apart."

Daniella paled. "But why? What does it have to do with anything?"

"It falls under MASHA jurisdiction to contain dangerous magical artifacts," I interjected, rising to all fours.

"Stand down, Safety Inspector Simarron. Don't you dare pull that jurisdiction crap with me," Voshawk snapped, cutting me off. "I appreciate your efforts to locate the haunted painting. However, we now know it was fake, a powerless imitation of the Soul Anchor. It's possible the killer was looking for the real Soul Anchor the entire time."

I sat down again, my mind reeling. He must have talked to Coroner Rin Heartbloom and come around to my single killer theory. Rin—did she already tell him that I took the Soul Anchor to destroy? No, Voshawk was focused on the Lyness family. What drew his attention in this direction? Then it hit me.

Manrik Skrift!

He'd been in the storage room at MASHA, and I suddenly doubted he'd had permission to be there. It was strange that I hadn't really questioned it at the time. Not strange—uncanny. Regardless, he must have found the files on the Soul Anchor and tipped Voshawk off, likely spinning his own sensational tale about the Lyness family that he was getting ready to publish at this very moment. I felt a sick vindication in my distrust of Manrik.

Daniella's voice cut through my spiraling thoughts. "I run a boarding house. I'm not in the magical artifact business. Whatever family history there is, it's just that—history." She crossed her arms.

"History has a way of catching up to people," Voshawk countered. "Especially when it involves murder." The light caught on his copper badge as he rolled his shoulders and clasped his hands behind him.

"Are you . . . accusing me of something, Captain?" she demanded, her voice rising with indignation and fear.

"I'm not accusing," Voshawk replied, his tone as sharp as flint. "But I am investigating. And if you're withholding information about the Soul Anchor's whereabouts, it could make you look complicit."

"That's enough," said Lilimari, dropping her spoon in a loud clatter. Her long curtain of dark hair quivered with the rage and fear shaking her body. "She's done nothing wrong. You have no reason to treat her like a suspect." The girl who fearlessly explored both the city streets and the boundaries of alchemy—who delighted in ghosts and never seemed afraid of anything—looked as if she might cry.

The captain ignored this outburst and switched tacks, his voice smoothing into a low rumble. "You're an upstanding wizard trying to protect your family's legacy, Wiz. Lyness," he said, gesturing to the faded grandeur of the room. "I understand, I do. But consider this: do you want your family's past mistake to drag you down with it? The Soul Anchor is tied to this murder investigation somehow, and I won't let anyone else become the next victim if I can prevent it."

A heavy silence fell over the dining room. I realized Voshawk wasn't acting out of malice but duty, even if his methods were a bit heavy-handed.

Daniella's posture sagged. She reached inside the neckline of her apron, then froze. Her hand patted her upper chest, her expression shifting to panic for a fleeting moment before she disguised the motion with a cough. My stomach flipped.

"I'm sorry, Captain, I can't help you," she said, her voice strained.

Captain Voshawk studied her for a long moment before nodding curtly. "If you recall where the Soul Anchor might be, or any information that may lead to its recovery, do contact me at once. Cualaith is compassionate to those who uphold the law, and destroys those who stand in its way or enable corruption," he said, sketching a symbol in the air as he spoke the goddess's name.

Without another word, he donned his hat and strode out of the Slant Row Boarding House.

Daniella sat down slowly, her hands trembling in her lap. Her earlier hints about her family's history with the Soul Anchor echoed in my mind. I felt a fierce urge to protect her, the matriarch of our home. The thought of her being implicated in the murders was unthinkable— it would destroy her and her reputation. I could already see the fallacious, sensationalist headline: "Soul Anchor Murders: a Respected Wizard Family's Dark Secrets Exposed." And then what would happen to the boarding house? No, I wouldn't let that happen.

"What happened to the locket?" I asked.

"I don't know. I'm sorry," she replied, her voice breaking. "I should have listened to you. Now it's gone."

"Gone? How could it be gone?" asked Lilimari, her mouth dropping open in shock, revealing her pointy teeth.

"I fear someone's taken it," said Daniella, her eyes filling with tears.

The guilt that had been wiggling inside me twisted into a hard knot. I should never have let her delay destroying the Soul Anchor, but I'd been swayed by her plea for one last moment with the family heirloom. At the time, it had seemed like a harmless gesture of compassion. But now the artifact was gone, and the crushing realization of my failure as a MASHA safety inspector settled over me.

I didn't know who had taken it, but one fact remained. If I caught the murderer, the one behind it all, the landlady could no longer be a suspect. *Wiz. Lyness*, I reminded myself. It was more urgent than ever to return to Château Gorget and uncover the truth. However, the watch captain had forced an unfortunate delay, and given how difficult it had been for Mina and me to reach the place in daylight, I doubted I could navigate there safely at night. I would rest for a few hours and set out before dawn.

Chapter Thirty-One

That night in my room, my mind incessantly gnawed at my decision to return to Château Gorget. Robbed of a restful night's sleep, I awoke many times before dawn. If Flit appeared, I didn't recall.

I finally jolted awake when the eerie blue glow of the pre-dawn sky cast a ghostly pallor over my room. Lurching out of bed, I lit a candle and I performed my morning ablutions, the cold water in my wash basin piercing my suffocating doubts and tightening my resolve. I then dressed for the long walk to Misty Vale.

I noticed a large envelope on the floor, looming in front of the gap at the bottom of the door. Reaching down awkwardly, I snatched it up. I brought the envelope closer to the candlelight, my hands trembling as I unwound the string from the button that held the flap closed. I pulled out the papers, surprised to see the Château Gorget case files. On top was a piece of handmade paper, its edges unfinished, inscribed by a beautiful flowing hand.

Dear Simarron,

I'm returning your case notes that I took from you that day at The Angry Unicorn. I was only interested in information about the minerals there, for my paint pigments. I never meant for any of this to happen. I felt awful about it, so I tried to avoid you after that. I hope you can forgive me, for I am going to forget you. When we meet again, let's start over and be friends?

—Tia

Paint pigments. My mind swirled as pieces of the puzzle snapped into place with painful clarity. How had I not seen it before? The haunted painting—so strikingly similar to Tia's sunset piece. A dark-haired woman, and behind her a surreal sunset of purple fading to pink unfolded in Tia's raw, organic strokes, each inch of canvas infused with emotion.

Mina's finding spell had shown the missing notes near a lake shore at sunset—Tia's painting! I leafed through my case notes and there it was, element X51, noted as an inscription on a stone near where I had taken a soil sample. Was this the mineral she sought for her paint pigments?

I clenched Tia's note in my fist, crumpling it, and winced as the edge of the stiff paper sliced a tiny cut into the inside of my hand. I could have kicked myself for missing the signs. Her anguish when someone —Professor Ashmin—had scraped paint off her debut work, the haunted painting. Her defensiveness during our discussions of the painting . . . and the murders.

Self-recrimination gave way to anger. I had trusted Tia, shared meals with her, and thought of her as a friend. Her theft of my case notes, her creation of the haunted painting—could she have been involved in the murders, too? The thought stung worse than the paper cut, spreading a deep ache through my heart.

I felt like there were suddenly two Simarrons, locked in a heated argument in my mind. One clung to the belief in her innocence, insisting there had to be an explanation; the other demanded answers and refused to let her betrayal go unanswered.

"She couldn't have done it," one voice argued in reasoned tones. *"She's an artist, not a killer. Just because she painted the haunted painting—the fake Soul Anchor—doesn't mean she's responsible for murder."*

"Oh, wake up!" the other snapped, bristling with indignation. *"She stole your notes, Simarron. She lied about it, and now she's confessing in this*

letter. If she's innocent, why didn't she return the notes earlier? She's only playing with your emotions by asking for your forgiveness now!"

"Because she knew she did wrong and was scared that you'd react badly!" the first voice shot back. *"She said so herself—she only wanted the pigments for her paintings. Artists need resources, and the minerals at Château Gorget are rare. That doesn't make her a murderer!"*

"And yet two people who knew about those minerals are dead." The second voice's tone turned cold, accusing. *"Lysandros Garbor and Kari Ashmin. Coincidence? You know better than that. She's tied to this, admit it."*

"Tied to it, yes, but not guilty of killing them!" The first voice faltered, but clung to its conviction. *"She's a liar and a thief, yes, but she isn't evil. Maybe she's being manipulated. Think about it—she left this heartfelt letter, didn't she? Evildoers don't have regrets. And it doesn't smell like the killer!"*

I sniffed the paper, the ink giving off an odor that was earthy, and a little metallic. It also smelled faintly of a rose bloom, withered to dust, as though it had long since given up on ever feeling the cool touch of water again.

"But does this letter sound like the whole truth to you? Does it explain everything? She implies she acted alone, with no interest other than art. Yet she doesn't mention her part in creating the haunted painting, which you know she did. It's just another layer of lies."

The realization hit me like a kick to the chest. Had Tia really collaborated with the killer? She claimed she'd stolen the notes to make pigments for her paintings, but this confession felt too neat, too self-contained. Who else might have been involved? Could someone else have used her—or worse, partnered with her?

"She might not have known how her art would be used," the first voice argued desperately. *"Who rigged the painting and hid it after the gala? She's not a member of the Kami-Nihkia Club, so how did she gain access? Who sent the malicious note to Professor Ashmin and erased the memory from the Witchy Whisk messenger? Tia couldn't possibly do all that, could she?"*

That final question hung in the air, silencing the argument. But then, something else gnawed at the edges of my thoughts, something I hadn't considered before.

How did Tia know to steal my case notes in the first place? I didn't remember ever telling my housemates about the Château Gorget inspection. Had she been sneaking around, reading my journal? Or had she *seen* me?

The thought unsettled me deeply. I racked my brain for memories of her red hair among the green vines, her rose perfume mingling with the crumbling dust of the ruins. But that day at the castle was a haze, my memories fragmented and unreliable, with gaps I still couldn't fill. Had she been there, watching me? Or had someone else told her about my visit and coerced her into stealing my notes? I didn't like how easily the landlady and Tia's ex-beau had pushed her around. Could someone have been pulling her strings? And how could she be planning to forget me?

Throttling my seething inner monologue, I blew out the candle and rushed out of my room into the hall. As I made my way to the staircase, a conflict waged within me. My instincts urged me to seek answers from Tia. Yet I hesitated, my fingers gripping the stair railing. Just then, the front door rattled gently as someone cautiously entered.

The hallway was steeped in shadows, the light having gone out. For a moment, all was still—until the lanky figure of a Helvenkin emerged, outlined faintly in the dimness.

"Kai," I greeted him in a loud whisper. "I need to have a word with Tia. Can you check on her, see if she's awake?" I felt uncomfortable confronting Tia like this, but she was closer with Kai.

"Has something happened?" he asked, his voice tinged with concern.

"She left me a note of a rather important matter."

Kai swept up the stairs and rapped firmly on Tia's door. He listened for a pause, then turned the doorknob and pushed the door open.

"She's not here," he announced softly. "I wonder where she could have gone? The Angry Unicorn should be closed at this hour."

I glanced down the dark hallway toward the door, frowning. Why was it so dark anyway? Of course—the meteor crystal light was missing, the one that had caused such drama during the storm! Tia must have taken it, planning to travel somewhere in the dark. Although she hadn't mentioned it in her letter, I suddenly knew exactly where she'd gone.

The trail began with the stolen case notes, which turned out to hold significant information about important minerals at the castle site with my casual note: "sample collected near stone bearing inscription 'X51.'" Was that the real reason Lysandros Garbor was so interested in Château Gorget? Tia's brush had fabricated the painting used to disguise his death, and Kari Ashmin's unfortunate curiosity about the mineral pigments used in the painting had led to the second death in this bloody path.

Tia's footsteps led all the way to the vanishing castle, the heart of the mystery.

"Château Gorget," I said. As the words left my lips, I felt the truth of them deep in my bones. There was also a powerful spirit at the castle that tampered with memories. It all pointed to one conclusion. My resolve to investigate the castle strengthened with a new sense of urgency. "That's where she will be."

I thought of the Magical Energies Detector, borrowed from work, but shook my head impatiently, deciding that I moved faster without its burden on my back. I dashed toward the door, then, turning suddenly, I ducked into the kitchen. My hooves clattered on the tile as I spun, searching for the lamp.

I turned my attention to the heavy wooden doors of the larder, shining the light on their contents. I began flinging open cupboard doors, revealing an assortment of dry goods. The cool air and scent of herbs greeted me as I swiftly scanned the stock. The shelves were warped under the weight of canned preserves, sacks of grains, and neatly arranged jars of pickled vegetables.

"Is Tia in trouble?" asked Kai, following close behind. He was no longer whispering, as I made little effort to minimize the noise of my activities.

"I have to stop her, Kai," I said. "If she's gone to Château Gorget, she doesn't understand the danger she's in."

"What's all this fuss about?" Daniella demanded as she appeared in the kitchen in her robe and slippers, hair wild, looking every bit the wizard who might command the elements from the comfort of her own hearth. "I serve two meals a day, and there'll be no raiding of the larder in between."

"Tia's gone to Château Gorget," I repeated, turning to face Wiz. Lyness. *I am going to forget you*, her letter had said, the cryptic words sticking in my mind. "She has . . . regrets, and she's going to visit the unohdus, the memory-eating ghost, at the castle."

"She wouldn't!" exclaimed Kai. "Except, of course she would. She mentioned the hungry ghost that morning when we read about Professor Ashmin's murder in *The Mercury*."

"That's not the only problem." I continued. "She knows about the unique minerals at Château Gorget. Two other people who shared this knowledge ended up dead. Regardless of her involvement, she could be targeted next. The murderer is very motivated to protect the castle from those who would uncover its secrets."

"No, I don't believe it. Tia isn't that reckless," Daniella protested, tears shimmering in her gray eyes, making the flecks of silver and blue seem to swim. In that moment, she wasn't our landlady or a powerful wizard—just Daniella, afraid for one of our friends. "She always wants the easy way."

But this was the easy path, wasn't it, if Tia believed she was protected from harm?

"What if she had protection . . . She must have taken the locket! But if she believes the Soul Anchor will grant her immortality or protection, she's mistaken. The Soul Anchor's power isn't what she thinks—it's a curse more than a shield."

I reflected on the night that I had brought the Soul Anchor home and realized that Tia had left the room in a huff, offended by my calling her painting a fake, before I'd revealed what it had done to its previous victims.

Daniella bowed her head and dug her hands into her white hair. "Oh gods, why didn't I destroy it when I had the chance? That thing will twist her soul!"

"But it's useless for me to go there—the unohdus could eat my memories again—unless I give it something else to feast on."

Daniella glanced at the larder shelves quizzically. "If you think my pickles and jellies will help, take them," she offered. "I won't need them, if I'm . . ." The sentence didn't bear finishing aloud: if she was arrested and jailed for her perceived interference with Captain Voshawk's investigation into the Soul Anchor.

"What do you mean? How could Tia possibly be involved in the murders?" Kai stepped forward, his hand reaching out as if to stop me. "Let me help, Simarron. She's a dear friend and I know she wouldn't hurt anyone. You go make sure the ghost isn't a floating safety violation, and I'll talk to Tia."

I looked into Kai's golden eyes. "No, it's too dangerous, and I'll run faster on my own," I said, forcefully stuffing supplies into my satchel. "If I don't return, tell Mina Hereswith at MASHA where I've gone."

Daniella wrung her hands on her apron. "Simarron, I hope you know what you're doing. Be careful, and bring back Tia—and that cursed locket."

I tightened the straps on my satchel and stepped out of the warmth of the boarding house into the chill of early morning. The wind bit at my face as I turned toward Château Gorget. The journey might cost me everything—my memories, my job, my life in this magical city.

Chapter Thirty-Two

I set off for Château Gorget in Misty Vale at a hasty trot. In the heart of the city, stone and brick buildings loomed, solid and unyielding, as though the city had been set in stone for centuries. But as I moved farther out, stone gave way to wood, the structures growing more haphazard and increasingly sparse. I hurried out through the city gates, past the staring watchtower, the rigid cobblestone roads turning to winding dirt paths.

Galloping on the open road beyond, I then controlled my pace as I began to climb the steep, winding track to Misty Vale. It was faster going without the oxcart or the Magical Energies Detector, but I estimated it would still take me two hours to reach the castle. My heart beat in my chest as my hooves pounded the dirt. I hoped I would catch up to Tia, but I wasn't sure how far ahead she was.

The sun rose and began to follow me, Hyperion a tiny dot creeping along in its wake. First a wan yellow glow on the horizon, it stained the clouds pink and orange before bursting into flames of gold. Its rays pierced through gaps in the trees, burning away the mist. The brisk air, heavily scented of pine, entered my lungs with each breath, fueling my muscles and clearing my mind. As my long legs devoured the final furlongs to Château Gorget, my plan took shape.

When I reached the familiar green iron gates of the castle, I saw that they were set into an imposing gatehouse that I didn't remember. Thankfully, the gates were unlocked and I pushed them open, entering the dense tangle beyond. Between two hills, partially reclaimed by nature, the stone walls and towers of Château Gorget rose. A sense of déjà vu enveloped me, an uncanny blend of recognition and distortion.

There seemed to be an echo in my mind, my present and past moments at the castle converging. I was now certain I had seen the castle before, but my memories danced just on the periphery of my consciousness, eluding my grasp.

My sole visual memory of the castle hadn't been a hallucination brought about by an acrid smell after all. In attacking me, the unohdus had permanently affixed that brief vision in my mind. My sense of smell was too primal to be erased, even by its memory-rending bite.

I set down my satchel in the courtyard and, pulling out a cloth, I laid out a picnic on top of a stone block that had tumbled down. The simple spread consisted of honey bread from Daniella's larder and her little wooden salt box. It looked like a miniature treasure chest, complete with a tiny latch, which I flicked open to unhinge the lid. Then I set out two cups and filled them with wine.

I settled down on my haunches, closed my eyes, and tried to recall that same half-dreaming state where I had connected with Flit, as well as Professor Ashmin's spirit in the courtyard. It was difficult at first with my heart beating so quickly. I took deep, calming breaths.

"Unohdus, spirit from the Underworld, I invite you to share this feast," I called. I only hoped I wasn't too late.

Before long, I felt a looming presence, the phosphorous scent of ectoplasm. The hairs on my withers stood up, and I recognized that the unohdus was here. I saw a shadow slide across the ground and fall upon the feast. Then it was gone from this world.

"What is this?" asked Vanadar, his voice coinciding with waves of malice, an acrid odor of dried blood and decaying wood that made my stomach lurch.

"This ends here." I opened my eyes, remaining calmly seated.

Vanadar sauntered toward me, but I straightened my back, refusing to feel threatened. Even sitting on my haunches, I took up a lot of space. If anyone should feel intimidated, it was him.

"Ah, you're that nosy safety inspector that I had to drain before. I didn't want to kill you, but then you had to poke your nose around the club and uncover Tia's painting." Vanadar held out his hands in a conciliatory manner, his shoulders lifting in a shrug.

"And now I leave you no choice?" I suggested.

"There is always a choice." Vanadar's lips curved into a sardonic smile as he sat down on a ruined stair opposite of me, the stone block bearing the feast for a ghost between us. He waved his hand over both cups, whispering arcane words.

"And what choice would that be?" I asked, not taking my eyes from him.

Vanadar's unnatural green eyes gleamed like a cat's. "Drink. Choose one of these cups and take a sip. I will take whichever cup you do not choose. One holds whatever fine vintage you poured into it. The other . . ." he paused.

"The other?" I prompted, my voice steady, although I was trying not to gag on the scent—that haunting, horrible smell that had plagued my investigation—assailing my senses.

Vanadar leaned forward, his tone lowering to a whisper as he leveled his deadly intentions at me. "The other now holds a poison."

I flicked my tail along the ground. "And why, pray tell, would I play this dangerous game of chance?"

"Ah, Safety Inspector, you misunderstand," Vanadar replied. "This is no mere game of chance, but a contest of wits. If you truly believe that your deductive prowess is superior, then this should be a simple decision."

My gaze remained locked on Vanadar's. "And if I refuse to drink?"

"Then you prove yourself a coward, a man who cannot take risks for the sake of truth."

I finally looked away, noticing the dewy grass springing up through wide cracks in the flagstones, the spears of light streaming in through holes in the ancient walls.

"Lovely spot," I said. "Too bad Lysandros Garbor can't enjoy it now. A bit far from the city for a luxury hotel and theater, though. Then again, that enterprise was never his real intent."

"A puerile ruse to disguise his interest in Château Gorget so that his rivals wouldn't catch on. You'd have to be stupid to not see that. You're stalling. Drink."

I looked back at Vanadar. "You're a clever man and willing to risk everything to gain prestige for yourself and the Van Adair family name, once a highly respected family of wizards in the city. You studied the past of this place, and also came to the conclusion that a hidden element lay in the minerals here. And you wanted to be the first to share that revelation with the world."

"Why shouldn't I, when I'm this close to isolating it? Lysandros Garbor may have purchased Andreas Hippolyte's castle, but he failed to improve Hippolyte's work on *panchromia*, which was dismissed at the time as an impure sample of chromium. I think *vanadium* has such a better ring to it, don't you? But enough about me. Make your choice."

"You suspect an element X, but you're not even close to isolating it, are you? My case notes held evidence of a strong spell being cast here —recently. You summoned an unohdus to drain Garbor's memories of his work here and set him back. But you needed a more permanent solution."

Vanadar sneered, but his eyes held a startled look.

"Spirits can't kill," I continued, "but you correctly assumed that a haunted painting would incite the imagination of the public and rumors of ghost attacks would confuse the City Watch. You were inspired by the legend of the Soul Anchor and had your lady friend Tia Larose create the painting."

He grunted at the mention of her name and I hesitated, hoping I wasn't putting Tia in further danger by revealing what I knew of her involvement. "You kept her in the dark, but Tia had been conducting her own experiments on your samples of rocks containing panchromia, hadn't she? You didn't count on her using the mineral in her paint pigments, which ended up connecting you to the painting. The art gala at the Kami-Nihkia Club, of which you are a member, presented the perfect opportunity to administer poison via a hidden compartment."

"You're even more nosy than that alchemy professor," he said, his voice low with threat.

"Whom you lured to a secluded graveyard on the night of the spring equinox, and again hoped the mysterious nature of the attack would divert suspicion from your actions. You needed an enclosed space for the poison gas, which the mausoleum provided."

"And when am I supposed to have done that? That night I was having tea with my lady—and you, if you recall."

"You set up a trap with wire and vials of poison gas, and disguised the scene with an arcane circle and necromantic runes. The storm that night helped cover your tracks, but you failed to remove all traces of your contraption. I found a bit of wire in the mausoleum. The truth is, you are a secret necromancer pretending to be an illusion wizard, and more importantly, a coward who poisons people!"

"And which cup did I poison? This is your last chance. Make your choice!"

With deliberate calmness, I reached for the cup on my right. "Very well, I shall meet your challenge," I said, casually swirling the wine by tilting the cup. "Actions bring results, right?"

Amusement danced in Vanadar's eyes as he picked up the remaining one. We held each other's gaze. I brought the cup to my lips, and he mirrored me. I then tipped my head back and downed the entire contents with a flourish.

"My, my, that confident in our decision, are we?" Vanadar mocked, wiping his mouth with the back of his hand.

"It's just salt," I said.

"That's where your deductions fail. I can assure you, your cup contained arsenic."

"They both did. But I also put salt in each cup—just a few grains ought to violate your pact with Arsenicia."

Vanadar's eyes widened in understanding. He flexed his fingers in a divine gesture, but nothing happened.

"No, Arsenicia, don't withdraw your power from me!" he cried, toppling to the ground, powerless.

I grabbed my satchel as I also fell to one side, sick. "The charcoal . . ." I groaned, bringing it to my lips as the world began to fade around me.

Chapter Thirty-Three

My eyes fluttered open and I blinked, trying to clear the haze from my mind. The last sunlight was fading in the castle courtyard, glinting dimly off the cups lying discarded on the flagstones. It was much later in the day. How long was I out? Was it still Copperday?

A breeze, carrying the earthy scent of the surrounding forest, sighed through the trees. I remembered Vanadar's sardonic smile, the cups of wine, the smell of coagulated blood and rotted wood, and the bitter taste that had stuck to my tongue. Panic surged through me as I recalled retrieving the activated charcoal from my satchel. I was alive —I'd merely passed out for a bit.

"But Tia could still be in danger," I reminded myself aloud, my voice sounding harsh and strange to my ears. Despite how she'd treated me, I couldn't help my concern for her. All my efforts would be for nothing if the killer took another life, even if she was complicit in his crimes. I staggered to all four feet and my head spun, but I didn't feel like I was dying, so the activated charcoal had saved me.

I scanned my surroundings, noticing fresh drag marks in the dust that led to the keep. I was certain Tia had gone to Château Gorget to have her memories eaten by the unohdus. And then what? She would have been found by Vanadar. He couldn't go far, deprived of the goddess's protection from poison. They both must be hiding in the ruins.

Somewhere deep inside, my adversary lay hidden. I knew that Vanadar would certainly have another trick up his sleeve, and I was armed with only my wits and my instincts. Each step brought me closer to a desperate killer and to a woman whose alliances were unclear.

As I passed through the inner gate, an intense pain stabbed my temples. I recalled coming this way before. I remembered a dark shadow falling upon me while gaunt fingers reached for me from behind. At the time, I had reared up and galloped away in a blind panic.

My hoofsteps clopped loudly in the entrance hall, echoes bouncing off the high ceiling of the interior. The last rays of the sun slanted in through arrow slits to shine on empty suits of armor. One lay on its side, a gauntleted arm pointing the way to a larger room—the great hall. Here I paused, letting the sounds of my own motion die away, trying to sense any small sound or faint waft of scent. I heard nothing but my pounding heart and continued on to a chamber with a collapsed roof. It felt strangely familiar, drawing me in. On the aged stone floor, the symbol for mystery element X51 was carved.

I approached a spiral staircase where the cobwebs looked disturbed, dusty strands flying free in the current of air as I pushed forward. My nose wrinkled at the smell of perfume. It wasn't Tia's usual rose scent. As I paused to examine the scene more closely, a silvery glint caught my eye.

There was a thin wire, strung tighter than my nerves, across the bottom of the stairwell. Stepping over it carefully with each of my four feet, I followed the wire to a hidden vial. Its delicate glass would certainly have shattered had I touched the wire, releasing its poison gas, but I now disabled it safely.

They had gone down the tight stairway, I determined with chagrin. I supposed it made sense, as Vanadar seemed like the kind of person who liked to drag everyone down to his level. He may be cunning, but he had trapped himself into a situation where he could not win. I would not let a narrow, dark flight of stairs stop me now.

I descended with the utmost caution, tapping each step with each hoof before stepping with my full weight, my hands pressed against the walls for support. There had been no torches lit in the castle, but now I smelled smoke, hopefully from a hearth. I followed the smell down to an underground passage, my forelock brushing the low beams of this cramped space.

Along the passage wall, I smelled the perfume again—familiar, yet also not. I paused, looking for traps. Sure enough, there was a concealed wire about a hand's breadth away. I carefully disabled it and continued on.

I stopped at a seam of light that spilled underneath a heavy wooden door.

Drawing a deep breath, I gripped the iron handle and eased the door open to a guard room. A gust of warm air met me, carrying the scent of burning wood mingled with coagulated blood. The flickering light of the blazing hearth illuminated the scene before me. Broken weapon racks hung with rusted spears and shields lining the walls, and in the center of the room, the figure of a man lounging in a high-backed chair, his silhouette hazy against the dancing flames.

He was being attended to by a red-haired woman, displaying a disturbing blend of servitude and confusion. A locket shone at her neck—the Soul Anchor.

"Tia!" I exclaimed. I closed the door behind me, in case Vanadar tried to make a run for it, but he remained in his chair, languidly poised. The fireplace blazed fiercely, filling the room with oppressive heat.

Tia looked up with a blank expression on her face. "Who are you?" She moved to set a bowl and cloth down on a half-rotted table. The action missed, and it clattered to the floor. It appeared I had banished the unohdus too late to save Tia's memories.

Vanadar fixed his gaze on me. "Dearest, it seems our inspector has come to arrest you for your crimes."

"Arrest me?" she said, stepping behind Vanadar's chair as if to shield herself from me.

He reached up and grabbed the chain of the locket, pulling her face close. "Not before I take the Soul Anchor, however. I had no idea the legends were true, much less that it was within my very grasp." Tia let out a strangled gasp, but didn't pull away. The chain held.

"Stop! I've come to arrest you, Vanadar!" I paused. *Have I?* "I suppose this is a citizen's arrest."

Hunched over the chair, Tia looked up at me with her unnaturally deep blue eyes. "I'm afraid . . . that maybe I am the one who killed the two alchemists. Maybe . . . I did it?"

"You don't know what you're saying," I argued, my gaze flickering between Tia and Vanadar. "You sought out the unohdus to erase your memories, and Vanadar is feeding you lies!"

"Don't worry, my little murderess, I won't let him take you. After all that I've done to shape you and your art career, do you think I'd let anyone take you away from me?" Vanadar laughed, then broke into a cough. His fingers slipped back into his lap, releasing the Soul Anchor's chain. His hair was now a dull brown, his eyes a muddy green. He didn't appear to have the strength to maintain his glamour spell over his appearance, or even move, yet his confidence seemed to know no bounds.

"Why would you even listen to this guy? The victims were his rivals in the search for element X, not yours. Your beau, your patron, whatever you want to call him—he's been using you."

"I just . . . I wanted my art to be recognized. And it worked, didn't it?" Tia asked. "Nobody is talking about that artist Xena anymore, are they? When I've been revealed as the artist behind the haunted painting, people will notice me," she said, sliding out from behind the chair and taking an unsteady step toward me. "Why are you here again? Oh, I think I messed up. Yes, arrest me, please?"

"No," I thought, but it was Vanadar who spoke the words out loud.

"Kill the centaur . . ." he slurred, his head lolling back in the chair and his arm falling limp to his side. A familiar glass vial slipped out of his fingers and smashed to the floor, releasing the garlic-scented gas trapped inside it. It was arsenic, I knew, but somehow made into a vapor.

My head pounded as the room spun around me, the shadows cast by the fireplace writhing like living things. *Oh no, I'm not going to die here. I am NOT ready to die.*

Tia grabbed a palette knife and took two more wobbly steps, then fell to her hands and knees and kept on coming. The sight of a two-legger crawling sent me scrambling back so quickly in fear that I felt I had exited my body and was now observing the scene from behind my own shoulder.

My MASHA training took over, and I noticed that the room was inadequately ventilated and there were no quenchfire orbs for safety. Goddess knows how long ago that fireplace was properly maintained, and it had no screen on it. No wonder Vanadar wasn't getting up and Tia seemed confused. Even without the addition of arsenic, we were all going to pass out and die from the poisonous air of the charcoal fire.

Snapping out of my panic, I swiftly grabbed Tia's arm just above her grip on the knife and wrenched her to her feet. As the knife clattered to the stone floor, I kicked the door open behind me. I lunged forward, snatched Vanadar from the chair and swung him up onto my back. Turning, I grabbed Tia's arm again and hauled both people out into the corridor. I kept moving toward the staircase without pause, without even thinking.

"Let go of me, Simarron!" Tia protested, stumbling along as I carried Vanadar up the staircase to the ground floor of the castle.

"You do remember me!" I released my grip on her, surprised.

"Certainly, you goof!" She rubbed her arm where I had grabbed her.

"But the unohdus—" I started.

She sighed. "I couldn't do it. Let it eat my memories. No matter how much I wanted to forget. But I pretended I did, so Van thought I was still under his control and wouldn't kill me."

The revelation hung in the air, as thick as the smoke we had just left behind. My instincts shifted from caution to a measured understanding.

"You double-crossing wretch! I'll end you!" Vanadar's voice cut through the tension. "Unohdus, I remind you of my command to drain the memories of any visitor about this place. Don't hold back anymore, take everything! Break them!"

"The unohdus is gone," I informed him.

"You won't . . . win," Vanadar croaked.

I snorted incredulously. "Says the man who almost just choked to death on his own schemes!"

As our strange trio emerged into the cool darkness of the castle courtyard, a shadowy figure swooped down from the sky to meet us. Steel needles flashed in the moonlight, then zinged through the space between us. Another trap?

Behind me, Vanadar groaned, and I saw the needles had been embedded in his arms and chest, through his clothing. He went unconscious, slumping against my back.

A pointy-eared man dismounted from the flying contraption—a broom. "When you two didn't come home, I got worried. Luckily, my knitting needles aren't just for show."

Tia's eyes widened in surprise. "Kai, Simarron, I know how this looks, but I had to play the part to survive."

"Are you all right, dear?" said Kai, brushing off Tia's excuses as he checked that she was unharmed. "What day is it? How many fingers am I holding up?"

"I'm fine," said Tia, gently pushing Kai's hands down. "I didn't let the evil wizard or the hungry ghost harm me."

"Thanks, Kai," I said. "Tia and Vanadar both almost died down there. Now you all can listen to me practice the MASHA lecture on fire safety on the way to the City Watch."

Tia's deep blue eyes flashed with fear, but she nodded in reluctant agreement. Surely, she understood the precarious nature of her situation.

"It will turn out all right," Kai reassured her. "Here, take my broom. I'm afraid it's been a few years since I was a Witchy Whisk messenger." He stretched his long legs dramatically.

Tia accepted the broom. "Vanadar's horse is tied up over there," she said, nodding toward a patch of trees obscured in the darkness.

"Good, the horse can carry its master," I said, shifting Vanadar off my back. He slid to the ground in a heap. "Let's find something to tie him up with."

Kai peered in the direction Tia had indicated. "That poor horse deserves better than to be mixed up in all this."

"I should have known better." Tia looked down at the broom in her hands. "After I took the locket, I went to work. By the time my shift at the tavern was over, I'd made up my mind. I went home, returned Simarron's notes, and took off again. Vanadar must have been watching the boarding house, though. He intercepted me before I even left the city. He said he'd 'escort' me safely through the dark, and the way he said it . . . I knew I had to play along."

"We'll take you back," I said. Suddenly uncomfortable, I switched the topic. "First rule about fire safety: you should be able to quickly and easily get to a quenchfire orb in a room where fire is used . . ."

Before long, we had to camp. I was exhausted from my near-poisoning, and we couldn't easily find the path in the dark, even with the meteor crystal light Tia had taken from the boarding house. We settled in a sheltered glade. The moonlight filtered gently through the canopy above, and the moss was soft beneath me as I settled into a comfortable position on my chest, with all four legs tucked underneath me.

I exhaled slowly and turned to face Tia. "I've been piecing this together, and I need to ask you something, Tia. When did you realize that Vanadar had used your painting for his nefarious plan? And more importantly, when did you suspect he might be involved in the murders? His plot required weeks of planning, the gears set in motion well before you stole my notes."

I had trusted her, and that confidence had been betrayed. I felt that I had taken a grand beating, a thousand licks to my heart.

"I think an unohdus ate my memories after all . . ." she hedged, her lips twitching into a smile that didn't reach her eyes.

I looked hard into those green-blue eyes, which had lost their other-worldly tint and now appeared as natural as a deep mountain lake with shiny flecks of minerals. Those eyes now flickered with a hint of guilt as she hesitated, dropping the false smile.

"Vanadar told me about the art gala coming up at the Kami-Nihkia Club, and that it was going to be attended by some of the most influential people in the city. He'd heard rumors about a certain haunted painting, and suggested that I could be the one to create it. He said I'd be the talk of the town, even if my signature couldn't be on it."

I felt an eyebrow straining upward with the incredulity of the statement. I glanced at Kai, who mirrored my expression perfectly.

"I know, I should have been suspicious," said Tia. "He said it was just the first step, that once my reputation as an artist had been solidified, I could reveal that I was the genius behind the haunted painting all along. I was desperate for recognition and I believed him. I didn't know his true purpose."

Taking a deep breath, Tia continued, "After Lysandros Garbor died, I had my suspicions, but I didn't want to believe it. It wasn't until that night when Kari Ashmin was murdered . . . Vanadar was acting strange, cold, and I broke it off with him at The Angry Unicorn. When we read about her death in *The Mercury* the next morning, that's when it all started to make horrifying sense."

Kai reached over and placed a hand over Tia's. "Oh, dear."

"I appreciate your honesty with me," I said softly. "You made a mistake by aligning yourself with Vanadar, and everything you did after that was to survive." *Including turning a blind eye until the last possible moment.*

She nodded, her face shining with a tentative hope that pained me. "Simarron, do you think we can be . . . friends?"

I looked away, unable to meet her gaze. It would be easier if I could hate her. I couldn't entirely forgive her for what she'd done, but I also couldn't condemn her as fully as I'd like to. Guilt chipped away the veneer of the rational, reasonable centaur I wanted to be. What kind of person was I if I couldn't see a clear answer here?

Looking up at the black silhouettes of trees framing the waning gibbous moon, it suddenly felt like a glimpse of hope in the darkness of the night. Where doubts caged me in, the moon hung steadfast, always shifting between illumination and shadow, yet never faltering in its progress across the sky.

"I think . . . we have to live together peacefully," I said finally. If I could extend grace to Tia, maybe I could forgive myself for not living up to my own ideals. "Don't take my stuff anymore."

"Take this," she said. From the edge of my vision, I saw her gather her hair and unclasp something from her neck.

"It isn't mine. When this is done, we need to destroy it." I refused to take the locket, even as my gaze was drawn to it.

"For once and for all," said Kai firmly.

The Soul Anchor struck me not just as an object, but as a symbol—chains forged from our own attachments. Whether to ambition, validation, or fear, it bound the living as tightly as it did the souls of its victims. Vanadar's obsession with its legend showed how desperately he clung to control. And Tia—her connection to it via the "haunted painting" mirrored her struggle for recognition, for proof that her art and her existence mattered. The Soul Anchor didn't just trap spirits; it seemed to embody the weight of our own patterns, dragging us down when we were too afraid or too blind to break free.

I was snapped out of my thoughts by the sound of Vanadar stirring, from where we had tied him to a tree. He would have to answer to the City Watch now, and Tia would as well. She had convinced me that she hadn't been a willing accomplice in his crimes, but Captain Voshawk might not see it that way.

I realized with a jolt that I'd likely have to advocate on Tia's behalf, and what an uncomfortable position that was. Yet I knew it was the right thing to do, even if I wasn't sure about our friendship.

Chapter Thirty-Four

I eyed the cup before me, filled with a dark liquid that mirrored the deep tones of the wood wainscoting that adorned the Ambrosia Coffeehouse. The aroma wafted toward me, reminding me of Professor Ashmin. Cautiously, I took a sip. The warmth enveloped my senses, and the smoky, nutty flavor danced on my tongue.

"Quite a curious elixir," I remarked to Tia, who observed my reaction with keen interest, smiling. I looked away, unwilling to engage further. Tensions still lingered between us, her earlier transgression casting a shadow over our friendship.

Although I was convinced of her innocence in the murders, I couldn't ignore the fact that she was still a liar and a thief. Trusting her felt like stepping onto unstable ground. What frustrated me most, however, wasn't just her past actions—it was how she let others, whether good people like Daniella or manipulative ones like Vanadar, push her around. Why couldn't she stand up for herself?

I resolved to keep a polite distance. But it was difficult, for despite everything, part of me still wanted to believe there was something good in her. Her artwork held so much beauty and raw expression—it hinted at someone deeper, someone I wanted to understand.

I turned my attention to her paintings, hung temporarily on the walls. Though the coffeehouse lacked the opulence of the art gala at the Kami-Nihkia Club, this was an even more exclusive event limited to just the members of the Slant Row Boarding House and our friends.

"So, Tia," said Kai, sidling up to her with a cup of coffee in one hand. He had used his connections to set up this event at the Ambrosia Coffeehouse, and was dressed as if this were the premiere event in the city. "You're our little ghost-painter, in more ways than one."

Tia gave a nervous laugh.

Kai continued, "You admitted to crafting the painting during the inquest, didn't you? Thankfully the City Watch believed that you didn't know it'd be used to cover up a murder. You have a charming naiveté." He shook his head. "But really, you need to start looking out for yourself. The murderer could have killed you, too, if Simarron and I hadn't come to your rescue!"

"You should really be thanking me for the character testimony," Daniella interjected, startling me. I hadn't noticed her at first, but then again, she always had a way of being right there, quietly listening, hadn't she? "I told the City Watch that you're artistic and impulsive, but completely incapable of murder. I even mentioned your ridiculous fear of ghosts—that you'd never risk being haunted by a vengeful spirit or becoming one yourself. I told them about how you still need a night light!"

Tia's face turned a shade of red that matched her hair. "You didn't say that."

"I did, and I had a few choice things to say about Horace Van Adair's character, too. Said he'd been sniffing around, dropping hints about your 'promising future' if you helped him. The entire inquest panel looked disgusted," she added, muttering, "I knew that boy wasn't right."

"Captain Voshawk was scary, though," said Tia, looking down into her cup cradled between both hands. "He kept pressing me about how I could not have known about Vanadar's schemes. But I can't blame him, can I? I must've sounded so suspicious, all my words running together, like paint spilling from a tipped palette."

"They needed character witnesses for a reason," Kai said. "You had people—us—who spoke for you. Vanadar's own family didn't even show to back him up."

"And they couldn't tie the mineral pigments you sought to the poison directly," I added. "That helped. The real evidence—the arsenic and the traps—pointed to Vanadar." I'd had a rather low opinion of Captain Voshawk, but I was impressed with how he'd handled the inquest. The watch captain was as dedicated to his job as Mina was to MASHA, begrudgingly earning himself a bit of my respect.

I thought back to that tense day at the inquest panel at Shetland Yard. The room had been austere, all dark wood paneling and heavy brass fixtures. The high windows let in shafts of bright light that illuminated the faces of the panel waiting in judgment. I remembered Captain Voshawk's piercing red eyes and even sharper questions, and the warm, steadying presence of Coroner Rin Heartbloom as she presented the cold facts about the two dead alchemists.

And caught between these opposing forces, Tia's fate had hung precariously in the balance. While I believed in her innocence regarding the murders, I hadn't been sure the inquest panelists would see it the same way. I'd been more than a little afraid that she'd be condemned for her artistic ambition and her susceptibility to the influence of stronger personalities.

Tia nodded, her shoulders relaxing slightly. "Captain Voshawk didn't make it easy, though. He kept going on about 'coincidences' and 'convenient ignorance.'"

"He'd have kept at you forever if Simarron hadn't spoken up at the inquest panel," said Kai. "His observations carried weight. The coroner trusts him." He paused. "Even so, you're lucky they decided you were naive, not complicit."

"Thank you," Tia murmured. "All of you."

Kai waved a hand dismissively. "You're welcome, but the next time someone asks you to paint a masterpiece based on a legendary artifact, ask a few more questions first."

"The coroner admires Simarron's ability to sense spirits," said Lilimari from a table laden with miniature sandwiches. She didn't meet my gaze, however, being overcome by how tiny and cute the sandwiches were.

"I don't know what you mean," I protested. Luckily, I was spared from questioning when a golden-haired woman approached, drawing me away from the group.

"Tia's art is beautiful. I have often seen the red-haired woman when she comes to the shore of Silver Lake to paint," spoke a voice reminiscent of a flowing stream.

"Aurelia?" I asked, recognizing the miniatures enthusiast I had met at the festival. "Elia Ariagwen . . . that was you, Aurelia, wasn't it? You posed as the foreign art collector and brought the painting to Tae Bellwyn for the art gala. Why aid in Vanadar's plot?"

"My full name is Aurelia Gwenia." Her shoulders sagged as she cast her eyes down. "The wizard told me of the new castle owner's scheme to develop the castle and our lake. He said the soul painting would convince everyone it was haunted and halt these plans, and I didn't see the broader harm until it was too late."

Soul painting . . . Vanadar had called it that. Such lengths he had taken to avoid dirtying his own hands, all to ensure that the secrets of the castle and its unique minerals remained hidden.

"You thought you were saving your home," I said softly. "You didn't know people would die."

Aurelia looked up, her sorrowful expression lightening ever so slightly. "No. I never imagined . . ."

She trailed off, her gaze wandering to the table of refreshments. She brightened as she noticed the tiny sandwiches, and she moved to join Lilimari.

I smiled at the pair of miniatures enthusiasts and turned to examine the painting Aurelia had been admiring. It depicted a dark forest glade bathed in silver moonlight. In the distance, the broken shape of a forgotten fortress loomed while wisps of otherworldly light floated in the air.

I sipped the rest of my coffee, feeling content, then crossed to the counter to set down my empty cup. My eyes narrowed as the "server" took it from me. He had the kind of face that fit in anywhere, but his movements lacked the smooth confidence of someone actually used to working behind the counter—and he smelled like newsprint.

I felt my tail lash out in irritation. Manrik Skrift. What had he heard, and how much would be part of his next article?

"The coffee's good, but you make a terrible server," I said.

The news writer shrugged, then tossed his towel down on the counter as if giving up the charade.

Before I could decide what to do about him, the bell above the door jingled, and the air shifted. The crowd parted slightly as a sophisticated woman entered, her tailored evening suit and confident stride commanding attention. Her silk tie matched her red lipstick. It was Mina Hereswith. I had invited her to tonight's event, but I hadn't been at all certain that she would come, considering how we'd left things at work.

"It reminds me of Château Gorget," she remarked thoughtfully as she approached. "You know, Simarron, when you first joined MASHA, I had my doubts about your . . . unconventional approach."

I glanced down self-consciously at my regular shirt and front kilt. I looked like a safety inspector, not a gala attendee. Yet, I found the cozy candlelit atmosphere here more comforting than the dazzling glamour of the Kami-Nihkia Club. And undoubtedly, I preferred the company.

"I know I came in like a dust devil on the plains," I confessed. "At first just a cloud of confusion, then moving with too much force."

Her red lips pressed into a tight smile. "Indeed. But sometimes, it takes a sudden whirl to stir things up. You've certainly shown you can uncover hidden truths, and your instincts have guided us well."

"Director Moosekind was right about one thing," I said. "People are far more concerned about a rogue necromancer than the everyday magical safety risks we try to protect them from."

"True," she replied. "However, the alchemists, even though they might grumble, should now see MASHA as a necessary oversight, not just interference. Vanadar had managed to produce a gas compound, far more dangerous than pure arsenic. And the wizards, who might have once scoffed at our efforts, can't dismiss us as a token agency any longer. We've made our presence felt, Simarron. Take the win."

She continued in a satisfied tone, "Not only that, but we've also managed to outshine Captain Voshawk, my old rival, showing him that MASHA is more than capable."

"Thank you, Administrator Hereswith." Her name felt formal and distant as it left my lips.

She paused. "Call me Mina," she said, her voice softening. The gesture disarmed me. It wasn't just the words—it was the way she said them. Her cold demeanor had melted and I felt that she was, once again, my trusted colleague and mentor.

As we conversed, Kai reappeared with a gleam in his eye, eager to glean insights. "Mina Hereswith, former Inquisitor of the Bureau of Magical Inquiries, I'm so pleased to meet you! I have to ask, what do you think about the resurgence of alchemy in the city? Can MASHA keep us safe with protocols and inspections, or do you think the Bureau's strict hand was more effective? By the way, I think Simarron acted so bravely, helping to catch that poisoner."

"Indeed, he did," Mina replied with a subtle nod. "As Administrator of MASHA, I must advise caution when tampering with forces that history has shown can be unpredictable and, at times, perilous."

"You know, I can respect that," said Lilimari. Despite her bored tone, I noticed that she had torn herself away from the table of tiny foods to join us.

I felt a warmth creeping up my neck at the attention and self-consciously rubbed the back of my neck. "Thank you, Mina. It means a lot to me." I silently vowed to approach future situations with greater thoughtfulness.

There was one thing left to do. The spirits trapped in the Soul Anchor still had to be laid to rest. The chatter and laughter filling the warm coffeehouse filled my ears, but it began to feel distant as I remembered Professor Ashmin's chilling words to Coroner Heartbloom: *To free my spirit, you must sever the threads that tether me to this plane.*

I could still see the coroner's warm brown eyes peering at me on the day of the inquest, silently judging me for taking the Soul Anchor. Guilt twisted in my chest, sharp and unrelenting. Or maybe that was the effect of the coffee. Either way, I had waited too long already.

Chapter Thirty-Five

Flames danced in the fireplace of the Slant Row Boarding House's parlor, its residents settled into an evening of quiet little projects. Kai was knitting, while Tia's chalk scratched across the paper of her sketchbook. Daniella was working on a piece of cross-stitching, which I recognized as the house rules that normally hung above the fireplace mantel. Across the room, Lilimari appeared lost in her book, although she hadn't turned a page in a while, suggesting she might be either dozing off or merely pretending to read while secretly observing the group. The cozy scene was at odds with the tension sizzling in my mind, however.

"Tia, why did you steal my case notes?" I asked finally, setting my journal down. "I want the real reason."

The pause stretched. Kai's knitting needles ceased their clicking.

Tia slowly dragged her gaze up from her sketchbook. "I wrote you that note when I was still planning on feeding my memories to the unohdus. I didn't want it to contain anything that would remind me of Vanadar or anything that happened, if you showed it to me later," she said.

"So that's why you didn't include the whole truth in your letter of apology. But if we are to be friends, I need to know why."

"Vanadar . . ." Her voice wavered, and she set aside her work and stick of chalk. The portrait she was sketching looked familiar to me.

"Vanadar was ecstatic when he found out that MASHA's new safety inspector was my housemate. I wasn't going to break into your room, but that day at The Angry Unicorn provided the perfect opportunity to take your notes. It wasn't just fear of reprisal that kept me from returning them, though." She took a deep breath. "I knew he was involved in something dangerous, and I thought if you had those notes, you'd keep digging around the castle, and I couldn't bear the thought of something happening to you."

Daniella let out a small gasp. Lilimari had lowered her book and was openly staring at us now. I could almost feel the gears in her mind whirling behind her dark eyes. I felt a twinge of guilt at dragging out this last bit of unfinished business here, in front of our housemates, but Tia and I had been dancing awkwardly around each other since our encounter at Château Gorget.

"So you weren't quite as naive as you acted at the inquest," I said levelly. "But in the end, you sabotaged Vanadar's traps by spilling perfume near each of them for me to find. I want to thank you for that."

"You have the whole truth now," she said softly, turning her palms out in a gesture of appeasement. "And I'm not going to let anyone push me around anymore. At least . . . I'll try not to," she added, glancing sideways at Daniella.

Kai caught the look and his lips twitched into a smile.

Daniella had returned to her work and was adding one more line to her cross-stitching: *The house is definitely not haunted, so don't mention . . .*

I turned my attention to Tia's work in progress. "It's Professor Ashmin, isn't it?"

A flush crept across her cheeks. "I plan to donate the finished portrait to the university . . . anonymously."

When I caught Tia's rose perfume, I felt the last of my resistance melt away. Then I realized that it wasn't her perfume that I was smelling, it was something more intangible than that. It was the emotional scent of Tia's happiness that had a faint rose aroma to me.

Deciding to come clean myself, I cleared my throat and raised my voice. "I have something I wish to share with all of you."

"Yeah, the spirit haunting your room," Lilimari blurted out, circling one hand in a "get on with it" motion. "Can we have tea now?"

"Who said anything about a spirit?" said Daniella, now flustered, setting down her cross-stitching.

"We already know about the ghost, Dani," said Kai, placing his knitting needles down and raising his hands theatrically. "That's why you can't rent that room and how Simarron gets such a steep discount."

"Oh, that ghost," said Tia, without a hint of surprise.

"You knew?" I was astounded. "Well, it's time to send away all the spirits. It's time to destroy the Soul Anchor." The two days Coroner Rin Heartbloom had granted me were up. If we didn't do it now, Captain Voshawk would likely be back here, demanding it back—not to mention that I would definitely lose my job at MASHA.

"There isn't a—anyway, it's my mother's locket," said Daniella, her voice heavy with emotion. She stood up from the settee and positioned herself between Tia and me. "I'll have it back now."

Tia removed a silver chain from her neck, the Soul Anchor glinting in the firelight. She had tried to give it to me before, but I had refused, wanting her to carry the weight of her actions until now.

"The Soul Anchor," said Lilimari, leaping up from her armchair to join us. "Can we open it? Please?"

Daniella gave a slight nod, and Lilimari's face lit up with a sharp-toothed smile as she undid the clasp. "Umb, the fake looks nothing like it, Tia. And it's so tiny!"

"I didn't know there was a *real* one," Tia said as Lilimari passed it on to Daniella. "Vanadar told me about the legend of the Soul Anchor, but he just thought it would be a good story for my painting that would grab attention."

"You painted your face over Kari Ashmin's, I presume, so I'll consider that an improvement," Daniella said as she examined it. "But it'll twist your soul, you know. You shouldn't have done that."

"I know, I'm sorry. I thought it would protect me," Tia replied, looking away.

Kai touched the amulet at his neck. "Let's destroy it before it has the chance to do anything else."

Holding the locket by its chain, Daniella bustled to the fireplace. "Yes. It's caused enough harm." The room seemed to hold its breath as the Soul Anchor swung on its chain like a pendulum. She hesitated, looking at the locket one last time.

"The original portrait was . . . my grandmother's," she whispered. "I believe my mother created it for her. And we all know how well that must have gone."

"Your mother was a genius," said Lilimari.

"She meant well, anyway," said Kai gently.

Daniella extended one hand toward the flames, the locket open and dangling at the end of its chain. She let it slip between her strong fingers and into the fire. We watched as the portrait curled, its visage flickering between that of Daniella's grandmother, young Professor Ashmin and Tia Larose, before flaking into ash.

Was Flit Daniella's grandmother? The ghost seemed impish to me, in that way that the very young and the very old can be, but I would never really know.

"Spirits of the Soul Anchor, I invite you to share our feast," I said, glancing from the fire to the special afternoon tea waiting on the sideboard in the dining room.

It was something I'd helped Daniella prepare earlier. When the spirits could not eat the food or drink the tea, I hoped they'd realized they were dead and find their way to the Underworld. There were fresh raspberries and fern fiddleheads that I had picked in the wild and washed in a small waterfall of snowmelt. Daniella had prepared bite-sized sandwiches of egg and watercress, and perfect miniature tarts topped with more berries.

The scent of roasted coffee hit me with a wave of bitter contentment, then dissipated, leaving a slightly burned flavor in the mouth. Kari Ashmin. She can't have wanted to leave the world of the living this way, but at least I had found her killer.

Flit was older, I think, their presence more faded. I usually only felt the spirit in my mind, but I associated it with a nostalgic scent, like baking bread. I reached out with my senses, but I couldn't feel Flit.

"I'm still here, thank the Goddess," Tia breathed, a hand resting over her heart.

"Are they gone?" Lilimari asked. "You can sense them, can't you, Simarron? Spirits?"

"Lilimari, I don't know what you're—" I began in an effort to downplay.

"I've seen you, reacting to things that aren't there. Or at least, things that aren't there for the rest of us. Why would you hide that? Do you know how useful that could be?"

I sighed. "It's not like that, Lilimari. I can't sense spirits, exactly. It's more like their residual emotions. I can smell . . . impressions like joy, loneliness, or malice. I keep it quiet because, well, I don't even fully understand it myself."

Lilimari nodded. "Since Kai already found me out, I may as well tell you all. I have decided to switch my area of study and continue pursuing the threshold between alchemy and necromancy that Professor Ashmin pioneered."

"I can tell that is your area of true passion," said Daniella, who began pouring out cups of tea.

Kai sighed dramatically, accepting a cup. "This bunch is shadier than an enchanted forest."

Tia laughed nervously.

"Not just anyone can summon an unohdus, you know," Lilimari continued, ignoring him. "How sad that Horace Van Adair was so ashamed of his necromantic ability while also trying to live up to the legacy of magic his family expected of him. No wonder he snapped."

While everyone was chattering and drinking tea, I took out my journal and re-read the letter I'd drafted to the Board of Alchemists on Gold Row. Remembering how the candle wax had mysteriously stained the Periodic System of the Elemental Metals where element X51 should go, I requested that the Board of Alchemists consider naming it *panchromia*—the name Andreas Hippolyte had chosen when he discovered it. I then turned to a new page and began to write.

"What's this, Simarron?" asked Daniella as she filled my cup.

"Oh, I started keeping a journal after my experience at the castle, to try to work through what happened."

"So, what are you working on next?" inquired Tia, peering over my shoulder. "Your sketches are beautiful."

Self-conscious, I snapped the journal shut, but a smile slowly tugged the corner of my lips. Although the immediate threats had been laid to rest, there was still work to do. I was a safety inspector and, even in a city of magic and intrigue, safety comes first.

The End.

Acknowledgments

Thank you to my friends and family who generously volunteered as beta readers—your support and feedback meant the world. I'm grateful to my writing group buddies for the accountability and encouragement along the way. Thanks also to my husband for doing most of the chores, so I could focus on writing. A heartfelt thank-you to my writing mentor, Gabriela Pereira, for the wisdom and guidance I needed to finish this book, and to my editor, Wren Helgren, for helping me make it shine.